THE
BRIDGE OF
PERFECT WISDOM

Rupa Monerawela

ISBN 978-1-78222-114-2

Book design, layout and production management by Into Print
www.intoprint.net
+44 (0)1604 832149

Printed and bound in UK and USA by Lightning Source

CONTENTS

CHAPTER 1

Liang Feng's Journey

She was a good citizen of the proletariat. It had taken three years to learn and be accepted to the new way of life. Things had moved so quickly she could hardly remember a time when she was allowed to be with her thoughts. Yet now between the time of leaving 'The Red Brigade Commune' and time taken to travel to Canton Railway Station she was giving in, almost indulgently, to thoughts that were truly hers.

Yet those thoughts were short-lived, abrupt as the silence that holds whirlwinds in moments of unnatural calm.

Liang Feng stood by the road before the railway station, her senses alert, as the wind ploughed the yellow dust of Canton, threatening and lifting, gushing whirls with deep whoops, dust and debris daring to lie in its way. Dragged in from all directions, the orbit of power strengthened as it whirled around her legs and around the building, yet giving a short break of abnormal silence. Steadying herself against this force she took a quick breath.

Growling winds blasted and blew fine grains of sand that clung and clawed her skin, sparing neither the living nor the inanimate as it held sway.

Shielding her eyes and clutching her little grey cloth bag before it too was pulled away from her hand, she rushed past the wind into the building. She heaved a sigh as she entered the formidable refuge which welcomed travellers going to Peking, on the second day of September in the year 1965.

The travellers to Peking stood in a long queue. It was a mixed group, as mixed and varied as the expectations they held in making this great expedition. For some, presumably now returning from lands that were really kicking them out, this had become a forced pilgrimage that otherwise would have taken place when their cremated bones were brought to rest in the motherland, and they stood with faces shadowed in gloomy uncertainty, feeling unwelcomed to the land they had abandoned at the time of civil wars and revolution. Though their faces were gloomy, their clothes were well tailored and becoming. The men wore smart cotton well-creased suits, leather shoes, and most noticeable were the heavy leather suitcases and the cameras in their possession.

In marked contrast to them were those residents of Canton taking this journey with bright happy faces, seeking a fulfilment to their most cherished dream of visiting Peking, the hallowed city where their revolution had been stabilised. In contrast to their bright mood of high expectations, their clothes were not flattering. The men and women, indistinguishable in a mode of dress shapeless and too out-sized for their figures, looked as if they had been battered by the storm! Now seeing their well-dressed kith and kin they drew back; standing stiffly, watching in disdain and envy, those who now dared to come to share their spoils. The bundles in their hands were large and clumsy and so were the cardboard boxes tied with strings which they dragged along the floor. But their pride in themselves slowly rose as the envious thoughts were overcome; they coldly surveyed the trappings of capitalist society that the new arrivals were importing to their proletarian culture. However they were all well-behaved despite such rebellious thoughts that sometimes rebelled. They were polite and disciplined as they took their place in a single queue united in that single dream of journeying to Peking, the historic capital of the peoples' Republic of China.

Liang Feng's eyes gently observed the faces around her. They were all strangers to her but she had a warm feeling towards all her new companions. It had not been an easy goal to achieve, to be granted permission to travel beyond the commune and to leave a district and go so far away, hundreds of kilometres from her original place of work. She was grateful to the kindness of all her colleagues in the commune and those authorities who had rewarded her with work that she longed to do in Peking.

She had tied to her back the sleeping bag that for many nights had given comfort in times of homesickness. Her own leather suitcase brought three years ago from Jakarta to Canton, had been taken by her husband when he was sent to join the exemplary Tachai Brigade. To be differentiated from the new society because of unacceptable bags and clothes irked her. She did not want to be noticed as a foreign Chinese in the land where her father and her grandfather had been born; she was glad she had got rid of her own foreign suitcase.

Liang Feng moved in the direction of the offices of the China Travel Service. It was steaming hot and crowded with passengers whose heavy breathing and perspiration added to the hot air of Canton. But the simple décor of the room, a table and three cushioned chairs gave a sense of order and clinical brushing which influenced the passengers to be on their best behaviour as in a doctor's surgery. The heavy cushioned chairs with antimacassars in lace, placed at head and arm rests, were neatly arranged, and acted to diffuse any rebellious thoughts in those who were impatient to get a seat on the train. They were uninviting to the proletariat, for people like her, to sit.

Like her, they all had that spirit of endurance as all those countrymen of her father's land, now waiting patiently in the queue. It was easier to endure all hardship, especially when their Chairman smiled at them, a benevolent father – a large portrait of Chairman Mao hung in the centre of the room, captivating all eyes with its brightness. The picture gave colour to that austere room. The bright green uniform with the red collar and armband stirred a sense of cheerful expectations in all their hearts. Yet, that was not the photograph that inspired Liang Feng in her greater aspirations! On the opposite wall was a portrait of Mao Zedong standing in a long grey mandarin dress amidst a cloud of mist of Hunan land. He was holding in one hand a paper parasol of striking beauty and, in the other, his now famous red book, 'Thoughts of Chairman Mao Zedong'. This was not an official photograph, yet it evoked in her the spirit of the freedom fighter, intellectual and idealist beneath the formidable exterior. Slender fingers held to his heart in all pride, 'The Book', the talisman that would preserve him in the imminent battle. The book, more potent than the sword for an intellectual struggle! Why did not others see this side of his character? For example, those critics in Jakarta who hurled angry words calling him a ruthless communist, making life intolerable for them? She glanced protectively at her bag; the book was carefully tucked into a corner and she hoped to read it on this long journey. She was agreeable to his philosophy of a great proletarian society.

Only the soft sound of patient shuffling feet in the queue was distinct in that otherwise silent room. Preoccupied with their own thoughts, showing no desire to share them with others, they inched forward to buy tickets. The train journey to Peking was going to take two and a half days. Preparing for such a journey, the travellers carried parcels and boxes of food. They seemed to put more faith in their own provisions than what would be made available in the restaurant car. Striking and thought-provoking were the large thermos flasks, each more than one foot in height, with covers of bright floral designs and aluminium. Like the 'Thoughts of Chairman Mao' everybody carried a flask in their hands for this journey. Liang Feng too carried a flask which, however, was less prominent because of its small size. It had taken a long time for Liang Feng to practice these new codes for good health and as in this case, to kill hunger by drinking hot water. She did not share her companions' need to gulp down cups of hot tea.

She looked round again at the faces of those in the queue, desiring to talk, but nobody showed any signs of obliging her with attention. Safe in their own thoughts, they ignored each other while silently gazing into the face of the Chairman. There was great desire in her to see Mao Zedong in real life. It was the wish of all her colleagues in 'The Red Brigade Commune'. He was truly the greatest leader of her country. He had made China a nation to be recognised in the world. A sense of pride now overwhelmed her, bringing tears into her eyes. There was also the desire to crush all that veiled criticism from those who left the country at the time of the Revolution. She had defended the system in China stoutly when confronted by friends who were sceptical of those achievements as propaganda that boldly encouraged other countries towards Revolutions. It was this loyalty that made certain authorities label her a Communist, and watch with suspicion the activities of her family.

Back in the country she had left, a new threatening attitude was adopted towards the local Chinese population in the belief that there were links with the Indonesian Communist Party. Only a few days previously the newspapers had reported the massacre of Chinese in Indonesia. She was glad to have left at a time when troubles were beginning.

It was a new life she and her father experienced in the Commune. Back in Jakarta, how horror-struck her friends had been at the mention of communes; with shocked faces they deplored the so-called terrible commune system where men and women were forced to live apart. She smiled to herself remembering how wrong they were; she had found a sense of belonging in the commune. Happy in sharing work with fellow members of the 'Red Brigade', she found the people on her father's land to be simple, understanding and hardworking. At first they had been a little unsure of her father who dressed in a lounge suit in the western style, and also frowned upon her unconventional short perm. Influenced by her peers in the commune she tried to look like them by forcibly removing the curly hair to make it straight and stiff, but it had taken many nights. Before a tiny mirror she had tried to straighten her hair watched by an amused and unruffled father. After five months of striving she succeeded in making her hair look like everybody else's.

As she moved forward, she saw part of her reflection in the unostentatious mirror that stood above a half-table against the wall of the room. She watched the passenger ahead of her giving it a troubled glance. Eyebrows emphasised the frown she adopted as she looked at her uncomplimentary appearance in over-sized clothes, she wearily sighed, and moved on. It was now Liang Feng's turn to look into the mirror, her hand automatically moved up to touch the fringe and strands of hair that had escaped her disciplined hand to keep it neatly tied in two plaits. She saw the half reflection of the passenger behind her trying to peep into the mirror. She could not help noticing the contrast of her colour and shape of eyes with the fair round face of the passenger behind her. Her large eyes shone brightly with enthusiasm, with the long lashes giving them a tilt up at the corners. Her pale brown skin had a deeper tan from exposure to the sun, while carrying out her work on the farm. She looked more like her Indonesian mother although she had her father's neat black eyebrows and high cheek bones. Her mouth was small and showed a row of half-hidden white teeth when she smiled, as Liang Feng found she was doing now.

The passenger next to her pouted, impatient for her turn to look at herself. Liang Feng, taking the hint, stepped forward quickly, letting her see her full view. Memories of her new life filled her with recollections of her own nature that had changed in the new environment. She was not self-conscious. The girls in the Commune had taught her to dress like the men and not be conscious of her sex when she worked with the labour construction team. She imitated the men, and gradually over the last three years, that quiet feminism which she had carried with herself to Canton, disappeared. Now she was a great believer in equality for women in all forms of work, which was once the monopoly of men. She remembered her own enthusiasm for this equality and had fixed a poster on the commune door – "Men and Women are now equal; criticise the idea that men are superior to women".

There had been a remarkable change after the Revolution in the traditional role of women. Their participation with the men in bringing about the Revolution had given them this equality, once the new Communist rule was established. This was a new experience to Liang Feng, coming from Jakarta where customs and religion kept women confined to homes. She was proud to belong to the new China where women and men worked side by side.

It was more than an hour since joining the queue. She looked at the woman who had tried to peer into the mirror, who was straightening the creases in her blouse. Seeing Liang Feng steal a glance at her, she straightened her shoulders and let her hand drop to her side. Liang Feng's desire to talk was not reciprocal because that comrade coldly avoided the glances Liang Feng was giving her.

Chuang Tsu who stood behind Liang Feng was middle-aged. She wore black trousers and a white cotton blouse reaching over her rather protruding stomach. As she stood straight and large she looked as if she could over-power the shorter Liang Feng. Sensing she was observed, her chin jerkily moved up, raising her nostrils and spreading an authoritative look on her rather flat broad face. Her lips, rather thin, were pressed together as if she held them tightly, controlling the muscle that was twitching to fall back into her normal relaxed expression. It amused Liang Feng to see this show of unnecessary hostility to a fellow countryman, but remembering the fair face behind her in the mirror, she wondered if it was her colour that prevented her from looking like the rest of her countrymen. It may be this that had made her neighbour assume an unfriendly air. Narrowing her shoulders as if not to offend her neighbour, Liang Feng tried to keep herself from any bodily contact with her.

Chuang Tsu on her part had not been unconscious of the glances Liang Feng was giving her. She observed her neighbour from that high position in which she held her nose, but when Liang Feng's back was turned, her eyes came down to a position to take a full view from a back angle. Chuang Tsu was curious; she could not establish Liang Feng's nationality and decided to dismiss her from her mind as a foreigner. But there arose a puzzling doubt as to why a foreigner dared to look in her face boldly as her neighbour did. She was almost taken aback when Liang Feng greeted her cheerfully with "Nii hao". The twitching in her lips ceased as they parted. She returned the greetings. It was not very enthusiastic. When she saw her neighbour's full front view she could not compromise; with a slight lift of her chin she mentally established Liang Feng as an overseas Chinese who would know only a smattering of words in her language.

Chuang Tsu had heard of the influx of displaced countrymen returning to the motherland, and also of those who prided themselves in coming back since October 1964, after China exploded the first atom bomb. She was critical of all categories of her countrymen now returning. They cared to return only when they realised the country was a world power in the eyes of other powerful nations. She regarded them as cowards who had left at the time of hardships caused by the Civil War.

Seeing the critical look on Chuang Tsu's face, Liang Feng smiled to herself. It was forgivable if her neighbour thought her an alien. But she and her father had got a special welcome from the mainland government. When the call was made to those living abroad to come back to build the motherland, her father had decided to take the opportunity to return with his daughter, saddened and disturbed by the attitude in Jakarta to the local Chinese community. They had both returned to the land her grandfather had abandoned. The gold they carried to the new land was also welcomed and ensured for them a special place in the 'Red Flag Commune'.

All these reflections on the past were rudely silenced when there was an outburst of loud angry voices in front of the queue. The voices were of officials handling the tickets to Peking and a white-skinned passenger standing before them. Speaking loudly in English the foreigner was saying angrily,

"I don't want to share my compartment with anyone. What does it matter if I buy four tickets for the two of us, you won't lose on the deal?"

The reply was controlled in faltering English, but there was annoyance in the tone,

"Yes, it matters to the Railway Authorities. It would deprive other travellers going to Peking on this train".

The official was trying to explain without completely losing his temper, and added with some anxiety,

"This train in already crowded."

The face of the foreigner flushed, emphasising the sharpness of his nose. The heat in Canton and his own body heat added to make him look like a spark of flame rising from the smooth circular lumps of coal which were however of a yellow hue. Those flat round faces all watched him with eyes that were mere slits and hidden in the high cheek bones disguising the emotions, if there were any. The foreigner, gesticulating with his right hand, was expressing strongly his

10

view on the matter. The fair-faced woman standing beside him was trying to restrain the man from exploding into physical violence. Her hand lay firmly on his arm, occasionally pulling him away from getting too close to the official. The foreigner's manner intruded on the calm demeanour of the rest of the passengers. Travellers, who had till then not shown any interest in their fellow passengers, now awakened to curiosity, peered with inquisitive eyes at the ill-mannered passenger. This was to compensate for their initial lack of interest in their neighbours. They engaged in non-verbal communication with each other, asking for assistance to explain the disturbance. All eyes and ears were now turned in the direction of the argument.

Understanding what the foreigner was saying in English, Liang Feng puzzled as to why he wanted to buy four tickets for only two of them. Her neighbour had got close behind her, breathing hard down her neck. She turned round and Chuang Tsu apologetically took a step back. But this was the break Liang Feng looked for, and gazing straight at Chuang Tsu's face she said,

"The foreigner wants to buy four tickets for his wife and himself".

The rather unfriendly manner of Chuang Tsu had now given way to a look of curiosity, with her eyes widening more and more as she listened to an unfamiliar tongue. She stepped away from the queue and stood beside Liang Feng who was listening interestedly to the conversation. Liang Feng's explanation made her take a deep breath of amazement, and once she recovered from the shock, she rose to the heights of disdainful anger. In her eyes all white foreigners were imperialists who upheld Capitalist governments, and the man's selfish motives confirmed without doubt her judgment. She said loudly, unable to restrain any longer the anger within,

"These foreigners, they only think of themselves. He may be having too much money to throw around!"

She had addressed Liang Feng, forgetting her former distrust; she was now overbearingly cooperative, and calling her for support, she exclaimed,

"Just look at him trying to grab four tickets, while we have been patiently waiting to get only one".

When Liang Feng did not give her full-hearted support by agreeing, Chuang Tsu made a little note in her mind. She was curious how Liang Feng understood what the foreigner said. There were many questions; of how and when she had learnt the language the foreigner spoke. But now, throwing away all those vexations that made her lips twitch, she kept them pressed together in cynical disdain. She smiled at Liang Feng. She wanted to know more of what the foreigner was speaking.

Glad at this disturbance breaking the silence, that had held all passengers to their own thoughts, Liang Feng said,

"He says he does not want strange faces to watch him and his wife", giving her own interpretation in a lighter tone,

"Maybe he wants to be alone with his wife".

This remark made Chuang Tsu explode in anger. Loudly forcing her breath out she sneered,

"No one will disturb THEM being alone together". She added in an acid voice,

"We have more important work than observing capitalist foreigners". Conscious of other passengers in front and behind her listening and showing their agreement with their eyes, she had spoken the truth. Rising to her height of authority, Chuang Tsu threw in her next words,

"We must NOT think only of our selfish desires especially in public".

There was pride in winning the attention of the other passengers, and self-satisfaction in rising to the defence of morals. Chuang Tsu had made a good speech, easily overheard by those near to her. In Chuang Tsu's eyes their silence was a show of approval, and now she wanted to maintain that attention. Picking her thoughts to exhibit her political knowledge, she quoted Chairman Mao,

"It is selfish capitalist thoughts to first think of oneself". Her speech was over, and gloating with satisfaction she smiled benevolently at Liang Feng.

Chuang Tsu was happy that she had quoted Chairman Mao and done better than Liang Feng who knew the foreigner's language. She did not want to be outdone by a foreign Chinese. She still thought of Liang Feng as one of those new arrivals. Liang Feng had listened to Chuang Tsu but, now hearing the thoughts of Chairman Mao, she revealed her own knowledge of his philosophy, and, with her face shining with enthusiasm, she quoted,

"When Capitalism raises its head, strike it down with Force". The camaraderie feeling of Chuang Tsu vanished like the enthusiastic first wave overpowered by the stronger waves that follow. In meeting her match she decided she had had enough of all foreign looking people. She quickly turned her back to Liang Feng and gave deliberate special care to study the rest of the passengers standing behind her.

Chuang Tsu's attitude jarred within Liang Feng and the argument of the foreigner heightened her impatience to purchase her ticket and board the train to Peking. She was looking forward to meeting new and pleasant countrymen in Peking. She listened to the foreigner with puckered eyebrows, astonished at the privilege he had, to talk back to the official. The official concerned with carrying out his duties, was now perspiring with indecision. So was the foreigner, as beads of perspiration stood on his temples and neck. He was the worst affected of the two, with the heat of the noon sun and more so with the heat he had worked up within himself in the argument.

The official's pale yellow face flushed pink while his eyes became anxious and troubled. He had to settle the issue before it could create unnecessary problems for him with his superiors.

Thoughts of historical events that had brought a period of foreign rule passed through Liang Feng's mind. Fresh in her thoughts was the Boxer Rebellion when the British Treaty had tried to favour their Nationals at the expense of the Chinese government and its people. With new hostility Liang Feng watched the arguing foreigner who was apparently a Britisher, trying once again to get better facilities for himself and his wife, while her own people languished uncomplainingly in a queue that was not moving.

Feeling the heat, she took out a fan from her bag and fanned herself. Becoming tired of observing the passengers Chuang Tsu stood scowling, sending darts of anger, as if that could unnerve the foreigner, in the direction of the arguing man. Liang Feng smiled with amusement; looking at Chuang Tsu, she thought: that passenger would never allow herself to be bullied and intimidated by any foreigner, unlike the last empress did when foreigners entered her country for trade.

It was Chairman Mao who gave them the courage to stand up to all this bullying from other nations, and she recalled the time when he proclaimed the People's Republic of China. She had been six years old and had sat down to a feast to celebrate the occasion. Yet the occasion was marred when her grandfather had refused to participate. Grandfather had been always angry concerning the changes in his country, calling the communists "cunning devils" whose propaganda won over the people.

Unable to conceal her silent disdain and anger, and hearing the continuing argument between the two men, Chuang Tsu spoke loudly, not addressing anyone in particular, but standing behind Liang Feng,

"I wonder if anybody knows WHAT the official is going to do NOW?" Feeling that the question was directed at her indirectly, Liang Feng, forgetting Chuang Tsu's obnoxious behaviour, turned round and said,

"The foreigner keeps saying he does not care for our rules, and he says he is not going to share his compartment with strange men".

Chuang Tsu's face was like a balloon about to explode. Burning passions of anger and hatred blazed in her eyes and mouth, and they hurled a tirade of abuse in Chinese directed at the foreign couple. Once she had emptied all those powerful words, she became calm. With controlled bitterness she recalled sulkily all the suffering she had undergone before Mao Zedong liberated her land.

Liang Feng was given the benefit of hearing the tragedies that had fallen on Chuang Tsu's family before liberation. Waves of sympathy now rose within her as she listened to poor Chuang Tsu.

Before long, two officials in khaki green uniform, walked in. They walked up to the foreigner in a very decisive manner and sternly said,

"If you foreigners cannot obey our rules, you can miss the train".

It worked; those stern decisive words had their effect on the foreigner who was trying to bring the clerk to submission. There was no uncertainty in the look he gave the khaki uniformed men. The queue behind him was pushing him to submit with their hostile looks. He did not want to miss the train. Everything was different in China. Travelling by another mode was ruled out. It was also not easy after such an incident to reach his destination without mishaps. Further it could affect his job as well as his stay in China. He had to capitulate.

Donald Brown, the new Attaché to the British Mission in Peking, spoke. He measured his words slowly, yet with a stubborn finality, and not accepting all their rules, he said,

"Alright", and then, "I will share, but I would do it only if you send two ladies". The argument was over, the uniformed men relaxed with relief at not having to use more threats to those carrying diplomatic passports. They smiled, showing their white even teeth, as if they had forgiven Brown.

"It is not a problem, we shall find you good company for the journey" they said, almost grinning.

Seeing the change in the foreigner's composure and an end to the argument, Liang Feng was glad that she could move forward in the queue. She turned round and noticing Chuang Tsu standing almost by her side, said calmly,

"The foreigner says he would share the compartment only with two ladies". Chuang Tsu almost tripped over as she took a step back with shock and excitement.

"What audacity these foreigners have to say such things in public", she snorted loudly and disdainfully.

"So the capitalist foreigner likes women's company more than men." Chuang Tsu's loud voice drew the attention of the passenger next to her and he piped up to defend all good males excepting those who sought women's company for other reasons.

"He is mistaken", he said. "No one is allowed to have concubines any more". Then looking at Chuang Tsu he minced his words,

"Chinese women are too manly to allow that". Chuang Tsu turned round sharply and gave him a look to seal his mouth from any further utterances.

Liang Feng enjoyed the conversation. She was glad at involving more people to break that unnatural silence that made her heart contract with panic at this journey to Peking. Trying to prolong the conversation Liang Feng said in a light tone,

"The foreigner may want to protect his wife from strange men". Her remark unfortunately did not have the effect she expected; it made the passenger who was already chastised by Chuang Tsu to step further away from both Chuang Tsu and Lian Feng.

The ticketing officer, his temper now ruffled, remained with knitted eyebrows and in a high sharp voice called,

"Next in line please". The faces of the travellers that had relaxed during that long argument changed, and once again with anxious eyes they watched the clerk hoping they would not be refused tickets to Peking. It was Liang Feng's turn to produce her identity card and railway warrant. Scrutinising the photograph and carefully reading the letter attached to the warrant he asked,

"What is your purpose in visiting Peking; you have been in this country only three years?" While she was preparing to answer he thought it better to consult his superiors and without waiting for a reply walked into a cubicle at the rear. She was indignant. Why should they be suspicious of her visit, and she heard the officer's voice and another coming from the cubicle. They were saying,

"This young woman is an overseas Chinese, now settled here and married to a citizen in Canton. She is 23 years old. The Red Flag Brigade has arranged her visit to the Foreign Language Institute in Peking". The rest of the conversation was lost as loudspeakers announced,

"The train to Peking will leave in half an hour".

CHAPTER 2
Chuang Tsu, the Deputy Director

Liang Feng was angry, it was an unnecessary delay in getting the ticket and she looked for sympathy to the passenger next to her. But that passenger, who obviously had heard the conversation, stood gazing vacantly over Liang Feng's head as if she had not heard anything. But there was a smile of self-righteousness on her face as she congratulated her own powers of detection regarding the foreign-looking Chinese.

The officer was back. He was endorsing his approval on Liang Feng's passport. He now gave her a welcoming smile; in fact it was his official duty to welcome those fellow countrymen now venturing to build up the mother country. Deciding to give a special privilege, he said,

"I have reserved for you a seat in the four-seat compartment." This was her first trip within China and it did not matter what kind of seat she was given. However she smiled back at the man and was about to receive her ticket, when the railway clerk recognised the broad face of the passenger standing behind Liang Feng peering inquisitively at him and the ticket in his hand. Her approving manner showed her gladness at the extra precautions the authorities were taking with new arrivals. The clerk's face changed to anxious politeness. He said quickly,

"Comrade Chuang Tsu, it is good to see you. I should not delay you any further", and as she smiled at him superiorly he said,

"Can you please give me your warrant". The smile he had given Liang Feng had been abruptly cut short as he handed Liang Feng her ticket without another glance at her. Comrade Chuang Tsu was now more important in his eyes. As Liang Feng took back the warrant in her hand, Chuang Tsu stepped up and was engaged in an animated discussion with the official.

Liang Feng walked away. She was thoughtful; she was now alone once again and her destiny was in her hands. But she was not alone for long. Chuang Tsu strode fast to catch up with her. She smiled broadly, almost with extra confidence; she was not going to leave Liang Feng alone. Liang Feng had heard the clerk say as he stamped Chuang Tsu's warrant,

"I will give you a comfortable seat to share with the overseas Chinese woman." Liang Feng, who had at first wanted to communicate with Chuang Tsu, was disappointed at this arrangement. She did not like Chuang Tsu's sudden change of moods and inquisitiveness and she had not shown any friendliness to her except to ask what the foreigner was speaking. Confronting her, Liang Feng now wanted an explanation from Chuang Tsu for this disagreeable arrangement. She said sarcastically,

"There seems to be a special arrangement for both of us on this journey." Chuang Tsu did not reply, she pulled herself up as she shifted her parcels to her left hand and walked briskly forward, while the wide legs of her black trousers fluttered in the wind. Her face was screwed up against all foreigners, and foreign-looking Chinese who intruded on her thoughts.

The People's Liberation Army stood to attention; their faces were alert while watching the rail track and the passengers carrying their luggage to the stationary train. The passengers were almost running, trying to get away from their cold scrutiny. They ran faster as they heard the train whistle. They were all keen to get a good comfortable seat in the compartments for the long journey. No longer did the faces of the passengers remain inscrutable and expressionless. They talked and laughed as they hurried along. Liang Feng stopped. She stared at the billboard mounted on a bright iron stand. It was colourful and large, covering the view on the other side and hiding the territory of the People's Republic of China. The faces on the board were bright and cheerful as they stood aiming their guns in the direction of the new travellers to Peking. "Workers of the world unite and fight Imperialism!" screamed the poster.

Liang Feng's heart beat fast. She was determined to find happiness. It was her dream as well as that of others who were making this journey, to see Peking, the place where the 1949 Revolution was consolidated by Chairman Mao. She was going to face a new life. Nursing these thoughts, with no more misgivings, she walked towards the railway carriage. There was enthusiasm and light-heartedness in her step.

Walking up to a carriage Ling Feng stopped abruptly. The number on the carriage corresponded with the number on the ticket in her hand. The large yellow numerals on a green surface almost mocked her. Her face changed from enthusiasm to disappointment. She stopped, hesitating to get in; she saw the two foreigners who had made all that unpleasant delay, seated in the carriage. She did not understand why she had been chosen for such mandarin treatment; only special people had that special privilege. The disappointment was further heightened; already she had the obnoxious task of sharing with Chung Tsu. But of course there were those who would throw away those ideals to grab a comfortable seat that was always allocated to officials and foreigners. Whereas an ordinary compartment would have suited her, to lose herself among passengers she would not know and cared not to know.

Chung Tsu was following her, elbowing her way through her vociferous fellow-countrymen, scrambling and pushing themselves and their possessions into the 'peoples' carriages. When Chuang Tsu saw the uncertainty in Liang

Feng's face, she got closer to the carriage and pressed her face on to the glass pane to get a better look at the passengers already seated inside.

CHAPTER 3

New Friends

Mr and Mrs Donald Brown sat within. Looking anxiously through the window, they watched the faces of fellow travellers peering into their compartment. They stopped they stared, and moved away. With rising anxiety Mr and Mrs Brown watched the faces of the passengers disregarding their carriage and getting into others. Since they had been forced to agree to share their compartment, they looked for agreeable companions. They were newly married, and desired to take the two and a half day's trip in the quiet intimacy of a six by four carriage without prying eyes. But now having to share their intimacy with complete strangers, they hoped that the two female passengers, as promised by the railway authorities, would be pleasant, and mind their own business.

It was a new experience for Donald Brown to travel by train to Peking. He chose this mode of travel to get a scenic view of a country he had read about. It was his first assignment in his new career as a Diplomat. The year being 1965, it was a time when Peking, the capital of The Peoples' Republic of China, was in the news; steeped in rumours mixed with some facts given by journalists. It was still a country that needed to be explored and that he was determined to do.

Donald Brown possessed the enthusiasm and spirit of his forefathers to deal with any situation. When he saw two women standing on the platform staring at his carriage he quickly got up from his seat. Summing them up in one quick glance, he decided that they would be the passengers who were selected to share their carriage. In his eyes they looked agreeable company and, taking the initiative, he opened the carriage door. With charming suavity he looked at the two ladies and enquired,

"Are you the two ladies who are going to travel with us to Peking?" His expectations and surprise heightened when the pretty younger woman answered in English, rather hesitantly,

"Our tickets have the same number as this carriage."

Now resigning to sharing the carriage with the foreign couple, Liang Feng added,

"I hope you would not mind us getting in."

Donald Brown eagerly replied,

"Certainly not."

Seizing the opportunity which he thought was a wonderful chance to make acquaintance with a Chinese who spoke English and undoubtedly would be able to give him valuable information about a country that was new to him, he became helpful.

Noticing the boxes in Chuang Tsu's hand he hurried to her side.

"Let me carry your bags and boxes," he said, and without giving a chance for a reply, he took the boxes from her hand and carried them into the carriage. Liang Feng followed them in.

Once settled, Mr and Mrs Brown sat facing Chuang Tsu and Liang Feng on the opposite seats. The cushioned seats with lace antimacassars were a luxury for both Chuang Tsu and Liang Feng. They enjoyed this comfort which the foreigners were entitled to.

Donald Brown, being the only man among the three women, now took charge. He knew his etiquette. Taking the large flask from the table placed between the two seats, he poured hot water into the four mugs. Green tea leaves were placed inside. He had made the first move in breaking the barriers, if they existed, among the four travellers. This opportunity was important to solve the many myths and rumours, mainly built by headline-seeking journalists about the people and a country that was out of bounds to most of them, he thought wryly. In a few days he would be renewing his friendship with his journalist friend Pierre Devon. He looked forward to this.

Liang Feng watched Donald Brown with interest. She noticed his strong hands as he carefully poured the hot water into the tea mugs. Chuang Tsu was also attentive. Her first opinion of the arrogant foreigner had changed. She was secretly flattered by his attentions. She was pleased when he had taken the boxes from her hands. In her family it was always she who had carried the heavy baggage, not the men.

But she became a little uncomfortable when he addressed her in English. Not wanting to look foolish, she began to busy herself with the crocheting she had pulled out of her bag. She was resigned to leave Liang Feng, who had showed her knowledge of the foreigner's language at the railway station, to attend to him.

Donald Brown spoke out hesitantly,

"I think it's better if we introduce ourselves, we shall be sharing our accommodation together for two days and two nights."

He looked at the faces of the two women, hoping it was acceptable to them. His eyes rested on Liang Feng, noticing her good looks as well as her nonchalant expression of firmly closed lips. He did not want to intrude and began observing the passengers entering the train.

He knew he had to break the ice to get the two women into a conversation as he was beginning to ponder how Liang Feng learnt English. Feeling his eyes on her, she translated what he had said to Chung Tsu. Unable to ignore the translation, Chuang Tsu said quietly rather inaudibly,

"I am Chuang Tsu, the deputy director of the Sachao peoples' commune in Kwangtung."

She lowered her eyes and went back to her crocheting. At the word 'commune' Brown's eyes lit up with enthusiasm, he blurted out,

"How wonderful! I want to know all about communes." He addressed himself directly to Chung Tsu.

Although she could not understand the language, seeing the expression on his face she giggled and her round body shook with suppressed laughter.

Liang Feng was secretly happy at Brown's eagerness to converse. He was a different man to the person she observed arguing with the railway official, less than an hour earlier. A new opportunity had opened up for her to practise her English after a lapse of three years. Taking courage to continue the conversation, she enquired politely,

"Would you be occupying the two upper berths?"

Before he replied, he glanced at his wife.

The small compartment consisted of two seats, on which four could sit, facing each other. A very narrow space was in-between. There were the two upper berths over the seats allowing more room to stretch one's legs. Four persons sitting together in those seats, with just enough space for two on either side, would be sitting in very close proximity to each other. This was a proximity which strangers would not welcome.

Sally Brown would not adjust herself to this forced intimacy with strangers. She had remained silent throughout the conversation, and having studied the two women had made a decision. She wanted to be alone with her husband. Sally responded to Liang Feng's question quickly,

"We'll use the upper berths while you can have the comfort of the seats." Brown's over enthusiasm to converse with the two Chinese women was making her irritable and impatient.

Sally's voice conveyed firmly her decision which Brown rather reluctantly accepted.

Stepping lightly on the side of the seat, he manoeuvred his body onto the upper berth and stretching his arm pulled his wife up. Liang Feng heard their laughter as Sally rolled over her husband when the train jerked to a start. Chuang Tsu had heard their laughter but was stony faced. She stiffened and pretended not to hear their whispers. If she looked up accidentally there was the chance she would accost their faces, and to avoid this embarrassment she rose hurriedly and sat on the opposite side, below the couple.

It was not very long before Brown came down and was seated beside Liang Feng. He was eager to delve into the hoary tales the western world was hearing of the communes and especially the forced segregation of the sexes. How fortunate that now he had the opportunity to obtain authentic information from a Chinese who knew his language. This was better than getting interpreters, who often twisted the translations from their own perspective.

Further, he could score over his friend Pierre, a journalist in Peking. The story would be a knockout he thought triumphantly, smiling at Liang Feng, who lowered her eyes in shyness.

The last letter Brown had received from Pierre had expressed his joy at the approaching visit. There was however a tinge of disappointment, reading between the lines, about Pierre's aspirations and career as a journalist. He had now accepted a teaching post at a Chinese University. Brown recollected with nostalgia their student days together. Pierre was from Marseilles, and had visited England as an exchange student. For four years they had attended the same school, but he had lost contact with Pierre for the last seven years. He was now looking forward to renewing their friendship. What bothered him most about the letter were the words, 'don't be disappointed if you find me a changed man'.

Donald remembered that even as a boy Pierre talked often about Socialist philosophy that neither he nor his other friends had understood or cared to make a subject for discussion. Pierre had enjoyed his own company and sought friendship with a few.

Chung Tsu, her eyes drooping with sleep, was adjusting her limbs; with both feet curled up on the seat for a good nap. Donald looked hopefully at Liang Feng to start a conversation. His eyes fell on *The Thoughts of Chairman Mao* lying beside her mug of tea. This was provocative and in a bemused tone he queried,

"Do you always read *The Thoughts of Chairman Mao*?"

She looked up at him with a start and conscious of his eyes and his mocking tone she abruptly said,

"No." she said with annoyance.

She did not like him to laugh at her. She had truly not read it daily as most others did in the commune.

Her thoughts were more on this journey to Peking. But having nothing to do in the train and being conscious of the foreigners in the compartment, she had opened the book. On the other hand, she was quietly enjoying Chairman Mao's sayings. They were short and terse and their ambiguity provided food for thought.

Her negative answer had no effect on Donald's smiling face. Hoping to crush him into silence, she hissed in a tone of superiority,

"But I do enjoy reading the Chairman's sayings, particularly when I am with disrespectful strangers."

His smile turned into a deep laugh. She had given him a curt reply. In fact it challenged him to retort.

"You are different to other Chinese here; you cannot be born and bred in this country."

She was exasperated. He knew too much, she thought, her eyes flashing angrily.

"This is my country even if I have lived in it for only three years, having moved from Indonesia".

Unwilling to disclose anything further she turned her face to the window.

A warm feeling of happiness soaked in as she saw the workers in the bright sunshine of the fields, halting their work to wave at the passing train. She waved back oblivious of Donald Brown. She liked the open fields although she got a little tired of the flatness of the landscape. Paintings of the mountainous landscape of China by master artists had always moved her deeply and filled her with a yearning to view them some day.

She looked forward hopefully to see similar scenery on this journey.

Peking too was said to have picturesque landscapes with pagodas and pine trees that reached up to the blue sky. There were also pavilions and palaces of the former emperors to visit. She was startled from her daydreaming when Donald, almost voicing her thoughts said,

"Peking is said to be a fascinating city."

His tone was encouraging and gentle. She wondered why he would not leave her alone but persisted in talking to her. He seemed to sense her thoughts.

She turned away from the window and looked into his warm blue eyes, now smiling with friendliness. She did not answer.

Donald was not willing to accept a lack of response, and wishing to break the silence said in a kind voice,

"Is this your first visit to Peking?"

Watching his face she replied cautiously,

"Yes this is my first visit."

Next she spiritedly added, as an afterthought, to his earlier statement,

"Peking had always been a beautiful city. I remember my father telling me that this beauty was destroyed when the imperialist British and French burnt down the magnificent summer palace."

She hoped her words would penetrate his conscience.

Donald sensed her disdainful anger and was regretful for what had happened hundred years ago. His voice was low and quiet as he said,

"Yes, I know about it. You must meet Pierre my friend who now lives in Peking. He knows the history of your land much more than anyone else I know. In fact he has accused the Western World of barbarity for destroying one of the most outstanding civilisations in our modern time."

She sat upright – his words and his tone surprised her. This was not the answer she had expected. It would have been more acceptable if he had defended his country just as she was doing hers. She looked at Donald with keenness and curiosity. In her eyes he was an honest foreigner. Such a reaction from her would have brought cries of 'unpatriotic' from those around her. The wall she had built against him was now slowly crumbling. Her voice did not fully reveal her pleasure as she said calmly,

"It is interesting to observe your understanding of our past history; I wonder if I could meet your friend, he sounds like a good foreigner."

This made Donald laugh; there was something naive in her quick replies to his questions. He wondered if it was the result of the education the Chinese population received. He had noticed this same quality in Chuang Tsu and even in the laughing and shouting Chinese passengers boarding the train. Liang Feng had already categorised him as a good foreigner as opposed to the bad.

The sympathetic and understanding tone of his voice encouraged her to say,

"I had a dream before I left Canton that I would find something I am searching for in Peking."

He was quite taken aback. It seemed incredible that a Chinese of the new communist state could dream or even talk about dreams. She sounded more like any ordinary person he met in his own country. He sat back feeling more relaxed in her company. He turned to her and said,

"Can I call you Miss Liang or Feng?"

A smile and a nod accompanied her.

"You can call me Liang Feng," she said, this time in her mind he was the foreigner going to Peking for the first time.

"You are the first Chinese I have really spoken to and also the first Chinese citizen to speak of dreams" said Donald.

Unable to control that teasing flippant tone whenever he spoke of Chairman Mao, he added,

"I believe that you Chinese are forbidden to dream of anyone except Chairman Mao."

Liang Feng was upset. He was an incorrigible man. She had to teach him a lesson.

Respecting the Chinese viewpoint and their Chairman Mao Zedong's philosophy, she took the roll of a teacher reprimanding a badly-informed student and said,

"Chairman Mao is the greatest leader the world has ever had. He has given millions of our people once held in poverty and bondage, the will to live. If he had not saved this land from warlords and avaricious foreigners, we would still be slaves of imperialist foreigners and feudal lords." The lecture was delivered with passion and sincerity.

She took a deep breath and sat back feeling a little deflated with her own enthusiasm. What was happening to her? Why did she feel her lecture sounded rather hollow to her, unlike at other times when she had an audience to cheer her defence of the system?

She blamed the foreigner for making her feel like that.

Suddenly, hearing the name of Chairman Mao, Chung Tsu was startled out of her comfortable doze. Her feet came down abruptly from the seat. Sitting stiffly, blinking her eyes many times, she questioned Liang Feng, her voice suspicious,

"What is the foreigner saying about Chairman Mao?"

Taking a deep breath Liang Feng replied tactfully,

"The foreigner says that Chairman Mao has brought many changes to our country."

She did not like to see the foreigner in trouble. He had been honest and good to accept the wrongs that his people had done one hundred years ago. She watched Chung Tsu's face slowly broadening into a benign smile. Her benevolence extended towards Donald, and looking into his face, she nodded her head approvingly.

From the expression on Chung Tsu's face, Donald guessed that something complimentary had been conveyed about him. He had not expected Liang Feng to defend his jibes about Chairman Mao with cover-up words.

He was beginning to realise that there was more to her then the naivety he had first observed; there was a depth and complexity in her personality. She had the sense to keep Chuang Tsu with her political connections as Deputy Director of a commune, out of their conversation. His idea of the stereotype communist devoid of any feelings and groomed only to labour and follow the party line, had been rudely shaken.

Instead he had found that these people could be human and sociable.

Chung Tsu had returned to her short snooze although one could wonder whether she really slept or was only pretending. Unfortunately for her she could not however understand the language being spoken.

Donald resumed his probing.

"Do you miss Indonesia where you were born?"

Understanding his over-eager childlike curiosity, she responded with a good-humoured laugh.

"I really do not miss that place, I came here three years ago and that is a long time, I have not had an opportunity to be alone to reminisce over the past that I left behind."

She was speaking his language after a lapse of three years and was savouring every minute of this wonderful opportunity. It was such happiness to express herself freely within the confines of the compartment without fear of others eavesdropping.

Chuang Tsu's inability to understand her words made her even more talkative.

"When my father and I arrived in Canton we were given a warm welcome by the officials in the commune. They said we must see the real China and not rely on what we had heard abroad. They were very understanding of our different ways and assured us that Chinese never fought Chinese. So, whatever mistakes we made were forgiven."

When Donald looked sceptical she added confidently,

"There was an official group in the commune to look after us and supervise our work and wellbeing."

The journey was monotonous and most of the passengers were now in deep sleep. Only Liang Feng's voice broke the monotony with excerpts of her past that had not been revealed to any one as there was no need for it. She welcomed the present and not the past. But Donald was showing fascination to know this past as it made him get a better understanding of historical events that moulds the character of a country's people. She went on,

"My father's talent for art was recognised and he was given work as a commercial artist, to paint pictures of the revolutionary cause. He made colourful posters for the Red Flag Brigade information unit."

Donald interrupted,

"What work did you do?" He was more interested in what she had done.

"I was given work in the factory to produce nuts and bolts for farm machinery."

With her voice lowered she said regretfully,

"I had never done manual work before, I only had an academic education and the commune authorities considered it was my bourgeois education that encouraged individualism – it was against the ideals of the proletariat society. My work was planned so that I integrated with the workers and peasants."

Donald looked at her hands. They were not red and rough as he had expected. Noticing his eyes on her hands, she said with laughter in her voice.

"But I did not work there for long." A note of childlike pride crept in.

"Do you believe that I can speak both English and French?"

Donald smiled,

"I guessed you were good at languages when you spoke such good English and I believe the authorities found good work for you to spy on foreigners."

She laughed and, picking up the red book beside her, she opened a page with slow deliberation and translated into English,

"All evil things in the world start from diversity of labour."

He however wanted to know more about her work.

"Did the authorities change your job to something you liked?"

"There was no question of liking the work, you had to do what was given to you."

"But, when they discovered I was too slow and did not show interest, they had a party discussion and allowed me to look after horses on the farm."

"I like horses, talking to them you cannot get in to trouble, don't you agree?" She said this with a meaningful smile at Donald, whom she felt had become a confidant to whom she could express freely her thoughts.

Donald agreed,

"Yes I do agree, I like horses too, they are less dangerous than humans," and laughed.

Elaborating on a happier time Liang Feng was now in a mood to reminisce.

"It gave me such joy to groom the horses, they were used to draw the wagons which collected the farm vegetables and took them to the peoples' market."

Donald was more interested in finding out the feelings of the people who did this forced labour and less about the work in the farm.

He thought of the hardships a family faced in adjusting to a new dogma. Looking directly into her eyes he asked,

"Did your father like his work?"

Liang Feng's eyes softened, and speaking slowly she said,

"He liked the quiet unhurried pace of life on the farm. My father did not mind his work painting posters but whenever he had leisure time he would paint scenes of the commune, it was different to the life in Jakarta, we had terrible anxiety; it was a terrible strain on the whole family when the local people started boycotting Chinese shops."

She continued,

"The time had come for all Chinese businesses to close down and leave the country."

The situation in Jakarta would have been worse than facing a communist life thought Donald.

In a sympathetic tone he asked,

"Did your father like the change from Jakarta to Canton?"

"Jakarta was less restrictive, but when you are not wanted there you had to change your life for better or for the worse, he liked the peaceful and quiet life in China even though we did not have the comforts we had in Jakarta; there were very few cars in Canton and no noise from traffic. Being an artist, he looked for the natural surroundings in Canton."

She was in a pensive mood recollecting the past events when Donald interrupted,

"Where is your father now?"

"Six months after he arrived he died of a kidney ailment. He had been suffering from this problem for a long period."

Donald was concerned,

"You must have felt very lonely in a new place with flimsy roots."

She replied stoutly, dispelling the softness from her face,

"At first I was lonely but the commune members, as I told you before, acted like one big family. They were keen for me to get married."

"What!" exclaimed Donald, "so in this new society too marriages are arranged, then it is not much different from the feudal system."

His eyebrows lifted as he added cynically,

"Did you love your political partner?"

She felt the sarcasm in his voice and was at a loss to reply. He waited silently watching her. He realised he had said something to hurt her. He did not expect her to be so sensitive, and at her abrupt silence, he grew anxious. But in a few minutes she recovered her composure.

"I can say in a way I did, and in a way I did not." She realised that after all she did not mind speaking to a stranger about her marriage. Trying to express her dual feelings she explained,

"Political marriages are arranged for people to share their thoughts with one another." Then remembering her lessons in the study class she added,

"Individualism is selfish, and it could threaten the new society."

Donald broke in sarcastically,

"Or it would save the state much money and inconvenience, having one member of a family watching out on any unorthodox communist behaviour by another in the same family."

Liang Feng did not feel angered by his tone. What he said was partly true.

She remembered her life with Wang Lee. Wang Lee was an exemplary party member. He was opposed to her reading novels written in French and English. He was suspicious of such books that she had brought with her from abroad to China. He had feared she could get him into trouble if she persisted in reading uncommunist material.

A smile of wry amusement came to her lips as she remembered Wang Lee reading passages from the 'REVOLUTIONARY ROAD FOR CHINA'S YOUNG INTELLECTUALS' and also from 'HOW TO BE A GOOD COMMUNIST' by President Liu Shaoqui, night after night.

She had had an excess of it and one night, and in a fit of anger, had flung them on to the floor. Her face clouded briefly as she remembered how calmly her husband seemed to react. He had not shown anger but had merely looked at her as if she had become insane. She thought the matter had ended there, but it had not.

To her horror a few days later she was called up before some officials and was lectured about how to behave as a good communist wife. She was also asked to attend extra study classes for three months.

Donald remained silent, as if he understood that she was absorbed in some private thoughts. To him, she was a person who would react passionately to situations. She seemed to have that sort of temperament. In a single moment she could swing from one mood to another of a totally different kind; from a pensive disclosure of her past she could immediately shift to passionately upholding the Chairman and the system.

Sitting back in her seat, Liang Feng's mind was full of reminiscence.

Memories concerning Wang Lee bothered her; he had behaved like a total stranger to her outburst.

In her mind there was the image of her husband, his face inscrutable, holding her a prisoner? She wished he had shouted at her but this he would not do. The expression in his face had been cold. He had started bringing food from the community centre, sharing it with her occasionally, while she sat silently watching him. He made her feel a total sense of guilt, and she dared not speak to him.

She was afraid of her own behaviour and, to dismiss the rebellious thoughts, had taken on extra work in the farm, taking long hours grooming the horses and looking after a new litter of piglets. While the horses grazed she had spent time reading 'Contradictions of Chairman Mao' as it appealed to her troubled spirit. She was beginning to understand the divisive feelings within her.

Chairman Mao had an answer to all these feelings and it was true that he expounded, 'What is called Nobility is the wisdom to know oneself'. She had begun to comprehend what would be expected of her, if she wanted to remain in the new society. Her own self-criticism had helped her to some extent in overcoming the individualism that had streaked out in selfish behaviour. She had blamed the society by which she had been nurtured. It was only when she realised that she could have got lost in her own individualism that she accepted the teachings thankfully. It was not wrong to experience contradictions, and as Chairman Mao said, 'Contradictions within a thing is the fundamental cause for its development'.

Donald at last decided to break into her thoughts and his voice brought her back into awareness of the present,

"Where is your husband now, is he in Canton?"

His voice was sympathetic and comforting to her ears. She did not mind his probing questions anymore and willingly answered,

"No, he was sent away to work in the Tachai Brigade in Shansi Province, it's almost a year since he has been gone"

Donald was alert with excitement,

"Is this the famous Tachai Brigade that has become an example of good work for all Chinese?" he queried.

"It is," said Liang Feng with amusement shining in her eyes at his enthusiastic expression.

There was almost a tone of pleading in his voice,

"Tell me more of the Tachai Brigade. I read a little about it in a magazine called 'China Today' when I was in Hong Kong."

The sound of snoring, coming from the direction of Chuang Tsu made Liang Feng aware of the long hours they had spent talking. Chuang Tsu was fast asleep on the opposite seat. Darkness had set in outside. Liang Feng's eyes turned to the window and she noticed a few stars in the sky. The monotonous sound of the train was making everybody sleepy.

Turning to Donald she said well naturedly,

"Everybody seems to want to sleep; I will tell you the rest of my story tomorrow."

Donald took the hint and rose from his seat. Wishing her goodnight he carefully placed his foot on the corner of Chuang Tsu's seat and, with agility, leapt up to the sleeping berth above the seats.

CHAPTER 4

Crossing the Yangtze Kiang

It was the second day of the journey. The horizon was bathed in a soft still light of dawn. Inside the train there were deafening bangs of cymbals and martial music accompanying songs of the revolution to greet the sunrise. The loud music brutally brought to attention the passengers who were still in a state of slumber. With the crash of cymbals they hurriedly woke up and sat up to attention when the loudspeakers above their seats screamed in fervent patriotic enthusiasm,

"Comrades, the train will cross the Xian Jung in a short time."

The train from Canton, as scheduled, would cross this tributary of the great river Yangtze kiang on its journey to Peking by mid-afternoon.

Soon there was a display of excitement by the passengers to whom a new dimension of the glory of this river had opened in recent times, with Chairman Mao commanding all good communists to swim the vast expanse of water to overcome all hardships. There was a cacophony of voices praising the Chairman.

The female announcer's task was to rouse the passengers into a fervour of excitement and patriotism; only a high-pitched female voice could achieve this.

Preparing for this event, the activity and bustle increased as the passengers hurried for their morning ablutions, competing with each other, in trying to reach the few toilets on the train. It truly became an ordeal for the passengers in the luxury coach, trying to share these facilities with the rest of the passengers from the peoples' compartment.

Sally Brown was up before the others in their cabin. She had made her way carefully down from the sleeping berth, except when she unceremoniously landed on the dozing Chuang Tsu. Chuang Tsu's startled scream woke up both Donald and Liang Feng. Chuang Tsu's cries and Sally's apologies established the first link between them. Now seated beside Chuang Tzu, Sally related with laughter,

"It was awful, the rush to the toilets. I had to stand in a queue with all eyes staring at me; with no smiles."

Donald heard Sally and interrupted,

"You are mistaken, that's how they all look at first."

A half smile appeared on Liang Feng's lips when Donald added,

"You have to know them well to see them smile."

Being in a talkative mood and encouraged by Chuang Tsu's benign smile, Sally picked up the crochet which was on Chuang Tsu's seat. Sally's admiration and complimentary words, although not understood by Chuang Tsu, kept her smiling. The non-verbal communication established a bond of friendship between the two.

Reaching the climax of this happy interlude made Chuang Tsu open her bag and pull out a box of eatables. She handed it over to Sally. The aroma of the delicacies was mouth-watering to the hungry group. There were fried shrimp balls, dumplings and glutinous rice balls filled with date paste.

"This looks like genuine Chinese cooking!" exclaimed Donald, putting into his mouth a shrimp ball.

They were all glad that they had stayed behind in their compartment rather than line up in the long queue to the restaurant.

Chuang Tsu enjoyed her role of hostess. Her generosity extended further when she opened another box and produced a fragrant crisp water chestnut cake and a soft lotus cake. She conveyed in Chinese to Liang Feng that she had made all this food to take to her daughter; thankfully she had made extra as she did not trust the restaurant car food. She was very glad the foreigners enjoyed her food. Liang Feng translated to Sally and Donald what Chuang Tsu had told her. Both Sally and Donald took Chuang Tsu's hand and thanked her for her kindness to them. Donald turned round to Sally and Liang Feng and said,

"I am so pleased the generosity of China has not dampened with communist ideology."

By mid-afternoon the revolutionary songs had increased to fever pitch. The female announcer once again screamed. This time she praised the long march and the terrible havoc of flood waters during the Kuomingtang rule. The faces of the passengers became solemn and Donald was puzzled by this change of moods.

"Why are the passengers with grave faces?" he enquired.

Liang Feng, also affected by this news, replied to Donald Brown bravely,

"The terrible floods during the Kuomingtang rule killed thousands of poor peasants."

But Donald quizzed,

"As far as I know there was a big flood in China in 1960."

Realising that he knew far too much of their country's history, she said slowly,

"It was not as bad as during the Kuomingtang rule."

She knew about that flood when Chinese living abroad had sent money for the victims' families. It was then that Chairman Mao had instructed all his countrymen suffering from the famine, to drink hot tea to overcome dehydration and starvation. Yet thousands had died. She looked at Donald watching her with eyes that seemed to mock her, and she turned towards the window. His gaze made her feel like a propagandist who covered up the truth under all circumstances.

In the brightness of the noon sun the fields lay golden and abundant with rice paddies. Red flags flew on poles on the boundaries of the fields that overflowed with workers, labouring in the hot sun. Their faces were hidden under oversized cooli hats.

Liang Feng's thoughts drifted to Wang Lee. Unlike Donald, who was always probing, Wang Lee was a slave to rules and regulations, and did not question rules that had no logical explanations. She was living in a vacuum during that time. On one occasion, just because she had delayed to be at the courtyard for the morning exercise and reading from *The Thoughts of Chairman Mao*, she was damned in his eyes for lack of self-discipline. To stop hearing his taunts, she had stuffed her ears with cotton wool. But this had gone against her when discovered by an official who assumed that she did not want to listen to Chairman Mao's Quotations blaring out during the reading. But, they were sympathetic towards her as they became aware of many others making wry faces when there were too many repetitions. It was ironic that Wang Lee was under criticism for his devotion to party rules. Contradictions were acceptable to most Chinese.

Donald had not forgotten the early conversation with Liang Feng. He was determined to know more and asked her,

"What happened to your husband after he went to the Shansi Province, does he write to you?" Before she replied she looked at Chuang Tsu. She was glad that Chuang Tsu did not speak the language she was using with Donald.

"He does not write to me, the party said he should not contact me as he is undergoing self-criticism."

"Wasn't he considered an exemplary worker?" questioned Donald.

"He had made many mistakes in his production team, He drove the workers too hard with his ambition and this was resented by certain officials," said Liang Feng. In a matter of fact tone she went on,

"Since you know quite a lot about our country did you know that there is criticism of Liu Shaoqui's profit-making agricultural policy?"

"I heard a little about it before I set out, but I would like to hear the real story from you," said Donald.

He had been too fascinated with China's past glories to study in depth its present political problems. He had left it to the time when he would be in China.

Liang Feng did not need any more coaxing to relate the story of her life. She enjoyed pouring out what she had kept to herself for a number of years.

She continued,

"At the inquiry it was said that the party cadre must first show concern for the workers before they extracted work out of them. They also said that his approach was building up hostility that was going against the communist goal."

Donald's response was unexpected,

"I can picture him suffering in a woeful labour camp."

The mockery in his voice made her want to rise up in defence of the system.

"No," she said sharply, "He was sent to learn from Tachai Brigade."

"Wang Lee did not win the hearts of the people in the commune, as he continued with the three bending downs."

Donald responded quickly,

"Did I hear right, did you say three bending downs?"

His puzzled look made her laugh; she was happy at his ignorance. It was time to give him a lecture on Chinese way of life,

"We call them pulling, transplanting seedlings and harvesting – the three drudgeries of women. The women workers, who were mostly against him, were angry that he did not respect their age and did not find ways to lessen their burden."

So involved were they in their discussion that they had missed hearing the announcement on the loudspeaker. But when the other passengers started singing loudly 'Sailing the Seas with the Helmsman,' Liang Feng stopped talking and looked out of the window. There was pride in her heart to see the vast expanse of the river.

The river was like an enormous golden dragon, lying stretched out in peaceful slumber – the sun's rays picking up from its muddy and yellow surface glistening scales of sunlight. It was this same peaceful creature throughout the centuries of the land's history, that had on several occasions grown violent, thrashing its tail and swallowing up thousands of people.

The music blared out "East is Red" at which all Chinese passengers, including Chuang Tsu and Liang Feng, stood up to sing. They were both unaware of their foreign companions who were taking photographs of the river from the window.

This show of patriotism was not enough for the female announcer, and her voice breaking in a rapture of emotions, she screamed,

"Chairman Mao has taught us to overcome all hardships with patriotism! Comrades, because he loved our great country he had the courage to defeat and overcome the flooding of this mighty river. He has promised to swim in its waters in summer next year."

As the people heard this they burst into applause. A chant of "Chairman Mao our great helmsman" resounded in all the carriages.

Tears were pouring down Chuang Tsu's face. Her eyes lingered reverently on the flowing waters.

The passengers fell into thoughtful reflection eventually when the scenery changed and the land appeared and river was left behind.

Liang Feng too was thoughtful and reflective as her destination was getting closer. She would experience its reality, from the dreams she had built up in finding a new life in a desirable and historical place like Peking. Moreover she had a family member, whom she had never met before to embrace and recapture the ties of kinship. She had heard of her great aunt Kwong, from her father, who had admired her courage to stay behind in China when the whole family had left to Indonesia. Before he died, her father had given her the address of this aunt who was affectionately called Wampu. Wampu had managed to stay in her own house even after the revolution. But it had a new name, commune number 302, situated in the outskirts of Peking.

Liang Feng suddenly felt lonely and isolated when Donald Brown returned to his bunk overhead. She liked him as she found in him a comradeship she had not felt for a very long time. She could not remember a time when she experienced such feelings except when her mother first, and then her father, had passed away. She hoped that in Peking she would be able to kindle this friendship that mattered to her.

She did miss Wang Lee on this occasion. It was best for her, the party officials had said, that he should be sent away to reform himself. They acknowledged that he had not treated her well. Also he had not treated the workers under him with consideration.

She heaved a sigh, remembering the agony he had put her through to be a good communist. It was the officials who had arranged her trip to Peking. They felt she would welcome this change since her father's death and parting from Wang Lee.

At her farewell the commune director had spoken highly of her obedience to the party rules and had declared,

"Liang Feng is a true communist; she has shown specially, her understanding of Chairman Mao's philosophy."

She had felt proud at these words, and in her enthusiasm had decided to change her last name to 'Feng', meaning revolution. She remembered with kindness the concern that the party cadre had shown her with kind acts.

Her loneliness was somewhat appeased by these recollections and she sat back more relaxed and begun to hum the songs that were hurled at them morning, noon and night from loudspeakers.

She smiled to herself when she heard the sounds of children's voices coming from the adjoining compartment. On her wedding day the party had given her advice on birth control. They had explained that new China needed only a few mouths to feed and all good communists should practise birth control. The women had giggled and whispered why Wang Lee had been sent away. There was a policy to separate newlywed couples. Liang Feng was not particularly disturbed by this separation. Even if she had lived together with Wang Lee they were separated by a barrier of misunderstanding which was often unbearable to her. She did not expect her husband to write to her, but when a letter arrived it was full of revolutionary slogans. The authorities had achieved their objective and Wang Lee had become a dim memory of the past.

CHAPTER 5

Arrival in Peking

Unlike in past years, the people in the capital were witnessing a significant change in the celebrations being prepared for October 4ᵗʰ, the anniversary of the Revolution. At the same time bitter dissatisfaction with Mao's agricultural policy had unleashed a series of attacks by other high-ups in the politburo; a clash between Mao Zedong and Liu Shaoqui was imminent. This was a phenomenon unprecedented in a communist society.

It was a bright sunny afternoon when the train from Canton pulled up at the Peking railway station. The place was a hive of activity as any busy station is. Yet there was a difference. Noticeable in that crowd were groups of young men and women arriving from all parts of the country. In the political climate of the city, their presence, together with their noise and agitation, seemed to trigger a revolutionary atmosphere. The railway workers, observing the scene, looked rather uncomfortable, hesitating to impose restraints upon the vociferous newcomers. The patriotic songs blaring out through loudspeakers heightened the feeling of excitement and tension. All these factors together contributed towards creating the air of a restless carnival.

Liang Feng remained listlessly in her seat, watching through the window the passengers alight from the train. Having arrived at her destination her emotions were strangely ambivalent, and she felt some trepidation to make a move from the safe sanctuary of the railway compartment into the unfamiliar world of Peking. Already her new friends of two and a half days made her think rather differently of her life. She was feeling a sense of loneliness at parting from them.

Chuang Tsu was excited; she hummed as she tied up her boxes to make a quick getaway to her daughter. She gave covert glances at the seated Liang Feng and the Browns pulling their luggage down from the overhead bunk. With no luggage other than the sleeping bag tied securely to her back, Liang Feng tightened her hold on the little cloth bag in her hand. She wanted to speak to the Browns before they left. She had liked their company and desired future contact. Even Chuang Tsu, whom she had regarded at the beginning of the journey as sometimes being obnoxious, had turned out to be kind and helpful. Chuang Tsu had really blossomed out in the fold of the compartment, becoming a gracious hostess generously feeding all her new friends. Her attitude to foreigners too had undergone a change. There was admiration for Donald which she expressed in the smiles she was giving him. Donald's gesture in carrying her bag had made him a hero in her eyes. Though she could not understand a word of what they spoke, she had watched them with a smile on her face. Chuang Tsu had given Liang Feng admiring glances whenever she spoke the English tongue.

"East is Red", the song Liang Feng had heard throughout the journey, was being played again over the loudspeakers in the station. Brown opened the door of the carriage and pushed out his suitcase. Liang Feng felt a pang of sadness in the knowledge that in a few minutes those links that she had forged would be broken. Two and a half days of sharing the compartment had endeared them all to her.

It was a surprise to her when Chuang Tsu, standing and surveying her seated figure, said kindly,

"Liang Feng, you are alone in Peking. It is a large city and you can get lost here easily."

Taking a deep breath, she continued,

"Why don't you stay the night with me and go to your relation's tomorrow?"

Taken aback at the unexpected invitation, Liang Feng hesitated. How could she make up her mind so quickly? The sight of Donald and Sally Brown preparing to leave the train pushed her to a decision.

"Thank you, Chuang Tsu; your invitation is very welcome," Liang Feng replied.

She realised she was no longer bothered about Chuang Tsu having any party connections. She did not fear reprisals as she herself did not have any questionable political ideologies. She had accepted the System with enthusiasm. She was relieved she knew at least one individual from among the four million inhabitants of Peking. This was more important to her at the present moment than waiting to find out whether she was amongst friends or foes.

It moved her to see Donald patiently waiting for Chuang Tsu to get off from the train, in order to speak to her.

He said,

"Liang Feng, it was pleasant to have your company on this journey, though those ear-piercing revolutionary songs wracked my nerves." Then taking her hand he said,

"I hope we'll meet again".

There was a twinkle in his eyes,

"It was superb getting all that information on China."

She smiled, looking at his open friendly face. Her heart was heavy at the thought that this new link of friendship was coming to an end at the railway station. Concealing her emotion she said lightly,

"I enjoyed practicing my English on you."

They stood on the platform. These friends of a brief encounter were reluctant to leave each other's company. Donald, already looking quite lost in the new surroundings, expressed his worries,

"I really don't know which way to go with all these signs in Chinese. I do hope someone has come to meet us." His eyes anxiously searched the crowd for a representative of the British Embassy.

Liang Feng was happy to put off the moment of parting and lingered with the group.

Chuang Tsu once again came to their rescue. On discovering the reason for Brown's helpless expression, she took the situation under control. Becoming the Good Samaritan, she instantly expressed her intention to hail a taxi which could take Donald to his destination. When Chuang Tsu's message was conveyed to Donald, he smiled with relief and thanked Chuang Tsu profusely. Beaming with confidence at this appreciation, words she could not understand, Chuang Tsu walked briskly across the road to the taxi stand. She was full of self-importance as evidenced in the brisk steps she took. Beholden to Chuang Tsu for her benevolent attitude, Liang Feng smiled wryly. Chuang Tsu would not let go an opportunity of showing her skills as the Director of her Commune.

Chuang Tsu's self-importance was short-lived. An old Ford taxi screeched to a halt beside Donald. A bearded man got out and hastened towards the group calling out Donald's name and paying scant attention to the crowds observing him. The newcomer hugged Donald warmly and embraced Sally in welcome.

Pierre Devon was of similar height to Donald yet with his broad shoulders appeared much bigger. He had a closely trimmed beard which appeared almost black in the evening light. His hair was curly and brown. His high receding forehead gave him a philosopher's aloofness. His arms were still around Sally when he noticed Liang Feng's scrutiny. The foreigner's demonstrativeness was embarrassing Liang Feng. He released his hold and turned towards Liang Feng, his eyebrows lifted enquiringly. Donald saw that look and stepping forward said warmly,

"Pierre, you must meet Liang Feng who was my interpreter and guide on the train". His voice sharpened with enthusiasm,

"It was great to have her translating all that jargon they broadcast."

Feeling somewhat uncomfortable, Liang Feng smiled shyly. Donald did not stop at that. Assuming a superior and challenging air and looking directly into Pierre's eyes he exclaimed,

"I now have more information on China than most people."

Taking the hint, Pierre smiled at his friend. Donald had not changed in the years they had been apart. But that remark brought a rush of blood to Liang Feng's cheeks. Her face was burning hot. She did not wish Donald to disclose to strangers what she had divulged about her life in the commune. She had once got into trouble with Wang Lee for questioning the new society's goals. Seeing her discomfited and understanding her embarrassment, Pierre stretched out his hand boldly and took her half-stretched hand.

Liang Feng found his clasp warm and comforting. Regaining her composure, she said in greeting "Nii hao" to which Pierre responded with "Nii hao."

Donald stared at his friend with amazement as he continued to speak in Chinese,

"I know very few Chinese ladies in Peking who speak English," Pierre said.

Liang Feng's eyebrows lifted unbelievingly. His calm deep voice was pleasing to her ears. He spoke Chinese perfectly. Forgetting her earlier embarrassment and with a tinge of flippancy in her voice she said,

"I know of no foreigner who speaks Chinese as well as you do."

She continued to look at him forgetting the others in the group. Still holding her hand he said,

"I know just enough to get around."

Chuang Tsu had seen the arrival of the taxi from the other side of the road. She had also witnessed the warm exchange of greetings. She waited, hoping that the taxi and the stranger would depart as suddenly as they had arrived. There was disappointment on her face as the greetings were prolonged. Finally, when it dawned on her that the taxi and the stranger had come to take Brown and his wife to their destination, her shoulders drooped and her face turned sullen. Her hopes for a mission of goodwill were dashed. She had lost the opportunity to impress on the foreigners the benevolence of Chinese hospitality. Chuang Tsu walked back dejectedly to join the group, but stood as far away as possible from any intimacy. She glared at Pierre from time to time when he looked in her direction. Then she pretended to busy herself with her boxes lying around on the ground.

Chuang Tsu was now restless. She wanted to leave the group. She felt left out and tried to draw Liang Feng's attention with bold stares. Liang Feng however failed to notice these non-verbal communications. Added to the unhappiness at her situation, Chuang Tsu's legs were also beginning to give her trouble; she had not felt those irritating pains while in the train, nor had she felt the unbearable weight of her legs. She had been especially happy with a new feeling of wellbeing after Donald had carried her bags for her and shown so much kindness. Not able any longer to control her annoyance, she now interrupted, her voice harsh,

"Liang Feng, we have to get the bus before the sun goes down." Her voice hissed in Liang Feng's ears though she had tried to keep her voice low so that the bearded stranger who knew her language would not surmise her mood.

The crowd that had collected at the railway station had now dispersed, leaving only a few uniformed armed guards on the platform. Becoming aware of Chuang Tsu's impatience, Pierre left Liang Feng abruptly, calling out to the Browns to

40

board the taxi. The farewells were short and quick, and to Chuang Tsu's relief the foreigners were gone from her sight, and hopefully from her mind.

With mixed feelings Liang Feng watched the taxi leave. It had been a new experience for her to meet the Browns, and the unexpected encounter with Pierre was no less remarkable. They were different to the people she had met in the last three years.

She was pulled away from her reflections when Chuang Tsu shoved into her arms one of the boxes, and led the way out of the station. She meekly followed the older woman who, showing off her knowledge of the city, elbowed her way with determination through a stream of cyclists and pedestrians crowding the roads and pavements.

The city itself was a magnificent sight. Lining the sidewalks of the broad avenues were rows of young delicate trees planted with great care and encircled with iron grills. A sense of discipline and order dominated the scene. Even the litter bins, painted green, stood spaced at every hundred yards, a reminder to keep the city clean.

Chuang Tsu increased her pace. She was eager, after a lapse of many years, to see her daughter again. The earlier disappointment was forgotten and her thoughts were now occupied with her family. Her face breaking into a broad smile, she turned to her new friend.

"My daughter has been given an apartment in the new block built for workers," Chuang Tsu proclaimed grandly. There was pride in this disclosure of the privilege her family was enjoying.

Shi Kai Ying lived in a block of apartments in Jianguamen Wai Avenue in the city. As they hurried towards it along Jianguamen Wai Avenue, through crowds of blue-clad workers, Liang Feng was surprised to see many foreign nationals walking among the local population. Her thoughts lingered on Pierre Devon. Pierre had held her hand warmly in a firm hand of friendship. She was happy he had spoken to her in her own language. In fact this had established a sense of intimacy between them, from which even Donald and Sally had been left out.

Liang Feng smiled to herself but soon her thoughts were interrupted when Chuang Tsu whispered in her ear.

"I wrote to my daughter I was coming to see her but she did not have the courtesy to reply." There was some anxiety in her voice. Liang Feng was unable to offer any reassurance and therefore sought a change of subject. She desired to know more about her new friend and suddenly remembered the railway clerk in Canton. She asked cautiously,

"Chuang Tsu, you did seem to know the railway clerk in Canton, is he a friend?"

This question came as a shock to Chuang Tsu whose thoughts were now only of her daughter. She took a deep breath.

"Liang Feng, don't you worry your head about me. He is only a party worker who happened to visit the commune six months ago."

Then in an attempt to quell any uneasiness that could arise from this disclosure, she laughed warmly.

"Liang Feng, I began to like you when, on the train, you translated to me what the foreigner said in English."

Liang Feng smiled back but there were many answers she was keen to obtain from her new benefactress. She reminded herself of how she had been warmed by Chuang Tsu's gracious invitation at a time when she had been feeling lonely amongst the new faces in the crowded station. Further, her preoccupation with the Browns and Pierre was such that it helped her to put aside any suspicions of Chuang Tsu's intentions. She dismissed quickly from her thoughts all unwarranted speculation.

She was eagerly looking forward to her new job in Peking. She reassured herself that there was no reason to fear Chuang Tsu. She herself was as politically important as Chuang Tsu.

As they neared their destination, rows of newly built brick apartments rose ambitiously to the sky. Liang Feng's eyes shone with pride on noticing the modern comforts for the people. The aspirations of the people themselves would rise with improved conditions she thought. Yet material comforts alone were not enough. She did not want any political party or any one particular class to gain dominance over the others as in the past. She desired a brand of communism which believed in greater individual freedom. Chairman Mao had uttered the prophetic words,

"The struggle between the Proletariat and the Bourgeoisie has not really been settled; the class struggle has to continue". Yet she knew that with such a struggle, innocent people too would have to suffer and sacrifice like her grandparents. When those fears were expressed, Chairman Mao had offered a philosophical explanation,

"Great storms are not to be feared".

Liang Feng gazed in admiration at the picturesque city. The rumblings of the impending storm were remote in such a benign landscape.

Peking unfolded itself in magnificent splendour before her eyes. Curved roofs in the traditional architecture of China were silhouetted against the light of the setting sun. The celestial globe of the old observatory was a reminder to countless dreamers like her, as it had been to the astronomers of the past centuries, of the closeness of heaven. For 600 years it had stood invincible in its splendid isolation within its stone fortifications.

Like a gentle waterfall a sense of tranquillity bathed the streets stretching across the city – north to south and east to west. For three thousand years the city had existed and withstood many storms. Such storms could reoccur, as Liang Feng, familiar with China's history, was aware. However, to her the iron grills encircling the newly planted evergreens were a symbol of protective forces, keeping away the destructive effects of such storms. The storms of agitation may fan the atmosphere, but would not be allowed to destroy the foundations. Liang Feng's renewed faith in the Chairman and his philosophy gave her the belief that China and its people were an indestructible power.

Gazing upon the scene, her eyes were drawn once again to the evergreen tree. She could not help but see that the delicate trees, dwarfed against the high rise buildings, were helpless and vulnerable.

Walking along beside Chung Tsu, Liang Feng's mind was full of China's destiny. She was almost startled to be pulled back to the present by her companion. They had reached their destination. Before them were identical rows of newly built apartments that displayed no characteristics of the traditional architecture of China. Outside the Chienkuo gate was an area where all architectural links with the past had been firmly severed. The apartments were of brick construction, block beyond block, monotonous in their uniformity. Between the blocks were narrow open strips displaying barren sandy grey soil.

Chuang Tsu led Liang Feng to Apartment Block 6, and they began the climb to the fourth floor. Chuang Tsu was breathless and panting heavily, more due to excitement than physical exertion. Within her there was trepidation at the thought of meeting her daughter who, by not acknowledging her letter, had become a stranger.

The two women had now reached the door of Apartment 41. Chuang Tsu hesitantly rang the bell, but there was no answer. Her face became stern and she insistently kept her finger pressed on the bell, its shrill ringing tone jarring to the ears.

When there was still no response from within, she became apprehensive and looked appealingly at Liang Feng as if seeking reassurance. Liang Feng was strangely moved to see the formidable Deputy Director of a commune now reduced to a worried and helpless middle-aged woman.

The piercing sound of the bell had some effect; the door to the adjoining apartment was opened by a female, face frowning in annoyance. She was middle aged, her greying hair tied in a bun at the nape of her neck, wearing the conventional black pyjamas of the older generation. Scrutinising the anxious face of the offending visitor, her eyes expressed recognition and her face softened. Her enquiry was to the point,

"Are you Shi Kai Yin's mother?"

Chuang Tsu nodded, her own expression stern again, as habitually. The woman's tone was apologetic.

"Your daughter and son-in-law are attending a political meeting and left this key for you."

She pulled out a key from the folds of her pyjama pocket and offered it humbly to Chuang Tsu, who however could not conceal her hurt and anger. Grabbing the key from the woman's hand she began a tirade of abuse concerning the ingratitude of children.

The neighbour noiselessly shuffled back into her own apartment and hurriedly closed the door, leaving Liang Feng outside waiting patiently for Chuang Tsu to have her say.

With a depleted audience, Chuang Tsu's fuel was soon exhausted. She opened the door and walked in followed by Liang Feng. Chuang Tsu's head was throbbing painfully and she was beginning to lose control again.

"This is not a welcome a mother should receive," she grumbled. But a quick survey of the room brought a completely different reaction.

The apartment was impressive. Though small, it was modern in its amenities. There was a pleasant living room, two small bedrooms with a kitchen at the further end. A white bust of Chairman Mao took pride of place on the centre of the main table in the living room. The grey walls were brightened by large new posters, the glossy red letters of their slogans adding a splash of colour to them. Her disappointment completely forgotten, Chuang Tsu unceremoniously laid her boxes on the table and sailed into a bedroom, her eyes appraising the comforts.

Ignoring her friend standing mutely in the room still holding a box, Chuang Tsu walked around, taking in everything. Her curiosity finally satisfied, she was now keen to see the view from the fourth floor, never having lived in a high-rise building before. She now beckoned to Liang Feng, who, quietly laid her box down on the main table and walked across to the window to stand beside her friend who was pointing at an impressive large grey building opposite Block 6.

The building across the road was an older type of building converted to numerous large apartments – the entire structure grey concrete. In that neighbourhood of impersonalised monotony, this building stood aloof and distinctive, imposingly walled in, a large iron gate manned by a sentry. Liang Feng and Chuang Tsu were impressed by the official manner in which the guard at the gate interviewed and examined those who were entering the building.

After she had washed and settled in her room, Liang Feng went over in her mind the day's events. She was beginning to realise that she may have unwittingly been drawn into the clutches of a political group she had hitherto been unfamiliar with. She was sharing a room and sleeping in the same room as Chuang Tsu who may have had an ulterior motive in inviting her to her daughter's apartment.

These thoughts now puzzled and worried her. It was a shock for her to read the slogans on the apartment's walls. They were different to any she had seen before, not being quotations or political thoughts of the leader, Chairman Mao.

The new slogan read "It is an illusion that Collectivisation will lead to Agricultural Growth". This was contrary to Chairman Mao's theory which believed that Collectivisation was the key to mass participation and the mobilisation of a greater number of people for agricultural development. It was the Chairman's policy to encourage collectivisation in forming Peoples' Communes as opposed to the line of Liu Shaoqui which encouraged private markets and material incentives. Liang Feng was disturbed and angry. She was revolted by the slogan above her bed which read "Hired labour is justified for economic growth". In the last three years she had studied only Chairman Mao's 'Thoughts' and she was not prepared now to accept anything contrary. She did not like this new twist to her dream of a perfect communist state. Her anger turned on the new politburo that was attempting to restore capitalism once again behind the back of Chairman Mao

She lay down on the narrow hard bed and tried to relax; but the loud posters surrounding her, in that enclosed space with the windows closed, threatened her peace of mind. On this, her first night in Peking, she could not sleep – she felt suffocated. Her enthusiasm for a new life in Peking had suddenly gone sour. In the darkness of the night she made a futile effort to analyse her doubts and fears, but she was afraid. The whispers of her colleagues who foresaw a new revolution, hints of opposition to Chairman Mao's 'Communism' – she had not taken them seriously before, but their meaning was now becoming a reality to her. Her own desire had been for more individual freedom for law abiding citizens like herself, as against the present party cadre domination.

The overpowering thought in her mind now was to get away from Chuang Tsu as soon as dawn appeared. Her longing for that grandaunt she had never seen was now overwhelming – more so because she felt her peace was now threatened. Her own weakness at having tolerated Chuang Tsu was distasteful to her. She watched with sullen anger the reclining shadow of Chuang Tsu in the adjoining bed. All the speculation which darkness evokes in a stranger's home was now gathering momentum in her troubled mind. She saw Chuang Tsu as the sinister counter revolutionary sneaking into Peking to undermine Chairman Mao's revolution. She felt betrayed by this new friendship.

The solace of sleep eluded her as the hours dragged by. The night seemed painfully long. However, as the soft light of dawn entered the room through the chinks in the windows her tension eased off and her surroundings took on a different perspective. Chuang Tsu, snoring in her sleep, her body bulky and helpless under the sheet, seemed pathetic and even comical.

Liang Feng smiled at the fears that had kept her awake. Dismissing them from her mind, she relaxed on the bed, as she snuggled on to the soft cushiony pillow.

As the welcome shadows of sleep drifted over her, thoughts of Pierre and Donald brought back a renewed feeling of hope that individual freedom, the kind of freedom most familiar to her spirit, would become a reality. There was sadness that her association with the foreigners had come to such a quick end. But as her eyes closed in slumber the last thought in her conscious mind was that perhaps she would meet them again.

CHAPTER 6

The Committee Members

Liang Feng opened the window. The morning air was fresh and cool as it touched her face. The nightmarish confusion of images that had troubled her in the night now seemed unreal, and the nagging doubts concerning Chuang Tsu were submerged by the memory of the vulnerable and rather comical picture she had unconsciously presented while asleep. She felt that her anxieties had, in the night, assumed exaggerated proportions due to her fatigue and perhaps even more due to the shock of seeing the sacrilegious posters. The revelation that there existed individuals who were cleverly side tracking the all-embracing communist goal which the Chairman was seeking to achieve, had been a shattering experience.

However, looking now at the scene outside through the open window and seeing a new society meticulously built over the relics of the old, her heart felt pacified. With the dawn of a new day and the expectations of a new career, her mind was eager to cast aside stifling doubts about Chuang Tsu. She was more excited about embarking on a new life in Peking.

New apartments crowded the landscape and many more were in the process of being built. Construction workers had resumed their work as usual at the break of dawn. Yet in contrast to all this modernisation in the city of Peking there still remained, visible to her window on the fourth floor, broken down dilapidated houses down small obscure lanes. They were the remnants of the feudal past clinging pathetically to a modern setting. There had been a time when magnificent abodes befitting the grandeur of the city overlooked and overpowered the cringing people living in their shadow. Liang Feng's eyes darkened with memories, remembering her own family home in Jakarta and the insecurity of living among those who had fled China at the time of the civil wars. She had heard them speak of going back some day to the motherland when the good old days returned. But since her return she had not heard of China's peaceful and prosperous past from any of her colleagues. Under their influence she herself had begun to associate the unsightly sights of the country with the past. Now as she gazed at the view, she only saw orderliness, with the lives of the citizens regulated by the state, the basic needs of life given to enable them to live in dignity. The city had abandoned all forms of night life, as had been done in the whole country since the Revolution. Her eyes, responsive to the harmonious order, rested gently on the old woman leading a group of tiny tots on an educational outing.

This order she now witnessed had been criticised by her grandfather who would sneer at the rigid lifestyle of the people of the new China. The old man had spoken proudly of the freedom he enjoyed in Jakarta; but she had often been critical of this freedom. In her opinion he abused it in order to make money. She had seen corruption and class distinction existing side by side in that atmosphere of freedom.

A new feeling of pride swept over her. She believed the Revolution of 1949 had ushered in an era of happiness for the majority of her people. Chairman Mao was courageously guiding them into the modern era. The needy of her country now received a measure of care and kindness not experienced before. Her friends in Canton had mentioned that the Chairman desired to grant the workers and peasants more participation in the country's political life. These reflections were interrupted with Chuang Tsu's sudden appearance.

Chuang Tsu stood by the door; her stern face seemed indifferent to Liang Feng's welcoming smile.

In the clarity of the morning sunlight she had lost the bouncing joviality displayed in the train. It was not only her manner that had changed; her clothes were also different. She was clad in a suit, manly in style and buttoned neatly down from collar to waist giving her an official air, her dress befitting her status as the Deputy Director of the Red Flag Brigade of Canton. The friendly benevolent Chuang Tsu who had entertained her friends seemed a person of the past. After clearing her throat she spoke stiffly,

"A message has arrived for both of us to report to the committee of the commune!"

Liang Feng stared accusingly at Chuang Tsu, forcing her to lower her eyes. The misgivings Liang Feng had nursed the night before rushed back to her mind, the air in the room seemed to suffocate her. The loathsome posters staring at her from the walls had taken on gigantic proportions. All the doubts regarding Chuang Tsu's political beliefs now returned.

Although grateful for Chuang Tsu's help, Liang Feng was stunned into anger by the invasion of her privacy. Her voice was cold in angry accusation,

"I thought my visit was unplanned."

Chuang Tsu's response was immediate,

"Nothing goes unplanned here."

According to her the matter was settled and she strode out of the room, flinging back an instruction,

"You had better make your way to the ground floor, that's where the washrooms are!"

Liang Feng muttered to herself, her voice thick with bitterness and resentment,

"I can see that everything is planned, even her kindness has a motive."

Her present dependence on Chuang Tsu brought tears of frustration into her eyes. There was an overpowering desire to escape from the apartment. She blamed herself; the momentary loneliness in the train when watching the Browns leave had driven her to accepting Chuang Tsu's unexpected invitation.

Now remembering the British couple and their natural warmth and openness, Chuang Tsu's behaviour appeared not only unpredictable lacking in frankness. It was that very same manner of behaviour in her husband, Wang Lee, which had alienated her. It had made communication with him difficult during their brief time together. Gazing stonily out of the window, the orderly scene below her was now flawed in her eyes; the docile manner in which her countrymen were getting about their work had become an irritant. Angry words came to her mind.

"They have no visions of their own. They speak out only what THEY want them to say," was all that she could say to the blank wall. However, her annoyance now in control, the feelings towards Chuang Tsu softened and she tried to reason out under her breath,

"Why should I blame her, the controls of the system make her act officially towards me?".

With these thoughts Liang Feng found her way down to the washrooms. At the entrance a group of women, their faces showing hostility at seeing a stranger, blocked her path. Plucking up courage, Liang Feng greeted them with a friendly "Nii hao", but there was no friendly response. But, as if to compensate for their rudeness, some children shyly peeping from behind their mothers chorused, "Nii hao," not just once but many times. The women seemed to relax and they burst out laughing.

A voice from the group cautiously enquired,

"Are you an overseas Chinese?"

Liang Feng sighed, not surprised at being taken for an alien. It exasperated her to be thus isolated and in a loud voice she answered,

"I am as good a citizen of the People's Republic of China as you all are," and then laughed shakily.

The silent hostility of the women was checked and their laughter accompanied hers.

But there were questions put to her before they showed acceptance. Liang Feng herself summoned up the courage to ask,

"Why do you not like us new arrivals?"

They were quick to respond. One said disapprovingly,

"They are unfriendly and are critical of our life here." Another blurted,

"We feel they want to maintain the class distinction." A voice said angrily,

"Some even despise manual work." Liang Feng had heard enough to realise that they all disliked the so-called, under attack 'bourgeois revisionism' of the new arrivals. Her experience in Canton had made her aware of such criticism.

Sensing an audience who would be receptive, Liang Feng conversed with them while attending to her ablutions, trying to convince them of her willingness to share their way of life. She found the women gradually becoming more and more relaxed with her.

Chuang Tsu's arrival in the washrooms broke up the discussion. Taking leave of her new acquaintances, Liang Feng hastily followed her, noticing how stiffly she walked, her round shoulders set in military rigidity. Before long the two women were entering the Commune Committee Room situated on the ground floor.

On the wall facing the entrance dominating the room were two massive portraits, one of the Chairman and the other of President Lieu Shaoqui; one alongside the other. This was an ironic reminder of their past partnership in building the 'New Nation'. Seated at the long narrow table were the officials who stood up to welcome them. The new welcome was warm and cordial as they were shown to their seats, and as customary on such an occasion one of the men poured hot water from the flask into the mugs which had been kept ready with tea leaves in them; and these were passed round to the guests and the Committee. Once the greetings had been formally exchanged the Committee got down to business.

Clearing his throat one of the officials who had been studying Liang Feng for some minutes said,

"We are given information that you have been sent here to further serve the progress of our Revolution."

This came as a surprise to Liang Feng; all she knew was that she had been selected to work in the Foreign Languages Institute because of her knowledge of foreign languages. Furthermore the train journey and the invigorating experience of meeting new personalities had removed temporarily her preoccupation with the revolutionary cause. For a moment her mind lingered on Donald Brown whose disposition had stimulated her to pour out her thoughts without undue inhibitions. A slight but a deliberate cough by the speaker pulled her back to the present to reply in a low voice, "Yes". The guilt that flooded her mind immediately was not due so much to the passive acceptance of the role thrust on her but more to the uncertainty regarding her ability to fulfil what would be expected of her.

Suddenly there poured into the room through the open window the tremulous treble of children's voices, guided by an adult voice singing "Homage to our great leader Chairman Mao." Liang Feng stiffened to attention till the song ended, as did the others in the room. With a surge of pride Liang Feng gazed at the portrait of the Chairman, her eyes drawn to the quotation engraved below the picture, "Serve the People and fight Self Interest". These words revived her spirit to serve the motherland. Her voice now deep with conviction she spoke out,

"I fervently hope the new reforms of Chairman Mao will benefit the people."

Those at the table looked uneasily at each other and Chuang Tsu burst out in laughter, with the others soon following her example. Surprised and hurt, Liang Feng stared at the group. She had only uttered words which had come naturally to her. Had not her colleagues in Canton repeatedly said to her,

"Chairman Mao desires a greater participation within the party hierarchy for workers and peasants?" She was distressed and disturbed that her reference to him should cause such amusement.

Chuang Tsu's laughter ceased abruptly and her eyes keenly looked at Liang Feng, a soft smile of pity playing on her lips.

Recovering his composure, the oldest of the three men said in a serious voice,

"What better deal do you want for the people, are they not content now?"

The cynicism in his voice and the obvious interest of the others prompted Liang Feng to retort in righteous defence of Chairman Mao,

"As the Chairman says, the time has come to concentrate one's fire in the exposure and criticism of those party persons in authority taking the capitalist road."

For a moment there were no visible sign of reaction from the Committee. The subject was cleverly ignored; assuming an amicable tone, the previous speaker said,

"You are a good communist; we have received excellent reports of your loyalty to Chairman Mao."

Chung Tsu remained silent, quietly studying Liang Feng. The Committee was clearly staggered by Liang Feng's undaunted support for the Chairman and now became precise in their questioning.

"Have you read President Lieu Shaoqui's 'Self Cultivation by Communists'?"

In fact the contents of that book were fresh in her mind because they had sparked off an argument with Wang Lee, and she said with conviction,

"Yes, I read it and once fervently believed in the 'Great Harmony' when all humanity would consist of unselfish, intelligent, skilled and highly cultured Communists."

These words obviously created a good reaction. An official spoke enthusiastically,

"We can still achieve this."

As if no interruption had occurred, Liang Feng continued with the words of Chairman Mao,

"From ancient times people who wanted an idealist state never succeeded because they were from the exploiting class and did not include the workers in such a society".

The Committee did not show displeasure at the answer, but glances were exchanged amongst them, and the next question seemed challenging,

"Do you suggest that there is Revisionism in our society?"

This was a tricky question to answer. It was only in Peking and in particular in Shi Kai Ying's apartment that a suggestion of Revisionism had crossed her mind. The posters on the wall had suggested the benefits of an incentive economy, and now, remembering once again Chuang Tsu's puzzling and disappointing behaviour, her voice was tremulous in accusation,

"I am convinced there is a group advocating a return to Capitalism and exploiting the weaker in society."

There was a stir of surprise amongst the Committee except from Chuang Tsu, who awkwardly shifted her gaze to seemingly study the table.

The next question was unexpected,

"Do you believe in a continuous Revolution?"

This was the first occasion in her new country when Liang Feng had been directly questioned on her political views and it disturbed her. Though she had been enthusiastic about the system, its novelty was wearing off, giving space to a growing interest in the study of China's past history. A new preoccupation had been kindled within her since her association with the Browns and since she had begun to seek individual freedom.

These forces, together with the doubts of Chuang Tsu's loyalty to Chairman Mao, prompted her to reply,

"Yes, I do, if there is injustice in our society."

The belief that 'Hired Labour is justified for Economic Growth' was, in her opinion, damning to the achievement of the Communist goal. The reaction to her reply was one of stunned silence, as the officials stared at her intent and angry face.

Chuang Tsu now broke her silence, and in a voice which sounded tired and sad asked,

"Then do you support the idea of 'constant revolution?'"

The weariness of Chuang Tsu's voice distressed Liang Feng, her sympathy overriding her suspicion. Yet, remembering the older woman's coldness that morning, she was afraid to reveal the softening of her feelings lest they again be carelessly treated. Turning expressionlessly towards the portrait of Chairman Mao, Liang Feng said quietly,

"Yes, I do believe in it if it can correct any existing wrongs in the society. Chuang Tsu winced as if in pain.

Uneasy at the disturbance her statements had created, Liang Feng said in forced lightheartedness,

"I believe as Chairman Mao does, that questions of ideology and controversial issues among the people should be settled by the democratic methods; by discussion, persuasion and criticism." These words, she hoped, would alleviate the unrest she had created.

Her objective was achieved and the associations of civil wars and bloodshed temporarily forgotten, but not before one official cynically said,

"I hope the ordinary masses are as enlightened as Chairman Mao in understanding these profound concepts."

The cross examination was over and there was a feeling of relief in Liang Feng that she had frankly expressed her views, especially after the night of fear and speculation. She was concerned that the Committee should be aware of the dangers in reviving the feudal practices again. With that weight off her mind she could look forward to her life in Peking. It was however difficult to make out what the Committee thought of her as they nonchalantly sat around sipping their tea.

Liang Feng was now restless to leave and the others seemed to sense this. The chief official looked directly at her.

"We have been in touch with the Foreign Languages Institute about your new job, but since the establishment is undergoing some changes, you will be suitably placed in another opening."

Liang Feng was visibly upset; she had looked forward to her work, and now unhappily she gazed at the speaker hoping he would clarify his words.

He continued,

"The authorities feel you should serve better working with foreign nationals in Waichia Talou."

This news was unexpected yet there was relief. Gladness flooded her mind at the remembrance of Donald and Sally Brown and their friend she had met at the station. Chuang Tsu had given her a detailed report of Waichia Talou the night before. She believed they could be located there, being the residential quarters of foreign personnel and embassy staff. The smile on her face caused an official to say,

"We see that you have accepted this sudden change with gladness, like a good loyal Communist."

But unfortunately these words reminded her of clashes with Wang Lee who had repeatedly criticised her for being a bad Communist. She had disagreed with Wang Lee's slavish devotion to the propaganda of the authorities. She remembered how she had tried to overcome her rebelliousness with a fervent devotion to Chairman Mao and his doctrine. She had welcomed the trip to Peking, hoping that she would at least catch a glimpse of the Chairman. Conscious of the group's scrutiny, she smiled demurely and remained silent.

The knowledge of her new appointment had caused a change of heart towards Chuang Tsu who was broodingly studying her. Ignoring her unfriendly behaviour, Liang Feng poured hot water from the flask into Chuang Tsu's cup. A committee member suddenly spoke out rather patronisingly,

"What did the Englishman tell you about our country?"

She felt betrayed. Anger and fear took hold of her. Had she exposed herself to suspicion by speaking to a foreigner? The entire group seemed to wait for her answer.

She did not want to disclose Donald Brown's frank comments. He had been kind and courteous both to Chuang Tsu and herself. In fact the honesty of his statements had appealed to her. Her reply was guarded.

"The Englishman was full of praise for the new changes in our country."

Those words had their desired effect on the three men, and they began to speak approvingly of 'good foreigners'.

Yet within her there was resentment about being cross-examined and treated with suspicion. The conversations between Donald Brown and herself had been spontaneous, though some of the foreigner's sarcastic opinions had upset her. However, in no way could such views brand him as a trouble-maker.

With renewed doubts and even bitterness Liang Feng stared at Chuang Tsu, whose relaxed face now revealed no hostility to her. She could not trust Chuang Tsu's smile, knowing it was she who had reported all that had taken place in the train. What a relief that at least Chuang Tsu could not understand the language they had spoken, Liang Feng thought.

Refusing to respond to Chuang Tsu's smile of appeasement, Liang Feng recollected with bitterness the incidents when Wang Lee had treated her in a similar manner. These incidents had been the reason she had lost confidence in him. Wang Lee had driven her to conceal her emotions and become secretive. She had despised his cold, unfeeling mind that was gradually killing her warm nature. Liang Feng had been unconsciously trained by him to be wary and cautious and that was why, on this occasion, she was able to say what the officials wanted to hear and not reveal her true self. She felt hostile to those in the room who had questioned her political views.

Suddenly Liang Feng wanted to get away from those people and from all those like them. She yearned to be in a place free from unjustified suspicion. A flash of relief swept through her as she remembered her grandaunt, living in the suburbs of Peking. She cautiously asked the committee,

"Before I start my new work, can I please visit my grandaunt in the country?"

She was unprepared for their reaction. They were full of praise.

"It is good for young people to be concerned about the old and to learn how people live in the country."

The bitterness Liang Feng had built against them crumbled. Yet she felt at a loss. She could not understand her own feelings. Faced with this inner conflict her mind sought Chairman Mao's guidance, and within seconds a familiar saying of his came to her which her lips gravely uttered,

"Resolute and unafraid of sacrifice we will surmount every difficulty to win victory."

The committee's smile of approval froze.

Liang Feng wondered whether she had again said the wrong thing. If they had been merely amused she would have quoted further from 'The Little Red Book' to convince them of the truth of Chairman Mao's philosophy. But she was now filled with self-doubt and confusion on realising that the entire group were observing her with compassion. Their pity unnerved her and she was relieved when Chuang Tsu, almost as if discerning her bewilderment, said gently,

"I think it is time we left; Liang Feng is still tired after the long journey."

Liang Feng silently followed Chuang Tsu out of the room, dazed by what had taken place. She despised herself for being open to mockery. It was a solace to feel the cool breeze on her burning cheeks; only the elements of nature were comprehensible to her. She took in a deep breath of fresh air, then gratefully breathed out, feeling the tension being released out of her.

Chuang Tsu accompanied her back to the apartment. Her smiling face and casual conversation did not betray her inner thoughts and her kindliness was in marked contrast to the mask of aloofness she had worn that morning. On being told of Liang Feng's intention of leaving immediately for her grandaunt's village, she purchased some delicacies for Liang Feng to have on the way.

Back in the apartment, Chung Tsu quietly assisted Liang Feng in preparing for the journey. The young woman was baffled by this kindness and touched by the concern, and when the moment of parting arrived, she impulsively took Chuang Tsu's preferred hand between both her own, pressing it in gratitude. Followed by the older woman, she walked down the steps of the apartment block to the public highway. From there she set off alone, turning back once to wave at Chuang Tsu who raised her hand in farewell, a thoughtful expression in her eyes.

Chuang Tsu's heart was heavy to part from her new friend, yet she could not understand Liang Feng's eagerness to uphold Chairman Mao's line of thought. She had herself come a long way from the days of the 1949 Revolution to hold the position of Deputy Director of the Red Flag Brigade in Canton. With the passage of time her zeal to uphold the Revolution's ideals had gradually waned. Although ashamed to admit it aloud, she was now weary of a frugal life style which concentrated only on the bare necessities for living, allowing no indulgences whatsoever. Like many of her friends, she too coveted quality items such as foreign-made wristwatches and imported clothes. Hoping for some reforms in the economic set-up, she welcomed President Lieu Shaoqui's new economic policy which encouraged to some extent a move from collective to individual enterprise, by allowing a system of 'private holdings'. In these holdings, or enclosures of land within the communes, the residents were able to carry on private farming and animal husbandry, deriving from their labours a cherished private income.

In contrast, the Chairman's call for self-discipline and constant vigilance against self-surrender to temptations associated with Revisionism was irksome to her, as it stood in the way of those who wanted to 'get on in life'. Chuang Tsu could not tolerate 'lazy' people as she chose to call those who did not show ambition to better themselves. Her own expertise had been gladly given to those who believed in self-improvement. With the welcoming reforms of President Lieu Shaoqui's profit-making schemes she desired to encourage her friends and family to pursue such a policy.

This visit to Peking was motivated not only by a desire to visit her daughter, but by a definite mission – to propagate her views. Being aware of the conflicts between Chairman Mao and President Liu Shaoqui, she was apprehensive that her hopes for a better future would be doomed by open clashes between them.

Her admiration for Liang Feng was genuine, but her heart was wrung with pity that the young woman did not have the correct insight to the present situation – a deficiency which to her was the result of a lack of experience. She sadly reminisced,

"Liang Feng knows only of the glorious aspects of the Revolution, not of the ugly side of death and deprivation." She walked back to the apartment, her mind preoccupied with thoughts of Liang Feng rather than of her own daughter whom she still had to meet.

Liang Feng however, walking down the road, was feeling a relief not only to leave but to put behind her remembrances of the interview with the committee. Her mind went back to Donald Brown and his amusement when she had quoted Chairman Mao's thoughts to him. Now her own people had laughed at her zeal for the Chairman's teachings. She wondered sadly whether her enthusiasm would waver under such mockery.

The sight of the city with its tree-lined avenues revived her fallen spirits. The city pulsated with life under a fierce red sun burning in a clear autumn sky. Red balloons and banners fluttered gaily in the breeze and the russet coloured roofs of the 'Forbidden City' gleamed brightly. Red was the dominant colour all around – its glory even echoed by the loudspeakers playing 'East is Red', and the melody vibrated on every pore of those in the vicinity.

There was a sense of freedom in the air she breathed, as she strolled along the vast Tiananmen Square. Alive to the constant clamour within her for individual freedom, she could not hold back the knowledge that there were those who had, before the Revolution, led lives of misery in lowly dwellings which had congested the area where the Square now stood. Their hovels had long been demolished and the freedom and pleasures the Square now offered made no distinction between the rich and the poor.

The atmosphere was festive. Already the rehearsals for the October Day Celebrations had begun and youngsters in khaki uniform were practicing military drill. Enjoying the sights, like herself, were groups of visitors, many of whom she recognised as Chinese from overseas. Many of them appeared hesitant as they studied the scene while staying close to their kinsmen guiding them along, their wide open eyes revealing amazement at the progress the nation had made after the Revolution. Yet there were others who displayed uncertainty in accepting the new way of life that would accompany this progress.

Suddenly Liang Feng realised that in her pride and happiness to be in Tiananmen Square she had almost forgotten her visit to her grandaunt. Seeing a crowded bus, only a few being available to the people, she hurriedly clambered on it. Packed above capacity with passengers, the bus swerved along, turning away from Jianguamen Wai heading towards the western suburb of Peking. It was along this route that her attention was drawn to the symmetry of the White Pagoda.

Partly hidden by a cluster of trees, Bai Ta, the famous landmark in Peking, rose majestically above the city scene. The bright red plaque on the upper part of the dome added to the mystery of the structure. Eyes shining with enthusiasm, Liang Feng exclaimed to a fellow passenger, a middle aged woman standing beside her and, like her, holding on to the rail,

"Isn't that a beautiful sight?"

The woman did not speak and seemed indifferent both to the sight and to Liang Feng's enthusiasm. The pagoda was stirring within Liang Feng a flood of memories of her life in Jakarta. She was reminded of temples she had visited there, but none had so enthralled or moved her as this.

Unable to contain her joy she instantly turned again to her neighbour.

"Are people allowed to visit that pagoda?" she enquired.

Surprised by this show of undue enthusiasm, the woman studied her carefully before giving an answer,

"Yes, people can visit the pagoda but are forbidden to use it as a place of worship."

Beneath the unemotional tone of her voice Liang Feng detected a tinge of remorse. The woman however seemed to be impressed by the stranger's keenness and curiosity in a subject which was obviously considered to be taboo. Evidently, the topic was something a citizen would fear to speak about. She murmured,

"You certainly are new in this part of the country." Liang Feng merely smiled, her mind still dwelling on the pagoda. Seeing an opportunity to offer some advice to a fellow citizen, and conscious of her civic responsibilities, the woman said,

"That pagoda was built in 1651 during the Chang Dynasty to commemorate the Dalai Lama's visit to Peking."

As the woman proceeded with further information, Liang Feng listened with fascination to the past history of her country. But very soon this information, given with a sense of pride, came to an abrupt end when the woman realised that there were other silent listeners displaying an interest in the conversation. Suddenly with her tone changing to one of derision, she said,

"What is the use of religion if it does not serve the people," and she looked at the others for their support. They were quick to join in the discussion and very soon religion had become the focus of critical condemnation.

Listening to their conversation, Liang Feng could not agree with what they said. The beauty of the pagoda moved her, enfolding her in a feeling of peace and tranquillity. It was making her forget her bitterness with Chuang Tsu and the committee. In Liang Feng's heart she knew the pagoda could help the people to forget the trials and tribulations of their daily life. In fact she herself was feeling its calming influence now.

The bus had left the city and was ambling along the uneven roads of the countryside. Liang Feng watched with a dawning sense of disappointment the grey and bare fields. The stretches of that barren landscape brought back again a fleeting sense of loneliness. This was not what she had expected when setting out from Chuang Tsu's apartment. The scenery became drab with no signs of any vitality. Solitary power looms stood like ominous ghosts in the centre of the grey fields. The atmosphere was stern and austere. The only touch of colour came from the red flags displayed on public buildings. New misgivings arose in Liang Feng as she viewed the passing scene. It was a different landscape that her father had described nostalgically when he had spoken of his childhood.

Liang Feng's grandaunt had decided to stay behind in China when the rest of the family left the country at the time of the Civil War. Unfortunately, her father was unable to, because of his illness to revisit his childhood home. In this drab scenery she could not envisage the kind of beautiful house he had described as being his family residence. The view from the window held no appeal for her.

In the present context she could not help being glad that her father had not returned to his village. Her own first glimpse of a suburb of Peking was not very heartening.

CHAPTER 7

Visiting Grandaunt

A narrow lane led to commune No. 303. The gravel path was dusty and uneven. Fields were on either side of the path and the greyness of the soil heightened the colourless scenery. The only inhabitants Liang Feng could see were a group of workers hoeing between rows of newly planted vegetables.

The workers had seen her. She observed them stopping their work and watching her without any show of friendliness or unfriendliness. The fact that she was a newcomer had not gone unnoticed in a place where strangers were a rare sight. She was compelled by their silent observation to walk up to them and dispel any doubts they had of her.

Making the first move she ventured,

"I am looking for the house of Wong Shu Cheng".

The workers showed surprise but, trying to keep a calm demeanour, they spoke in one voice,

"Do you know her?"

"Yes," was her hesitant reply.

Liang Feng said,

"She is my grandfather's sister."

Her reply ruffled them and, dropping their hoes, they surrounded her. Seeing the anger in their eyes she became nervous. They knew Wong Shu Cheng. They also knew she had no family to visit her. Wong Shu Chang lived all alone in the commune. Surprise had turned to suspicion and she felt menaced by their silence. A sharp voice from one member of the group demanded,

"Are you coming from another part of the country?"

Liang Feng hesitated and said,

"Yes, I am travelling from Kwang Yung Province".

Those words increased their hostile displeasure. Kwang Yung was too far for them, and they had not met a resident of that place in their lifetime. They, the workers, had never ventured beyond the commune. There had been no cause to motivate a visit to the capital. They could not think of anyone travelling from far off Canton, except for some urgent political work. Silent eyes scrutinised the stranger angrily. Though she was dressed differently and not in trousers, they could not identify her political affiliations.

The workers were aware of rumours circulating in the commune that a new Revolution had been launched by the Chairman with young people in the forefront. One woman in the group spoke hesitantly,

"We have heard that young people have embarked on a revolution and they are expected to arrive in Peking. Are you a revolutionary?"

Distressed, uncomfortable and taken aback at their unwarranted suspicion of her, Liang Feng retorted,

"I don't belong to any political group; I have come only to visit my grandaunt."

But they were not convinced so easily. There was still reason to doubt her words. Realising she had to provide them with a bona fide identification, she pulled out from her bag a photograph yellowed with age, and held it before them. Momentarily forgetting their suspicion, they gathered round her and peered at the photograph. A middle-aged, well-dressed woman sat on a chair holding a child on her lap, and another little boy stood by her. Identifying the face in the photograph one women exclaimed,

"I recognise the face of Wong Shu Cheng. She is much younger here, but she had the same proud face."

Turning to Liang Feng with new interest, the workers were apologetic for their behaviour and, with a show of friendliness, the woman who had recognised Wong Shu Cheng volunteered to accompany Liang Feng to her grandaunt's home.

Relieved that her grandaunt was still alive and evidently keeping well, Liang Feng went along silently, her mind full of emotions. The woman beside her was asking too many questions about her family and she was reluctant to answer. She recalled the cold reception she had received from Chung Tsu's commune members who had mistaken her for an overseas Chinese. She was short with her answers. Her father had described the house of her grandaunt with pride but what she was seeing were only poor peasant cottages huddled together on the roadside with no signs of the luxury she had visualised. Everything was grey amongst those houses – grey tiles and grey walls sadly bringing to her associations of poverty.

They arrived in a compound, where a group of men and women were seated on low wooden stools, relaxing in the afternoon sun. Some of the older men in the group were smoking cigars while the rest sipped tea. The house in the compound was so far the best Liang Feng had seen. Its roof was curved in the traditional design, tilting up at the corners, giving it an ornamental appearance. Unlike in the cottage, the grey-coloured bricks were well pressed. A veranda ran between the wooden pillars. The narrow centre door was kept closed while a curtain drawn across covered the glass panel of the door. The path to the house was paved with smooth stone slabs and large porcelain jars stood on either side with lilies growing in them.

A woman walked up to a member of the group; in a respectful voice she said,

"Ma Wampu, this is Liang Feng who has come all the way from Kwang Tung to see you." Liang Feng's eyes rested on the figure with interest. The woman was dressed in black silk trousers and a long-sleeved mandarin blouse. Her hair was grey and held at the back with a clip. There was dignity, even an arrogance in the manner in which she held herself. Not wanting to arouse suspicion, Liang Feng once again pulled out from her bag the photograph, and presented it to Wampu saying,

"You are my grandfather's sister."

In these new surroundings she wanted to be accepted without reservations and immediately by this member of the family. She lowered herself beside the stool and said,

"I have come to pay my respects to you."

Wampu, holding the photograph in her hands, was keenly inspecting it. Her face lit up with a smile. She was delighted to see a relative after so long. She had given up hope of ever meeting a member of her family. Her front gold teeth glistened as she smiled warmly at Liang Feng. She exclaimed,

"You are Cheng Po's daughter; I lost contact with the family after they left for Indonesia." The group surrounding Wampu were showing warm interest as Wampu recounted her family history. Feeling proud and excited, Wampu introduced her grandneice to the group.

"I am terminating the meeting early today," she said in a rather authoritative tone.

Turning to Liang Feng, her tone now softened, she continued,

"I have something to celebrate. My grandneice has come a long way to see her poor grandaunt."

The group clapped their hands showing their approval, and Wampu, rising slowly from her stool, clung on to Liang Feng's arm. They left the group with Wampu hobbling unsteadily down the road, holding firmly the arm of her relative.

They came to the old cottages Liang Feng had observed before. A crowd of children had followed her down the road. Suspicious of a stranger in the commune, the children stood staring with hostile eyes as Wampu and Liang Feng entered the compound of the house. Wampu raised her hand and shooed them away. They relaxed and giggled; they knew the stranger was acceptable, and waiting for Liang Feng to smile at them, they ran off.

Inside the house it was cold and dark. In the centre of the room was a small rectangular table on which the family photographs were placed. Liang Feng's eyes wandered around the room. The cottage walls were blank and held no photographs of the Chairman as in other homes she had seen in Canton. Wampu had gone straight to the kitchen and was preparing tea for her. Carrying a small flask back to the room, she poured water onto the tea placed in the cups. Liang Feng was curious to find out why Wampu had remained behind in China while the rest of the family left for Indonesia.

"Wampu, do you like this life of isolation?" she asked.

Wampu paused at her task and replied thoughtfully,

"I have lived alone since my youngest son left for Hong Kong ten years ago." She added quickly,

"I can manage alone; the people here are good to me."

There was pride in that disclosure although the voice trembled. Remembering the house and garden where Wampu had conducted the neighbourhood committee meeting, Liang Feng brought out once again the photograph and, looking at it carefully, murmured,

"Wampu, I can see a resemblance between the house in the photograph and the one I saw just now."

Wampu gave a short deep-throated laugh,

"You are clever. That was my family home before the revolutionaries took it over." She added thoughtfully,

"I'm glad I no longer own it – I have no headaches looking after it; I like to live like the rest of the people in this newly converted commune house."

After tea Wampu, holding Liang Feng by the hand, walked into a small inner room. She chuckled to herself as she made her way to the covered objects in the corner and removed the old mat that was on top. With twinkling mischievous eyes she lifted the embroidered quilt and exposed two exquisitely carved rosewood chairs in the Ching period style. Two Pekingese dogs were carved on the arm rests. Liang Feng's eyes opened wide with amazement. It was the first time she had seen such grand furniture in a commune house. She traced the delicate outlines gently with the tips of her fingers. She sat down on its red cushions. Wampu, watching Liang Feng, murmured happily,

"My grandneice likes luxuries like her grandaunt."

Liang Feng rose quickly from the chair and said in a serious, troubled tone,

"Wampu, when I left Canton I heard about the new movement. They are threatening those who try to cling to capitalist ideas." Seeing Wampu's untroubled face she added,

"I hope they would not consider chairs as capitalist goods."

Wampu laughed and said,

"That's why I keep them covered."

Her mood changed and she became serous and philosophic,

"Liang Feng, the common people would envy me if they saw these chairs. When only a few have good things it arouses envy in others who plot to destroy them. Anyway now I am an old woman, what can they do to me even if they discover these chairs?"

Still worried about the possible discovery of ostentatious goods in her relative's home, Liang Feng questioned,

"Why must you keep them Wampu, if you don't use them?"

Wampu's tone was apologetic, and with nostalgia she said sadly,

"It is easy for people to say, get rid of everything, but I need something to remember the family."

Liang Feng did not want to question her further.

Looking out of the window she saw the flickering lamps in the houses of the commune members. Like fireflies they faintly glowed in the approaching darkness. Wampu continued talking as Liang Feng stood watching the evening meal being prepared on the little clay cooker kept on a built-in brick stand. Wampu said,

"I do my own cooking; I don't eat in the commune canteen because I have three mouths to feed."

Surprised, Liang Feng looked around her; she wondered who else lived with Wampu. Seeing the questioning look on Liang Feng's face Wampu smiled. Bending down, she pulled out a basket from beneath the brick stand in the kitchen. Three kittens nestled there together. They raised their heads at the disturbance, and hearing Wampu's familiar voice, stretched up and got out of the basket.

"I have taught them not to cry loudly," said Wampu.

"I don't want my neighbours to know I keep them."

It was surprising to see Wampu defying the authorities. The rearing of pets was not encouraged as the authorities deemed it wasteful to feed animals when people were in want.

The quietness of the surroundings brought out a desire in Liang Feng to find a place to rest. She relaxed on the kang that served both as a bed and a seat in the house. As darkness fell the house became increasingly cold. She called out,

"Wampu, how do you keep the place warm in cold weather?"

Wampu had finished cooking the meal, and carrying back to the room the little clay cooker in which the lumps of coal were still burning, she knelt down and pushed it under the kang. Smiling, she explained,

"You are new, a southerner who does not know the northern way of life. I will pile up more coal in the cooker and push it under the kang to keep us warm all through the night."

Just as Wampu had said, the kang became warm with the heat of the cooker. It was making the room cosy and comfortable. Placing the dishes on the kang that now also served as a table for their meal, they sat cross-legged on the kang for their meal. It was her first meal in Wampu's house and Liang Feng enjoyed the cabbage soup and steamed manto (northern bread). The aroma of the food drew the kittens onto the kang, and Wampu kept them beside her, feeding them occasionally with pieces of dried chicken liver that was the speciality dish for the occasion.

Wampu was quick to notice the tired face of Liang Feng and said,

"In the country we sleep early because we have to rise with the dawn for the farm work. Was it the same where your grandfather lived?"

Wampu was keen to know the life her brother had led after leaving China.

"It was different, Wampu" Liang Feng replied.

"Grandfather was not a farmer, he was a businessman. We always had late nights, some people gambled till the early hours of the morning and the restaurants and cinemas were kept open till late."

Thoughtfully she added,

"No one seems to have late nights in China anymore."

Wampu said quickly,

"The old bad habits were rooted out with the Revolution. I remember the days before the Revolution when life was different."

After decades of restrained speech, now in the security of the four walls, in the company of a relative she disclosed,

"Sometimes I like the old capitalist life. My sons must be happy in Hong Kong, while their poor mother lives a boring life in a commune."

Feeling it was unwise to encourage Wampu to become nostalgic about the past which Liang Feng herself wanted to forget, the younger woman interrupted,

"But there were many who suffered at that time, Wampu. It is all far removed and different from the bright lights one imagines capitalist life to be."

Trying to convince Wampu she added seriously,

"I myself gave up that life to come here. I am much happier now."

There was firm confidence in the words she spoke.

That night, lying snugly beside Wampu on the kang that smelt of warm earth, Liang Feng felt happy and secure.

CHAPTER 8

The Sand Storm

Liang Feng dragged herself out of her sleep. It was an effort to keep her eyes opened. Although it was morning she did not see the light as the window and door were securely closed. She had slept soundly on the spacious kang beside Wampu. It was only now that she felt the fatigue of three days of travelling. She looked around the small room that Wampu was keeping so neat and uncluttered, with only family photographs on the side table. The absence of posters and any pictures other than the family photographs was restful to her eyes.

As the day brightened outside, sunlight crept into the room through the crevices of the wooden door. The coal cooker lay by the side of the kang, only a heap of cold ash now left in it. The soft sound of Wampu's feet came from the direction of the kitchen. The smell of cooking oil had floated into the room and remained clinging to the wall and roof and was now heavy over the kang where she lay. Liang Feng quickly jumped out of the bed and opened the window.

The horizon had turned yellow. The glow of sunlight pushed itself through an invisible screen. A thin flimsy veil of dust and fine yellow sand spread gradually in all directions blotting out the view of the fields, trees and houses from the window. The air was heavy and stuffy with no sign of wind or breeze. The smell of cooking oil hung heavily within the room.

Liang Feng called out anxiously,

"Wampu, the sky is changing colour. There is sure to be a storm!"

Wampu ran to the window and, taking a quick look at the sky, pattered back to the kitchen. She pulled out the cloth bag hanging on a hook on the kitchen door and was out of the room, and the house. Wampu's anxious movements caused the kittens to leave their basket. Behind the hurrying feet of Wampu they too ran but it was too late, the door closed firmly and Wampu was gone. They sat by the door crying softly, watching the streaks of light seeping through the base of the door. They then clustered around Liang Feng's feet, rubbing their bodies against her ankles and continuing to whimper.

She sat by the window unable to take her eyes away from signs of the impending storm. It would disrupt the work in the fields. The workers, putting aside their hoes, scrambled to the shelter of the trees bordering the field. The sharp touch of the air, gritty with dust, made Liang Feng aware of the change in the atmosphere. The sky was now a jaundiced yellow, and like a disease spread evenly enveloping and suffocating the trees. In the hazy visibility before her the trees cringed, bending in all directions, submitting to the increasing force of the wind. Her heart beat with anxiety. It was as if she was witnessing her people bowing and bending before absolute rulers as they had done for generations. Complete mastery by the wind, however, seemed to be checked by rows of newly planted trees on the borders of the field. They stood firm and courageous, breaking the force of the wind and thus preventing the extent of destruction that had resulted in the past.

The wind was blowing particles of dust into Liang Feng's eyes. The fine grains of sand choked the air. She coughed and grabbed at the white surgical mask Wampu had pulled out of a box and advised her to wear. She stretched it taut across her mouth and nose, fastening it at the back, as she watched in fascination the dust storm gathering speed.

The dust that had been trampled for thousands of years and had remained unnoticed climbed up with a triumphant roar like those who had risen to power to control the destiny of the land. The storm had the wind in its clutches and even the red glowing sun was obliterated in that moment. The wind flew about with the ferocity of a new freedom. The workers in the field, seeking shelter under the trees, lay crouching against the ground, covering their heads and faces with their coats and scarfs. They waited patiently for the terror to blow over. The cries of children could be heard close to the house. They ran along the pathways trying to get in through any open door. The shutter of the window beat furiously against the wall, as she tried to pull it to shut out the threatening wind. She blinked as the dust blew on her face and hovered over her head before clutching at her hair. It was a traumatic time; Wampu had run out in a flash while the howling wind thrashed outside the house.

Unseen, the dust had entered the house through the closed door, forcing itself to take on every nook and corner. It had invaded the tables and chairs; nothing was left untouched. All objects in the room were covered in a fine yellow powder. The kittens had climbed onto the kang to escape the blasts of wind coming through the door. Wampu's grand chairs that had remained uncovered were getting a beating and had turned grey with dust. Pitying them as she would pity the rich, Liang Feng took the quilt and the mat and covered them. She then crouched on the kang cradling the trembling kittens on her lap. Her anxiety for Wampu increased when remembering the abnormally tiny child-like feet of her grandaunt. Moulded feet were a distinction of the old society in which women's feet were bound tightly from childhood to prevent their growth. These thoughts brought furious anger against the fetters of feudalism. She was glad the revolution had stopped all such discrimination against women. Unable to bear her anger she said aloud to the kittens now rolled up on her lap,

"Wampu's feet might be her tragedy in the storm".

66

At this moment there was a faint knock on the door. Rushing to open it with the kittens following behind, Liang Feng stared in astonishment at Wampu. She was unrecognisable, looking like a ghost in a yellow robe with dust covering her white body and concealing her features. Her fingers helplessly tried to brush away the dust choking her mouth. Liang Feng quickly pulled her coat off her body and with the help of a bowl of water washed the dust from Wampu's face. Wampu smiled with gratitude for the attention and help she was receiving from her grandneice. It had been a long time since she had had people to attend on her. She said quietly,

"I could not beat the storm today, I tried to get to the shop before the storm struck, but I could not run."

Her eyes fell accusingly on her deformed feet as if to say

"You failed me this time".

In anguish Liang Feng cried out,

"Wampu why did you allow them to treat your feet so cruelly?"

Wampu sat on the kang and removing her shoes, thoughtfully replied,

"It was not thought to be a cruel act at that time to make women's feet small and beautiful; we women had to compete with many others for a good husband."

Liang Feng said angrily,

"Did you not know it was done to keep women prisoners in their homes!" and as an afterthought added

"I am glad for the revolution that has wiped out feudal slavery of women."

Liang Feng's fierce face reminded Wampu of all the angry young women in the commune who had joined the communist party, and had spiritedly told their parents that in the new China they would not continue practices such as the three bowings to parents, husbands and sons. Bringing a mug of hot tea for Wampu, Liang Feng sat beside her in the kang. The storm raged outside. Wampu said,

"Liang Feng, I hope this is not an inauspicious beginning to life in Peking."

Liang Feng spiritedly retorted,

"Wampu, I don't believe in premonitions or of Confucian teachings."

She did not like to talk of premonitions; she had often heard her grandfather talk with foreboding of every natural disaster. She also disliked her grandfather's rendering of Confucian laws of obedience.

She knew that in Chairman Mao's new China this type of slavery to outdated philosophies had been rooted out. Wampu shook her head sadly.

"I am sad to see my grandneice talking like the new young in the commune. They don't respect the elders anymore."

Liang Feng quickly took Wampu's hand; she did not want to quarrel with her and said,

"Wampu, it is not with you that I am angry with but with the old system, don't you see there had to be dust storms if there is a desert lying on the other side of the great wall."

She spoke convincingly and brightly as her teacher had done,

"We must not let natural disasters break our spirit, we must plant more trees."

Wampu remained silent. Thoughtfully she stroked the frightened kittens on her lap.

Liang Feng was angry with herself for speaking harshly to Wampu. The storm reminded her of revolutions, that they were unpredictable and cruel to some, while others benefitted.

She hoped the trees that were getting a beating outside would not succumb and fall. The commune had only a few newly planted trees which provided not only shade but beauty too. More important was the belief that the trees would act as wind- breakers to lessen the damage done by dust storms. She was surprised when Wampu said,

"It is true the storms have not been too bad in the last few years, I remember the time when houses of the peasants were blown off by strong winds that could not be controlled."

Liang Feng said warmly,

"Wampu, I am so glad you can see the good side of the revolution, I know that you miss your sons but they will come back when they are tired of life outside these shores." Wampu shook her head. Liang Feng's words did not comfort her.

"No Liang Feng, they will not return. They often said to me, one system of autocracy is replaced by another."

As Liang Feng listened with eyes that questioned her, she added,

"My sons were ambitious young men who saw the stagnation in the economy when they could not use initiatives to better themselves."

Liang Feng was annoyed by Wampus's sons' attitudes and took an instant dislike to them. They had behaved like their grandfather.

She said thoughtfully,

"I am glad the people who live here truly love the land".

The storm had passed over. Wampu smiled and said,

"Liang Feng, you have been very well educated in the last three years. I am still stubborn and have not learnt the new philosophy."

Liang Feng quickly looked at Wampu. If there was any sarcasm in her voice she could not discern it on her wrinkled face and inscrutable eyes. They seldom gave any indication of her thoughts. But Liang Feng was uncomfortable when Wampu referred to her political education; in fact it made her realise she was full of words and slogans which she would cleverly render at an inopportune time to stone-faced listeners. The phrases she learnt in the study class were always reverberating in her subconscious as a defence against revisionism. Liang Feng said,

"Wampu, I saw hundreds of trees newly planted in the city. They were indeed an elegant sight standing against a background of high rise buildings."

Wampu replied in a sad voice,

"I have never been to the city in the last ten years. When you are as old as I am there never will be a chance of going beyond the village."

Liang Feng was upset to hear Wampu's words and was quick to comfort her,

"Wampu, you must not feel this way, we must stand up for our rights," and she added quietly,

"The new movement will put things right; this is what my friends said to me in Canton."

Seated on the kang, the two women ate their night meal of boiled kidney beans. Watching Liang Feng's stern countenance, Wampu understood the fierce anger of the young for fair play. Her grandneice was speaking rebelliously of old customs as her two sons had done. She was herself reconciled to the changes because of the inner strength she had cultivated as a child, from the teachings of the Buddha. She smiled, remembering that she had not given into changes as easily as her grandneice would think. She had accepted the changes in her own way. She was the only member of the commune who had not seen the necessity to hang pictures of the new leader in her house, or to repeat like a parrot the sayings of the revolutionaries. She chuckled to herself remembering her own obstinacy to continue her way of life with little interference from the commune authorities who in fact put up with her because of her "grey hairs" as they whispered to each other in her presence. The size of her feet gave her no worry except when she was caught in a dust storm or for that matter in a revolution. In fact she was embarrassed seeing the large feet of the younger women who dressed like men and worked side by side with them, sacrificing their womanly charms. She looked across at Liang Feng eating her beans thoughtfully. She did look pretty with her large expressive eyes and delicate mouth. She did not believe such young pretty women should only read *The Thoughts of Chairman Mao* and walk in parades screaming revolutionary slogans. She had heard of her grandneice's marriage and was sad it had not worked out. Nodding her head she spoke out her thoughts,

"I wonder if the present generation has soft enough hearts to fall in love."

Liang Feng heard her. Pausing at her meal she said softly,

"Yes Wampu, they do."

Wampu served more beans to Liang Feng. With a smile on her lips and with the wisdom of old age she asked lightly,

"Liang Feng, do you support the new movement against the so-called bourgeoisie?"

Liang Feng immediately became the good student of the revolution and said fervently,

"Yes Wampu, it is necessary to put things right. Many things have not worked out the way the Chairman had wanted."

Wampu's face went stiff and she did not say another word, but getting up from the kang poured herself a mug of tea. Returning to the kang, she said, this time with concern in her voice,

"I know they talk these days of letting a hundred flowers bloom, but I have seen with my own eyes what happens. Only the flowers they like are allowed to bloom, while the rest are destroyed."

Liang Feng said with confidence,

"No Wampu, it will not happen; only poisonous weeds would be plucked out, the Chairman says."

That night Liang Feng, lying beside Wampu in the kang, was critical of her own behaviour towards Wampu. She admonished herself,

"I am critical of Wampu but I myself have bourgeois weakness. I am surprised at myself for wanting to visit the white pagoda. I am losing my spirit, I am afraid for myself."

Peking and its sights did affect Liang Feng, and memories of the past brought nostalgia. She thought of Pierre, whom she had met at the railway station. She closed her eyes as if to shut out his face from her mind.

"I must not let emotions over-ride reasons and facts," she said firmly. After three years of living in China, she had found both Pierre and Donald outspoken and appealing. Her present life sometimes showed up contradictions between her natural emotions and the theories instilled into her. However, such a thought brought a sense of fear and guilt, and she crept closer to Wampu.

CHAPTER 9

The Bridge of Perfect Wisdom

The bright blue sky next day gave no indication of the storm that had raged the previous day. Yet on the ground lay twisted branches and leaves wrenched from the branches by the ferocious wind. The newly planted trees had withstood the beating, but the hapless trunks were bent as evidence of the ordeal.

Angry yellow dust covered the horizon in grey yellow smog. The yellow powder suffocated the pathways, trees, houses and fields.

The neighbourhood committee had got down to the task of cleaning up the dust and it had turned out to be a social event, giving an opportunity to Liang Feng to meet the residents who showed friendliness and respect to her just as they treated Wampu.

Wampu was cautious with her friends, giving no opportunity to them to visit her in the house. She had confided in her grandneice that she feared an outbreak of jealousy if her background and the chairs were discovered by them. She had looked at the chairs with sympathy and had gently dusted with a feathered brush. Next she placed a quilt over them. With a mischievous smile she had brought a weather beaten old mat and placed it over them as a camouflage.

Once again the commune had returned to normality after the storm. Liang Feng left for the city to report her arrival at the Foreign Language Institute. However, it did not turn out to be an eventful occasion except to notice a sense of uncertainty and restlessness among the workers.

There were rumblings of an imminent movement by Chairman Mao to rid the headquarters of those planning to sabotage his ideology. Liang Feng was walking into this environment unwittingly. She would witness a revolution which her father said had happened in his life time. She noticed the divided loyalties between the older generation and the younger at all work places. She wondered if a second revolution would benefit her or persuade her to leave her country of origin as her parents had once done.

To her relief she was given to work in Waichia Talou that was called by the locals 'foreigners' big building'. On the opposite side of the building was the peoples' commune flats which was obviously strategically placed to 'keep an eye' on the foreign community.

Next morning, after leaving the institute where she was interviewed, she arrived at the Behai Park. The Pagoda was high in the places she wanted to see, especially after her bus ride and the discussion of religion. Her face lit up with animation as she stepped quickly, holding back her joy remembering that she was in a China that no longer encouraged spiritual beliefs.

The land before her was unfamiliar but there was the keenness to comprehend its historical past. In the study classes what she had heard was the horror of building such edifices on the blood and sweat of the poor. But now viewing the past grandeur filled her with a sense of pride and happiness to be part of history.

These mixed feelings were a secret close to her heart; a precious jewel was guarded against those who were bent to destroy it. How many like her must be walking beside these wonders of a rich ancient past but hidden in passive unemotional faces. Happy with life, Liang Feng walked through the formation of rocks cunningly arranged by skilled artists; the lake itself reflected the blue sky in the waters, the willow trees were gently caressing the surface forming ripples that were like the ripples of dreams that surfaced and passed away.

The park gates were opened to the public. However, it being a holiday, there were only a few people on the hill where the tall pines grew. She ascended the steps leading to the top of the hill after crossing the Bridge of Perfect Wisdom. The Pagoda, a dome of peace in her eyes, blazed white under the soft mellow light of the morning sky. It was a wonderful sight. Its contours and its pinnacle were in contrast to the octagonal structures of the traditional Chinese pagodas that rose to many storeys. The scenery before her intensified her own desire for freedom and inner spirituality. Millions of Chinese had venerated it at a time when religious faith had held people in spiritual sway. Since there was no patronage from the state or the people, there were no worshipers at the site, only sightseers.

The Pagoda was abandoned and had become a monument of oppression of the poor. Nevertheless, there were those who trekked daily to view it only from a distance, permitted by the authorities. In order to erase this feudal slavery as it was referred to, there was a bust of Chairman Mao placed symbolically and distinctively on a large marble stand which had served once as an alter to the divine. Chairman Mao's smiling face was to greet all pilgrims and acted as a constant reminder to them where their loyalties should lie.

With conflicting thoughts, Liang Feng yearned for a kindred spirit to share her thoughts. There was no one she could trust in a place where people bottled up their feeling for fear of being branded a counter revolutionary.

There was a sudden realisation that she was not the lone person on top of the hill.

On the eastern side of the pagoda there were three men, grey haired and of a reverend old

age, concentrating on tai chi chuan with hands outstretched before them. They were in absolute silence as they synchronised each movement of hands and legs.

72

The men had not heard her footsteps as she walked around the peak. She stopped on her feet; she became aware of someone running and her attention was drawn to a jogger running across the arched marble bridge towards the Temple of Everlasting Peace. The sight of him was lost, only for a moment; again emerging crossing the garden and advancing up the hill to where the Pagoda stood.

Next, it was in full view, and she recognised the runner as Pierre Devon, introduced to her at the railway station by Donald. Her heart beat fast with joy and nervousness but was gladly concealed under her padded warm coat. She did not move but saw him taking a deep breath with his hands on his waist. He joined the three men now relaxing from their tai chi and was talking to them in Chinese. Then they all resumed their tai chi together.

She watched him, reminiscing on his handshake at the station. It was warm and friendly. His eyes that watched her while Donald introduced her were dark brown and communicative.

Now studying his face, his half-closed eyes enhanced his peaceful expression that she liked. His high forehead was framed in thick wavy hair, dark brown in colour. He had a sensitive bearded face and looked distinguished. Fascinated, she observed as she had never attempted to watch someone without that person not noticing her. He was tall like most men she saw in Peking but was more heavily built.

He opened his eyes and looked at his watch and once again continued with his tai chi. Liang Feng too looked at her watch and decided to leave, but was worried her footsteps would disturb the group. She began to worry that if he saw her he would think she was like most of her people who would rudely stare at anyone who looked different to them. She had experienced such behaviour when she had arrived in China.

She picked up courage and tiptoed softly from the hill to the path moving away from the summit of the hill.

It was only after she had covered some distance that Liang Feng decided to glance back at the four figures on the summit. The pagoda seemed to have increased in height, dwarfing the men. After a few more steps they disappeared from her sight. The joy of her experience was short lived and with a feeling of her loss and now aware of her own personal looks hidden behind a camouflage of baggy blue trousers, the oversized blouse, rough and creased, she disliked her appearance.

There was a sudden feeling of nostalgia for her calf-length skirt that she had worn on the train. But in Peking's cold weather no one was wearing such clothes. Her thoughts flew to Sally Brown. Sally had worn such well-fitting clothes that made her look more beautiful in Liang Feng's eyes. In fact she had worn them all the time in the train, making the other Chinese feel inferior. She could not help comparing herself to the shabbily dressed peasant women in the commune. A rebellious feeling overpowered her; she did not have to look like them. Her pace quickened as she made to the city. She was haunted by the face of Pierre Devon and decided to look her best. Before long she was boldly pushing the glass door of the largest department store in Peking.

Once inside, she paused hesitantly, letting her eyes take in the displays in the glass cases. She stood there, thinking; then with measured steps she walked along the counters peering at the goods inside the cases. Her heart beating fast she walked into the women's department. Inside the glass cases there were a few cosmetics for dry skins.

A saleswoman stood in an embroidered silk blouse and grey trousers behind the counter. She looked aloof, showing no interest in the few customers coming into the shop. Her arms were folded and she kept on looking at her watch from time to time. To her, the shoppers were only sightseers who made no attempt to buy what was on offer. The times had changed and those who patronised were now afraid to do so because of the new ideology of the Red Guards.

One glass case caught Liang Feng's eyes; bending over the glass top she peered, eyes shining with pleasure. This was what she wanted she told herself as she gazed at the tube of lipstick lying beside the jars of facial creams. This single tube of lipstick seemed to have escaped the attention of all customers as it was an object that was taboo in the eyes of the new ideology.

The sales woman become aware of Liang Feng, and walked up to the container with the cosmetics. Doubtfully she scrutinised Liang Feng from the corners of her eyes. Picking up courage, hesitantly in a rather inaudible voice Liang Feng asked,

"Is that a tube of lipstick?"

A disdainful look appeared on the saleswoman's face and, without bothering to answer, she nodded her head. Building up courage Liang Feng asked,

"How much does it cost?"

There was no answer, but coming closer to Liang Feng she looked directly into Liang Feng's face. It was unfriendly and overbearing and made Liang Feng look at the next counter. After a few seconds of silence the woman replied in a matter of fact tone,

"Only five yuans." She disdainfully moved on to the farthest end of the counter as another customer had arrived and was pointing her finger to a parasol on the shelf.

Rooted to the ground, Liang Feng waited patiently until that customer left with her parasol. This time she approached the saleswoman, with her purse half opened and rather boldly said,

"I want to buy the lipstick." The saleswoman with an irritated look waited for a while and sharply replied,

"Did you say you want to buy the lipstick?"

Her discourteous tone made Liang Feng wince. And looking around with uncertainty she nodded her head.

There was a change in the saleswoman's face as she meticulously went over her skirt delaying the reply and surveyed Liang Feng's clothes haughtily. But noticing the half opened purse, she came closer and whispered,

"You are bold to buy lipstick at this time," and looked suspiciously at the other customers in the shop.

Liang Feng was uneasy; she wanted to get away from the store and hurriedly pulled out five yuans and placed it on the counter. The saleswoman became talkative,

"I never thought the day would come when someone would come along and take away this anti-revolutionary lipstick which would have put me also in trouble."

Her voice was cynical as she handed over the bag to Liang Feng.

Clutching the small bag of her purchase, she moved towards the mirror on the wall in the store. Feeling courageous she pulled out the tube from the bag and ran the lipstick swiftly over her lips. The reflection smiled back, congratulating her appearance. She applied another coating, but it was too bright for her liking. She gently rubbed off the excess. Fascinated, she watched her transformation; her thoughts flew to Sally Brown. She had seen Sally peering into a compact case and applying lipstick to her lips that were already pink. She had watched Sally with curiosity and admiration. In fact, when Sally had ventured out of her bunk she was well-groomed and was in vast contrast to the dishevelled Chinese passengers.

Satisfied with her looks, Liang Feng walked slowly upstairs, to the second floor of the new department store. This floor displayed shoes and sports goods. Taking her own time she lingered, postponing the time when she had to face the crowds in the street. Her joy was short-lived when she heard loudspeakers denouncing revisionists. She remembered Wang Lee who had said,

"A woman no longer needs to degrade herself as a slave with artificial aids in new China."

On her arrival in Canton, she had thrown away the cosmetics she had brought her from abroad after being intimidated by the posters in the commune which said "Women are equal to men". The women no longer needed to show their femininity which had risked exploitation in the feudal times. Her husband sometimes acted as her teacher and repeated the sayings of the revolution which he had learnt in the study classes. This thought brought a wry smile to her lips as she did not consider him a champion of women's rights. He was a bundle of contradictions and his behaviour towards her was that of a bully.

There was a sudden realisation that she had been walking round and round the glass display cupboards; brought her to an abrupt halt. The sales staff watched her with suspicion. She said, in an outburst of anger,

"I don't care what Wang Lee thinks."

The sales girl closest to her started laughing nervously. Liang Feng realised she had said something aloud. Leaving the place quickly she reached the mirror by the staircase. She liked her new look, pouting she exclaimed quickly,

"A little colour cannot change my belief in Chairman Mao."

She suddenly remembered her intention to visit the store. Turning back again to the store she went to the shelves where shoes were displayed. She was keen to buy a pair of shoes for Wampu as she had noticed the worn-out pair she was wearing. She went to the children's rack and picked up a pair of black cloth shoes. They were soft and pliable in her hands. Wampu would be delighted to have a new pair of shoes for her tiny feet she thought happily as she paid the yuans to the suspicious looking saleswoman.

The woman was puzzled. She looked at Liang Feng's feet, but shrugging her shoulders she said,

"You will have to bind your feet to get into this pair of shoes."

Liang Feng did not reply but with a smile she left the place and came down the steps to make an exit to the street.

She stopped as she saw a threatening crowd in the street and saw them moving towards the store. Liang Feng hesitated and, with a pang of guilt but with determination, she walked up to a woman coming in to the store and thrust her bag with the lipstick into her hand. The surprised woman, discovering the item in the paper bag, pushed it from view into a corner of her shopping bag.

Standing by the roadside Liang Feng heaved a sigh of relief. With her head held high, she walked slowly to catch a bus. Her head was throbbing with the words,

"I don't need artificial aids to look my best." The commune members had taken to her because she was clever and was willing to learn a new way of life. These were consoling words at a time when she was tempted to throw away those values. She had fervently believed they would build up a great nation as the Chairman propagated.

With night approaching, the streetlights were lit. It was a cold night and under the padded coat she shivered. She hugged the shoes to her breast to give more warmth. There was a long queue at the bus stop. Few buses plied between the city and the outstations. Most people used their cycles to reach their destinations.

While in the bus the platitudes that had acted as a balm to ward off temptation were uppermost in her mind. But although they were consoling thoughts she held back the tears clouding her eyes. She analysed the consequence of having the lipstick and the thought of possible accusations as a capitalist that would put Wampu into trouble as well. This would have made life difficult for her when she was just beginning her new life as a loyal communist.

CHAPTER 10

The Cultural Revolution

Working in Waichia Talou was pleasant at first but troubles were brewing on the horizon and threatening every work place. There were more problems with the staff employed as cooks and amahs to foreigners. In many instances the older domestic workers had to be reprimanded for their laissez-faire attitude to rules. It was known that they indulged in eating at foreigners' apartments and cherished imported chocolates and meat products.

In January 1966 the Russians were singled out as imperialists and organised demonstrations against them began. It was a time when Chairman Mao fell out with the Russian leadership on ideology. Things became worse when technical staff and aid were withdrawn by Russia.

It was also a time when there was disagreement in the Chinese politburo. Mao realised this and diverted the masses from divisive domestic problems to unite them against a foreign enemy. Organised marchers walked along the main road chanting 'Down with Russian imperialists'. In Waichia Talou Liang Feng was besieged by anti-foreign propaganda.

Things became worse for Liang Feng when any action to defend foreigners was taken for harbouring bourgeois ideals. In May that year the 'Cultural Revolution' was unleashed by Chairman Mao.

There was something unusual about the crowds that gathered on the roads and sidewalks in May 1966. They were mostly young people in a festive mood, flaunting as their special mark of distinction, bright red armbands which matched the red books in their hands. Red flags and red drums added to the buoyancy of their jaunty mood as they thronged the capital. Ironically the festive mood was not shared by the onlookers who heard in the beat of the drums the gloomy reminders of a new Revolution. They shrank from close contact with these young revolutionaries but moved their lips in joining the chant "long live Chairman Mao". If there were any protests amongst the crowds, they went unnoticed and unheard.

Whether it was in the commune, factory or house, no one could escape those waves of chaos and destruction when they struck peoples' lives. The young Red Guards shouting the slogans demanded the loyalty from the people to the new political message. Liang Feng heard that call, but she was now more inclined to close her ears and be alone with her own thoughts. As the Cultural Revolution unleashed its daily broadcasts of propaganda, not only was it deafening to ears but a threatening intrusion into her privacy. Standing amongst the crowds that day, Liang Feng wondered if there were others like her becoming disenchanted with the propaganda.

There seemed to be no escape from this demanding and merciless persecution. No longer were the nights restful; political broadcasts continued throughout the night! The message was the same, but taking various forms – speeches, slogans, poetry and even song. During the three years she had spent learning to adjust to her new life, she had trained herself to suppress any nostalgia for the past in Jakarta, but now there were occasions when she let her mind indulge in memories of her old life. The procession of Red Guards by paced her but their voices were unable to drown the waves of thought rising, falling and fading away, yet to reappear with added force. Suddenly she wanted to see Pierre Devon. There was an urgency of a surf rider to ride those waves of thoughts that had no written rules, and experience liberation. She ran to the house of Wampu's neighbour and borrowing a bicycle, she rode out of the commune on to the street and turned in the direction of Behai Park.

On a carpet of fallen leaves Liang Feng rode through the tree-lined avenue reserved for cyclists. The faster she rode the quieter the leaves fled away from her path. There was a feeling of liberation. Turning to the south gate of the park she alighted. The sight of the Pagoda of Peace calmed her and she entered the grounds of Bei Hai Park.

On her previous visit she had discovered in this haven of peace a place for her solitary reflections. But today she had a dual purpose for this visit. There was this new desire to see Pierre Devon amidst the surroundings of the park. She joined eagerly the rest of the travellers attempting like her to reach the summit of the hill.

Climbing the steps winding up the hill Liang Feng gazed with wonder at the pine trees aesthetically grown on the slopes. In her eyes they seemed to stand in majestic serenity, a sign of veneration. She was experiencing new emotions. Overtaking the other climbers, she hastened to reach the summit, her heart beating anxiously.

The sight of the Pagoda brought a sense of tranquillity to Liang Feng, so deep that she whispered,

"I wish I could see him to share this joy." But looking upwards it was not Pierre Devon that she caught sight of; an elderly woman had reached the hill before her. Crouching by the Pagoda in intent concentration, this woman was surreptitiously burning some sticks of incense while glancing with fearful eyes over her shoulder.

How had this woman, faithful to an old religion, obtained forbidden incense to carry on with a custom that was strictly prohibited? Scent of the burning incense wafted all round, making Liang Feng nervously strain her ears, fearful of those who were following behind her. But the woman herself, wary of being discovered, put out the faint glow of the incense with her fingertips and hid it in the pocket of her trouser. Disturbed by what she had witnessed, Liang Feng turned her eyes away and deliberately moved to a position that concealed her from the view of those arriving on the summit of the hill. She quietly waited there looking out for Pierre, and to her joy it was not long when he came with a group of young people onto the hill. She guessed they were his students from Xin Hua University. She watched them settle themselves down on some steps to observe the view. Her eyes rested on Pierre, who was sitting quietly letting his students do the talking. His expression seemed gentle and calm and there was an air of solitude surrounding him.

Becoming conscious of a pair of eyes focused on him, Pierre instinctively glanced in her direction and his eyes met hers directly. It was not difficult for him to recollect the large dark eyes and the tanned complexion so different to the fair complexions and narrow eyes of the local inhabitants. Leaving his students, in a few seconds he was by her side.

"Aren't you Liang Feng, whom I met with Donald Brown at the station?"

Hiding her nervous hands within her lap she looked up at him and said,

"Yes, I saw you another day too, engaged in tai chi chuan."

Her eyes were bright with obvious admiration for him and, feeling rather embarrassed, he said lightly,

"Do you hide behind rocks to watch people?"

She laughed. He sat by her on the steps. His voice was deep and its warmth relaxed her. Remembering his intent expression the previous day as he had gazed at the view from the hill, she said quickly,

"Do you come to Behai to watch the Pagoda?"

She secretly hoped he would say yes. But Pierre answered,

"I like to watch the clouds from the top of the hill, it is a beautiful sight early morning."

Liang Feng hoped he would go on speaking. As if he could read her mind he continued,

"Participating in tai chi chuan on top of this hill has a special meaning for me. There is such a feeling of tranquillity which conveys a sense of wellbeing to me."

His open manner of speech appealed to her. As she listened she felt a sense of sadness towards her own nature that had stopped expressing her dreams and hopes. Even her natural feelings had been suppressed in fear of being misunderstood. Had she dared to voice her own views she would have been forced to follow extra study classes.

Once when Liang Feng had quoted Chairman Mao, "Let a thousand flowers bloom", Wampu had said sarcastically,

80

"Yes it's a good idea to let people express their thoughts but it is also the way to eliminate those opposed to the Chairman." This had happened some years before but had not been officially disclosed.

Pierre spoke of the men who had stirred his interest in tai chi chuan,

"It helps me to relax for the rest of the day", gesturing with his hands in the manner of 'flying with cranes'. Her lips twitched in amusement even as her heart quickened to observe the strength and supple grace of his arms. She remembered the warm clasp of his hand at the railway station. His hands were attractively masculine. The new feelings awakening within her were disturbing and she shifted her gaze to the distant trees.

Pierre's remark made her uncomfortable and she could not reply.

"You are different to the other women here," he continued

"Aren't you afraid to speak to a foreigner from the West?"

She felt her cheeks burn. How could she explain to him that it was meeting the Browns that had compelled her to cast aside some of her inhibitions and look for people she desired to communicate with.

She always had a sixth sense to judge those who appealed to her. Her mind a confusion of thoughts, she told herself,

"Why should I be afraid to speak to him, I have been waiting all these years to meet someone like him?"

When Donald Brown had spoken of Pierre to her, curiosity had been kindled. The chance meeting at the railway station had transformed the idle curiosity to a deep desire to cultivate his friendship. She had felt that since the time her young mind was forming its dreams and fantasies, influenced by the books she had read in Jakarta, he had existed in bits and pieces like a jigsaw puzzle in her imagination. No more a restless traveller, she longed to discuss his interests.

"Why do you say I'm different to the women here and why should I be afraid to speak to you?"

He laughed; he could not believe what he heard. This was the first occasion he had heard a local woman speaking so boldly to him.

"You certainly sound different in this setup," he said laughingly, concealing his admiration.

"My students show no fear to those who come from the communist countries, but they do not feel at home with others."

She interrupted,

"But they do talk to you, I observed them today."

He reflected: his hand cupped his chin, and he answered her,

"I'm their Professor, but I know they still worry about my habits."

With feigned surprise and her voice tinged with irony, she inquired,

"Do you have bad habits?" She remembered the condemnation of unhealthy foreign influence in the study classes.

Noticing her irony he grinned,

"The only bad habit I have is my individualism".

She took a sharp breath. She was herself developing this so-called 'bad habit' which the authorities criticised. In fact, the authorities had blamed her foreign education for this misfortune. Feeling uneasy, she did not want him to perceive her conflict and said nonchalantly,

"Individualism can become very bourgeois, I learnt this in my study classes." She had defended the stand of the authorities, but there was a hollow feeling within her after the words had escaped her lips.

Surprised by her own use of clichés, she reminded herself the pleasure she had derived from translating *The Thoughts of Chairman Mao* to Donald Brown. She quickly turned her face away from Pierre's close scrutiny. On the other hand those words had come to her assistance to cover up emotions ruthlessly. Silently Pierre studied Liang Feng who had uttered all that rhetoric.

Pierre's curiosity was aroused to get to know her further, but his students were watching him. Their faces were inscrutable. He stood up. He wanted Liang Feng to meet his students, and led her towards them. Their welcome was however not cordial and they chose to ignore her presence.

But Pierre said,

"Liang Feng has come from Jakarta after getting tired of capitalist life."

This approach went well with the group. Their eyes widened with surprise; they were full of curiosity but they had many questions to ask her before they accepted her to their circle. Amongst them was Han who seemed to hold a special place in that group. Han was tall and thin, with an extremely thin waist giving him a delicate look. His eyes set far apart gave him a child-like expression. Pierre seemed to communicate more often with him than with the rest.

Allowing his students to freely question Liang Feng, Pierre observed her with increasing interest. Pierre had an affable relationship with them. He had arrived in Peking three years after abandoning his career as a newspaper journalist in Marseille. It was during a short period in Bhutan that he had experienced a new surge of life which had given him new perspectives. Throughout, being intrigued by the events in China and aroused by curiosity to study Chairman Mao's society, he had snatched at an opportunity to work in Peking. Won over by the idealism of Chairman Mao, he was now keen to help the new society progress, his main aim at present being to encourage the conservation of the environment during this drive for modernisation. It was with a sense of dedication that he had accepted to work at the Xin Hua University on environmental studies. He was interrupted by his students. He answered their question and turning to Liang Feng, saying in French to the annoyance of his students,

"Do you like to visit my house? We are going there shortly to discuss the painful subject of industrial pollution."

His tone was intimate when he spoke his native tongue.

"Yes," her reply came with a rush. She was overjoyed at this invitation, coming so soon after a brief meeting. There was also a longing to know his reasons to live in a land that was also new to her.

It was only after she had accepted his invitation that Liang Feng had some misgivings. She wondered if he was merely being polite. She had observed such courtesy in Donald Brown as well. Unlike Donald's rather patronising attitude to her people, she saw in Pierre a genuine understanding and kindness which was reflected in the calm intelligence stamped on his face. However, his face showed his obvious gladness at her quick acceptance of his invitation. Dispelling her doubts and with some boldness she said,

"Visiting you will give me an opportunity to see how foreigners live in our country."

Her formal words brought a twinkle to his eyes and made him teasingly reply,

"I live like a warlord in a house that once belonged to a capitalist Chinese."

He repeated his reply in Chinese for the benefit of his students and they burst out laughing. They knew too well he would not. Warlords and capitalists were criminals in their eyes. They had accepted Pierre as a member of the proletariat and they respected him for speaking their language and so readily adopting to their way of life.

He was looked up to as a special friend of the nation. Pierre had openly acknowledged his happiness at the improved condition of the masses after the revolution and also the present drive to democratise the party structure. He too viewed elitism within the party with the same suspicion, thus proving his support of Chairman Mao.

Pierre lived among the local population, unostentatiously. "In the midst of life" he called it. The authorities had given him a residence previously owned by a member of the nobility. Hidden among the simple dwellings of the masses, his house was distinctive in ornate architecture, and its beauty belonged to an earlier period in history.

The students were in a hurry to get on with their plans and set out with Liang Feng in their company. The group descended the hill. As they approached the Bridge of Perfect Wisdom, Liang Feng's lips lifted up to a quiet smile. Was she influenced by the appellation of perfect wisdom to let that inner self steer her in a new direction?

With Pierre's directions written in her mind, she left the group to find her way to Pierre's house on her bicycle. The route lay along the winding path bordering the wall of the Forbidden City. The sight of the giant edifice from where in 1949 Chairman Mao had proclaimed the Republic of China brought her to a halt. She remembered China's previous history when absolute rulers from these ramparts had flung their proclamations at the officials cringing and kowtowing in the courtyard below. Around her were the sightseers strolling along, their heads held high, and Liang Feng felt a surge of relief that those evil days were no more.

She stood and surveyed for a few minutes by the entrance to the towering fortress guarding the Forbidden City, the marble bridge, her eyes marvelling at its beauty as it glistened in the sunlight.

This reminder of the past era still on her mind, she continued on her way along Thiananmen Avenue. It was into a narrow lane that she now entered. In the heart of Peking often such lanes criss-crossed through the newly built avenues. This peculiar lane, although it had no name, was special in her eyes with a surface paved with cobbled stones.

Doors set along the wall marked the individual residences, a glimpse of low roofs behind them, a traditional architectural design which remarkably guarded the privacy of those living in the houses.

The door that opened to Pierre's house distinguished itself in its colourful appearance as different to the other doors on the wall. Those others were grey and colourless whereas his door was painted in bright red, with gleaming brass nail heads forming a motif on the surface. The tiles of his house were of an unusual green, in contrast to the grey rooftops of surrounding dwellings. In keeping with the style of roofs in China, it curved up at the corners.

Within the garden was a pine tree, its leaves green and luxuriant – clearly a welcome breath of freshness and beauty in a background of gloomy rooftops.

As Liang Feng stood outside the door, her glance taking in the distinguish house, she saw the figure of Pierre approaching the lane and turning towards his house.

His dark beard made him conspicuous among the smoothly-shaven students. Liang Feng felt an inexplicable sense of welcome as he smilingly took her hand in his.

CHAPTER 11

A House in a Hutung

It was another world that unfolded before her eyes. Liang Feng gazed with astonishment. She could not believe that the objects of grandeur before her eyes could be associated with an ordinary household.

The magnificence of ancient China paraded boldly in her imagination, which identified such rich delights only with museums and public buildings. Such treasures belonged to renowned periods in history when the dynasties of the Sungs and the Tangs amassed fabulous wealth which had survived centuries of political disasters to feast the eyes of a proletariat culture of the twentieth century. It was all there before her eyes.

In every visible place in the house there was something that belonged to the past. Rich red wall plaques displaying the four seasons in ivory, adorned the eastern wall. Two gold dragons, blowing fire, guarded that wall while holding daintily painted silk lanterns in their mouths. The light that entered the house shed a soft glow on the ornaments. In the absence of large windows, the court-yard in the centre enabled the sunlight to enter the house. Liang Feng was drawn to this courtyard. She gazed at large blue and white porcelain jars reaching up to her shoulders. She remembered the ancient practice of such jars being used to collect and hold rain water. Walking through the brick red pillars of the corridor, she entered the inner rooms in which the ceilings were painted in gold and white, giving them a special brightness.

Entering the adjoining area, she paused to admire the intricate carvings on the chairs inlaid with glowing mother-of-pearls in a floral design. They appeared proud and grand, standing on a blue and white Peking carpet covering part of the brick-tiled floor. Her feet sank into it as she walked around the room. She had seen such carpets only in grand public buildings.

Liang Feng was enjoying everything in Pierre's house. As she gently took in her fingers an egg shell porcelain vase, she was aware of his presence by her. There were countless porcelain vases lying around, large and small; there were also painted snuff bottles protected in glass-fronted cupboards and on high ornamental stools. She did not speak as she moved around, and Pierre, feeling somewhat uneasy, said,

"I don't think we can have our discussion in a room filled with the trappings of old China".

He waited for her to reply in the affirmative as all his students had done. The students, with Han leading the way, had walked through Pierre's treasure house without a glance, and were happily seated round the table in his study that was bare of all ornaments. Liang Feng, however, softly said,

"I have never seen a house with such a collection of China's past." With eyes full of wonder and admiration she added,

"I like to see a house with beautiful things."

Reassured at her answer but still wanting to minimise the grandeur he said lightly,

"I'll leave you to become a capitalist in this room while I join my impatient students in the proletarian set-up."

She laughed and he joined in, amused at his own quip. This made it easy for him; he was glad she could see his sense of humour. He remembered Han, when he had first walked into his house. Poor Han! He was afraid to look around him and had pretended to be blind to the objects in his living room. Han had walked briskly past the objects into the courtyard where he breathed with relief and stood gazing at the sky above. It was as if Han had been expressing relief that his soul had not been tainted by capitalist temptations. The reactions of other students had not been much different. It was as if they all feared that this ornamental cage could trap their minds. He had tried to make them comfortable by making fun of their seriousness. Yet they had watched his face intently with those black slits of eyes which showed no signs of emotions. He had given up teasing them, and had got down to the serious task of teaching the eager students his knowledge of environmental preservation.

Left to herself, Liang Feng slowly moved around the room. Her thoughts were on Wampu's chairs that lay covered in a dark corner, while Pierre displayed boldly his ornaments before all eyes. In the glass bowl before her, the gold fish flaunted their mandarin richness. Their bulging eyes strained to capture the world within and outside the glass bowl. They swam slowly, constrained by the limited space, reminding her of the lordly occupants of those fabulous houses in bygone days, concealed from the envious eyes of their poor neighbours. Yet that glass bowl had shattered as the revolution swept through the courtyards and palaces. Pity for Wampu swept over Liang Feng. Wampu too would have preferred to see her chairs displayed and admired by all, and not kept hidden.

The place was becoming oppressive for her, hastening her departure from that room. She entered the gallery where the paintings of China's old masters were hung. The soft delicate lines of the cranes and the pine trees soothed her eyes. The pine trees breathed life in the detailed exposure of their glorious branches and magnificent roots. There were also paintings of cherry blossoms and apple blossoms etched delicately beside finches and sparrows. It was delightful to see the fine strokes of the brush vertically executed, to make mountains grow in extent and depth.

86

The paintings were mounted on scrolls. With surprise Liang Feng observed a painting of Quibishi hanging boldly between the illustrations of landscapes. Quibishi's works were now condemned; they had become revisionist in the eyes of the authorities. Yet Liang Feng was unable to discover any signs of revisionism in the painting of the cock bird with its comb of dazzling red, beside a creeper of water gourd.

Pierre's paintings too hung on the opposite side of the wall. She admired his brilliant splash of colours. His sea was a dazzling blue, his earth was a diverse mixture of reds and browns; his red fiery mountains and earth resembled a scene at the time of creation. The landscapes were open and spacious as they stretched horizontally, blending well with the background of the white wall. Pierre's paintings reflected varying moods. Liang Feng was drawn to an artistic impression of the dawn, its soft colours reminding her of the view from Behai Pagoda. All his paintings mirrored a paradox of startling vitality and a hermit's solitude.

Realising that she had lingered too long, Liang Feng hastened to the study. The students were absorbed in a discussion and, quietly drawing up a chair, Liang Feng sat away from the group. The animated discussion was about methods of preventing sewage flowing into waterways. Pierre was logical in his approach,

"I have always maintained that the central authorities should implement standards before development is planned."

A student objected hesitantly,

"But it is too costly. We cannot put rules and then start an industry."

Pierre's response was,

"Why not? Under a popular leadership it is much easier to have correct laws from the beginning than under a capitalist state." He became conscious of Liang Feng's presence as she watched him with interest. She herself was in agreement with what he was saying. She knew of countries with free economies callously allowing the land to be poisoned in a greed for wealth. She had been enraged by the hypocrisy of those economists who turned a blind eye to those wrong practices and then unapologetically spent vast sums of money in eradicating the evil consequences. In her eyes, democracy was a failure in the nations that professed to be democratic. The voice of the silent majority was powerless while the voices of persuasion, force and power triumphed. Self-interest was more in vogue than democratic practices. Even if Chairman Mao wanted democratic communism, there would always be discontented elements hindering its effectiveness. Pierre was saying,

"I have seen the dangers of pollution in the western world; I hate to see it happening here too."

Moved by his words and feeling courageous, Liang Feng quipped,

"Yet everybody is in a hurry to catch up with the developing countries. They seldom see the dangers."

Han said,

"I know there are some who think economic leaps can solve all problems."

This comment was sarcastic because party leaders had now become the focus of criticism. He was hinting at the ideological clash between Mao Zedong's political revolution and Lieu Shaoqui's economic programme.

Liang Feng was quick to notice that the stigma attached to foreigners and western imperialists had not affected the students' confidence in Pierre. She realised that they found Pierre more approachable than some of his Chinese university colleagues who held revisionist ideas and would readily conspire to restore the old society, with all its class divisions.

The discussion gradually slipped on to the problems of the students.

Han again said,

"The new policy should combine manual work with academic work."

"Yes," chorused some others.

Han continued,

"The old-fashioned professors cannot see this point of view and prefer to retain the old system."

Pierre interrupted,

"It is a good idea, but there should be a fair basis of selection to the Universities."

Another student said,

"I believe Chairman Mao is right in saying our education is too old-fashioned, it should be changed to a more proletarian one."

Han's response was enthusiastic,

"That means children of workers and peasants would have a good chance to enter universities."

Pierre said sharply,

"But is it correct to pick out a student because of his parents' past?"

He supported fair play and would not justify discrimination at any level. In deference to Pierre's opinion everyone, including Han, cried out,

"It should not happen!" and more vehemently,

"We want democratic communism for all!"

Han's next statement surprised Liang Feng,

"I agree with Pierre but unfortunately those students who oppose the new system are critical of him. Behind his back they call him an interfering foreigner."

Pierre laughed amicably as all eyes scrutinised him. He was not angry with those students. In fact he wanted to help them to think more democratically. Liang Feng interrupted quickly,

"When people cling to feudal ideas of discrimination, revolutions are inevitable."

Agreeing with Liang Feng, Han said,

"You are right, it is not democracy or socialism that they want, but to go back to feudal times."

Pierre had seen in the university a slow emergence of intellectual elitism, those who hankered after privileges for themselves and their families. Mao Zedong feared elitism creeping into the party structure and had said, "I do not like to see today's peasants becoming tomorrow's rich peasants."

Mao Zedong was suspicious of any move to restore the old feudal society. To overcome those fears he had ushered in the Cultural Revolution to stem the thoughts of revisionism. He also encouraged the Red Guards to criticise those in power, before power made them corrupt.

Mao's call to the student body to visit poor villages and to get to know the peasants was resented by those who did not like to undergo the hardships of country life. Pierre did not blame those students; he himself had seen and experienced the difficulties of living in the country. The manual work was tedious, and added heavily to the burdens of the struggling agricultural workers.

Reflecting on this, Pierre turned to Han,

"Do you think combining manual work with academic work is beneficial to students?"

Han replied stoutly,

"Oh yes, some professors know only to grow rice in books."

Everybody laughed. Liang Feng interrupted,

"When I arrived here the authorities criticised my bourgeois education. They said I possessed only book learning."

With confidence she continued,

"But now I am capable of practical work. I really enjoyed my farm work once I learnt how to deal with the farm animals."

Her words appeared to have impressed Han who said admiringly,

"It is really not only the fault of education; I see faults in our society as well."

Liang Feng was rather surprised to hear such bold criticism expressed by a student. Gaining courage from this and also feeling secure within the walls of Pierre's home, she ventured,

"Yes, it is really our society that is to blame. It is still steeped in feudalism and Confucianism."

Han was gratified; he stood up and declared excitedly,

"I agree with you. The hierarchy of obedience has its roots in Confucianism. We have begun a campaign to discredit Confucian philosophy."

The others applauded and their approval was as fuel to his suppressed rage, and he burst out,

"Confucius has too long dominated the minds of our people and they fear even to think of any new ideas that could oppose the confirmed social hierarchy."

Liang Feng's spirit was kindled by these words and she said,

"Even in the 20th century Confucianism is stronger than the socialism that Chairman Mao represents."

Glancing at Liang Feng a student who had so far remained silent commented,

"Most people don't know that the weaker in any society gets exploited. It is because of this reason that Chairman Mao wants us students to criticise the professors."

Pierre laughed, and said in a teasing voice,

"Go ahead, criticise me. I'm your professor."

Han was emphatic,

"But it is not the same Pierre, you are different. You allow us to question and argue with you, but the other professors do not let us do this."

Pierre once again laughed. "That's why I am getting criticised."

As Liang Feng listened, there was a feeling that she was living in a different world where they all had the right to complain and criticise. Yet she knew that none of them would dare to do so outside Pierre's house. The expressions on the faces around her were so different to what they had been when they critically watched her at Behai. Her thoughts went further back to her irritation with Wang Lee on being forced to listen to his readings on communist ideals from 'The Revolutionary Road for Young Intellectuals'. She had already accepted the changes with keenness, anticipating a democratic communism. What she found especially irksome were the platitudes.

She was jolted from her reminiscences by Pierre's voice, this time speaking only to her as his speech was in French which only she knew,

"Liang Feng, do you feel any restrictions in your life here?"

He had obviously been watching her and had guessed the direction of her thoughts. There was curiosity in the faces around her. Taking a deep breath she said firmly, "No!"

She had justified in her own mind that the restrictions she suffered in the new society were far better than the insecurity she had experienced when the family's business had collapsed in Jakarta. To her family the limited freedom of speech was worthless in the face of financial insecurity. Reluctant to speak of her family in the presence of outsiders, and also not wishing to create suspicion, she continued in Chinese trying to explain her reasons,

"Even in the free world, poverty and insecurity restrict one's freedom of movement."

Pierre's voice was grave,

"I agree with you."

She however felt the hollowness of her own words which she had just uttered. She realised she was afraid of her own self. She did not want to admit that the society she had adopted was also making mistakes. But she could not avoid noticing them when a force within her sometimes prompted her to dissect the new system as if combing it with a fine tooth comb. Since meeting Donald and Sally Brown this had become a frequent occupation. She had that uncomfortable feeling that she did not feel free with herself as they were with themselves. Sometimes Liang Feng was afraid of the invisible wall around her. Often she had been startled out of her sleep when that wall trapped her in her dreams. She sometimes feared that the wall would suffocate her life if she did not break through it. Pierre's watchful eyes had seen the conflict within her. She hurriedly turned her face away from his gaze. It was a dilemma she did not wish him to comprehend.

Rising from his chair, Pierre led the students to his kitchen. He indicated the cooker. "If you light a fire for me, you can have the benefit of cooking a Chinese meal with me," he said jokingly. Showing keen enthusiasm, they trooped into the kitchen. Pierre said to Liang Feng,

"What I detest in this house is this large brick monster. I should have insisted on a modern gas cooker."

The object that attracted all eyes was the large brick-built coal cooker. It covered nearly half the space in the small kitchen. The wide funnel rose up, opening out through the ceiling and the roof. Han exclaimed,

"Pierre, this cooker can prepare a ten course meal at the same time." Pierre lifted the large round iron covers. Stooping low, Han pulled out from the space underneath the brick stand, a basket of coal, and emptied it into the opening above. One basket was not sufficient and he added a second, but the cooker was still only half filled-up. Once this was done the students crowded around wondering what the next step would be. Han struck a match and held it onto a lump of coal, but nothing happened. Only a streak of thin smoke emanated from the burnt matchstick. Finding an iron funnel, Han blew on the coal till his face was flushed with exhaustion, but in vain.

Standing by, Pierre was watching with some amusement, surprised at everyone's inability to light the fire. Finally when the room was getting uncomfortable with smoke, he came to their aid saying,

"Come, I'll show you a much easier way to light this monstrous hog."

Taking a bottle of paraffin from the kitchen shelf, he sprinkled it on the coal, next he lit a match-stick and threw it on the coal. There was an instant burst of fire and the coal started to burn. The students clapped their hands in approval and pleasure. Watching the flames, Han murmured,

"We must find easier ways to help the people and we must discontinue the old-fashioned way of life."

He was thoughtful and serious. In agreement another said,

"Such inconveniences increase the burdens of the poor."

Liang Feng, standing by the door watching the whole episode, said,

"It is women who suffer most with no help from the men."

Han interrupted with an eager face,

"But now things are changing; the Revolution has given true equality to both sexes."

Unable to listen to Han's ignorance of the real situation, Liang Feng sarcastically said,

"They say women are equal to men, but the women are paid less for the same work the men do."

Han showed surprise at this disclosure. He listened with disbelief when Liang Feng elaborated,

"I was paid much less than my male colleagues though they did the same work as I did on the farm."

Disappointed at what he saw as an injustice, Han said vehemently,

"We must change this, that's why the Chairman says,

"It is up to the people including women to be vigilant and expose injustice".

He was a keen exponent of Chairman Mao's philosophy. He held the attention of the rest as he continued,

"If the proletariat becomes apathetic then capitalism will slowly take over."

His colleagues cheered Han and one young man, speaking for all, declared,

"*We* are supporting the continuous revolution till everybody has equality and justice."

Pierre smiled hearing the frank disclosure of views. He was glad they had no fear of expressing their ideas in his house. As if he wanted them to reflect on a special subject, he spoke thoughtfully,

"Exploitation by one class of another has always happened from the beginnings of the so-called civilisation of man. I wonder how this can be stopped".

The students were silent as each one reflected on what Pierre had said. The room was getting heated with the burning coal and, noticing the time, Pierre's mood changed to lighthearted banter,

"Come on, you can reflect on what I have said after eating, now help me to prepare the food".

The meal was cooked by a happy group of students with help from Liang Feng and Pierre. The green capsicums cut in cubes and mixed with well browned pieces of chicken was Pierre's favourite. He was served a generous helping as they sat round the circular table for the meal. Liang Feng's preparation of fried fish with a hot sauce, which was especially enjoyed by everyone, blended well with the pale egg noodles. It was a happy meal, after which the students hastened home.

Liang Feng was now alone with Pierre, who sat cross-legged on the couch facing her. This was the first time she had been alone with a man since Wang Lee's departure. Surprisingly she was relaxed and at ease, as he was. She had known him only a few hours but their companionship seemed long. There was a peaceful silence between them.

It was Pierre who opened the conversation; he wanted to say something about himself to her. "I have been in this city for three years; it has been home to my spirit." After a brief pause he continued,

"I like the absence of sophistication in my students."

As Liang Feng remained silent, listening to him, he went on,

"Isn't it wonderful to be with people who do not have too much driving ambition."

It was as if he was asking for her opinion and she said,

"It may be because there is no competition here." With a nod in acknowledgement Pierre said,

"I can see how the Chairman's mind works. Competition unleashed would inevitably make one group ambitious and ruthless, while the other gets exploited and apathetic."

It pleased her to hear a foreigner commend Chairman Mao's philosophy. Donald had not been exaggerating when he said his friend was knowledgeable of China's history. Pierre went on,

"The criticism against the Chairman is that he has put politics before economic progress, but I can see his point. He wants everybody to equally share, not the benefits alone but also the hard work." His voice held conviction,

"I wish everybody around him would comprehend the true meaning of Mao's ideology." She was moved by Pierre's understanding and said thoughtfully,

"Yes, he fears President Lieu Shaoqui's economic leap that would reduce the status of the less able to hire labour, and shackle them in bondage to new masters."

Smiling now, Pierre said,

"Liang Feng, I see you are very enthusiastic for the new changes, but I also see you have a questioning mind."

She realised that he had an understanding of the thoughts in her mind, and looking at him she reflected,

"I like him to talk to me, it makes me realise I am not all alone in the quest for a just society."

Pierre too was glad that he had found it easy to communicate with Liang Feng. He did not feel awkward to carry on this frank discussion with her. Attempts at such a conversation had sometimes upset his students who did not encourage his criticism concerning the lack of individual freedom.

Remembering Donald and looking for a chance to change the subject, Liang Feng said,

"Your friend told me that you liked living here."

It surprised Pierre that she remembered a reference to him at a time he was a total stranger to her. He laughed,

"Oh, Donald is a good diplomat, he is charming and he will not leave any stones unturned to get at information".

His next statement however held a tinge of sarcasm as well as a desire to assess her,

"He would have found you an invaluable source of information." Her reply was defensive,

"I was happy I found someone to speak with in a language I had not used for three years." Recollecting her pleasure at the time, words now rushed out; her voice earnest and appealing,

"I had no reservations in speaking to him about my life in the commune. I could trust him, I felt my opinions were safe with him and would not be disclosed."

She then spoke more quietly,

"Later I wondered whether I misjudged him, whether he really understood."

Pierre said quickly,

"Donald can sometimes appear patronising, but that would be typical of most foreigners here. I have advised him of this, and that it would not win the people's good will." He was attempting to make her understand a foreigner's attitude.

"You know how it is, when a foreign community isolated from the rest, get together. One may say authoritatively,

"Hey, do you know the latest queer saying? Everybody round that chap will start laughing at what he has to say. Anything that happens here which they cannot understand is queer or strange to them."

Liang Feng laughed to see him imitate his own people. He continued,

"Donald thought I was an odd Chinese, but I did enjoy speaking to him of all the things he was dying to hear."

He did not consider the manner of her reference to Donald as an exaggeration. He felt it was characteristic of Donald to be so enthusiastic in his quest for information. He laughed.

In a serious tone Pierre said,

"I wish they could live like me among the people, they would then not consider their cooks and amahs as the typical representatives of the Chinese."

After a pause he went on,

"They make such sweeping statements on everything; my arguments to the contrary are futile."

Liang Feng, listening, saw Pierre the foreigner trying to assess the revolution and the people in an understanding manner. Pierre went on speaking,

"It is these sweeping statements that finally make headlines in the press; the exaggerations distort the facts and always makes sensational news for readers."

This seemed to remind him of his own previous career as a journalist. "I was happy only as a freelance journalist and not when I was working for any particular newspaper. But the money is always in sensational stories."

Liang Feng interrupted with some hesitation,

"Yes, Donald did appear to find the commune system a source of startling information."

Pierre laughed as he too had heard fascinating stories about the commune system. Feeling that he himself was not without blame for holding mistaken views, his voice became gentle. "Donald is a good chap, he is a good friend, but he is too inquisitive of many things".

Pierre recalled the shared years at boarding school with Donald who, even when Pierre knew only a smattering of English, had gone out of his way to be his friend. They had lost touch for many years until Donald had contacted him by letters when he had got the appointment in Peking. Remembering him with affection he said,

"He is a charming fellow, it is the service that makes him an enigma." Liang Feng said quickly,

"Yes, I found him very agreeable."

Pierre was surprised at himself, that he had spoken so easily with someone who had a few hours earlier been just a stranger, about himself and his friend. His brown eyes, observing her, smiled as he said "I enjoyed talking with you. I hope you will come to see me again."

To dispel any awkwardness on her part she quickly added,

"You are a journalist and an environmental expert who can help our country. I like to know how you can influence the authorities to accept correct views."

Pierre said in a personal tone, not wanting to discuss his work,

"I am more interested in the people in this environment as to what brought your father and you to Peking to face a new lifestyle here."

His words had brought a flush to her cheeks. She too wanted to see him again though she could not give expression to this wish. Dusk was approaching, the hours had sped by and it was time to leave but there was reluctance in her. It had been a long time she had felt as relaxed as in his company.

Seeing her rise from her chair, Pierre said,

"I know it is getting dark and you have to be back in the commune." Following her to the door, he took her hand in his and she felt the warmth of friendship towards him. He had awakened within her the first real stirrings towards a close human relationship. She stood by the door awkwardly waiting; she did not want to leave him.

The silence between them was becoming uncomfortable. Liang Feng felt dazed at the intrusion of emotions. To recover her composure she murmured inanely,

"I hope to come again to practice my French with you."

His laughter broke the uncomfortable silence as he replied,

"This would be a good opportunity to practice my Chinese with you."

When he opened the door she stepped out with a smile to him and a strange lightness in her heart.

Cultural Revolution destroys religious idols

Buddha images are removed from temples

Embassies under attack

Celebrating May Day with the 'Red Book'

In Waichia Talou from above

Foreign friend reads from 'Red Book'

Entrance to Waichia Talou (foreigners' building)

Employees reading 'the book' at the start of the day in Waichia Talou

Damage done by Red Guards to an Embassy

Inside an Embassy building

Cultural Revolution brings changes in the Army uniforms

The young Red Guards

Celebrating National Day with Mao Ze Dong in the Forbidden City

The drums roll in for street demonstrations

Effigies, effigies of foreigners

CHAPTER 12

Waichia Talou

Waichia Talou was an old impressive building. Walled in from all sides with two massive iron gates at the entrance and exit, it housed the majority of embassy personnel living in Peking in the year 1966. It was here that Liang Feng again met Donald Brown and his wife who had an apartment in this 'foreigner's compound' as Waichia Talou was generally called. It was pleasant for her to renew her friendship with him and she would meet him almost daily when he walked through the compound of the apartment block on his way to the British Mission. His openness and curiosity still brought a smile to her face but the keen enthusiasm which he had displayed on the train was now tinged with sarcasm; and therefore the relationship was somewhat strained by Donald's constant insensitive remarks on the 'Chinese System', which he blamed whenever he could not understand the country and its people.

Waichia Talou could easily have passed off as a new block of apartments, yet there was something special about the place. A uniformed guard stood at the entrance and another at the exit, keeping a careful watch on the locals entering and leaving the building. The guards first checked the workers' identity cards and their humble possessions before they were allowed to pass through. However the little cloth bag a worker carried, the only item allowed to be on his person, would hardly encourage him to smuggle anything through. There were the cynics amongst the foreign community interpreting this safeguard not as a means of protection granted to them, but as a measure to restrain the locals from surrendering to any foreign temptations.

It was a routine practice for the sentry to check Liang Feng's identity as she passed through, on her way to work every morning despite his acknowledgement of her as the new interpreter attached to the administrative office for the maintenance of Waichia Talou and its residents.

Her work became complicated when politics started to interfere. Misunderstandings in communication between workers and employers became common when international incidents occurred and affected the People's Republic of China. Significantly, misunderstandings between the workers and their foreign masters would correspond with hostilities between the countries of the foreign personnel concerned, and the government of Peking.

In the early months of 1966 there was a notable increase in the number of domestic clashes between workers and their employers, and Liang Feng was often summoned to mediate when the cooks or amahs deliberately disobeyed instructions given to them. Her task was made more difficult by the Service Bureau keeping a vigilant eye on her and encouraging the employees to dissent. In the eyes of the Bureau the incidents of Chinese nationals being harassed and ill-treated abroad could not go disregarded. The workers themselves were under two masters, the Service Bureau being the more powerful of the two. The wages earned by the cooks and the maids were controlled and handled by the Bureau who incited the workers to disregard their conditions of work stipulated at the time of employment.

All citizens of Peking and especially the workers at Waichia Talou were well informed of international events that affected the government of Peking. The local Chinese newspapers, the radio broadcasts and the study classes kept the citizens politically alert, with interpretations given by the authorities of events abroad.

Beginning with the demonstrations against the Russians, other countries followed in the table of enemies of the People's Republic of China. Indonesia was next in line to receive such hostile treatment. It was a novel way to hurt the personnel of those countries by getting their domestic staff to express their anger by giving the, tit for tat treatment. The Service Bureau that controlled the Waichia Talou employees' wages instructed the domestics to abandon their house work at most the vulnerable times such as cooking, shopping, organising official receptions or looking after children. This hit their masters who had come to depend on the Chinese staff for good work and trustworthiness. The strong condemnation levelled by Peking's government against foreign governments did not stop there. Demonstrations were organised for the workers to have hands-on experience. There were instances when the cooks would even leave the food to burn in the saucepans to join sporadic demonstrations by the gates of Waichia Talou. There were the leaders, leading these demonstrations who stopped by the gate to shout 'Down with imperialists' and next read from Chairman Mao's Quotations while brandishing the 'Little Red Book' vigorously. Very often the diplomats would come on to their balconies to listen with curiosity to the tirade of accusations that increased when they appeared. But amazingly no one felt really threatened. The rumour was that the authorities were in full control and used these means to divert the peoples' attention from facing the economic hardships in the country.

The number of countries accused of unfriendly acts towards Peking increased daily. Despite the influences of the Service Bureau, some of the workers in Weidatalo were finding themselves in a dilemma. Their sense of justice impelled them to doubt the fairness of their own provocative behaviour against their employers who treated them with kindness and consideration.

Donald Brown's apartment was behind the main building where the British diplomatic staff was housed. In the main building a large portrait of Chairman Mao adorned the doorway to the building. The Service Bureau was on the ground floor of this building. Donald Brown often said jokingly to Liang Feng,

"Each time I pass through this doorway I salute the Great Chairman whether I like it or not."

The teasing sometimes irritated Liang Feng as she supressed the accusations that rose within her.

These were the occasions when the past misdeeds by imperialists clouded her judgement. Not caring to argue in the current anti foreign wave of demonstrations against all foreigners, she silently swallowed his insults, angrily muttering to herself on his departure,

"He has the same patronising manner his people adopted towards our last Empress." Her eyes would turn pleadingly to the portrait of Chairman Mao, silently appealing for courage. It was only Chairman Mao who could give the citizens the confidence and pride to stand up to such bullying.

Pierre too was not happy when his friend singled out the local people for ridicule. After an evening with Donald, Pierre mentioned to her with some distaste,

"Donald annoys me, he easily forgets the past. I am ashamed of the West when I remember that they were even willing to make war in order to force down opium on the Chinese. They are quick to forget their own wrongdoings and accuse the Chinese of being full of vices."

It moved Liang Feng to see Pierre, a foreigner, defending her people. Pierre was strongly critical of the ridicule directed against the Chinese system by the foreign community.

Pierre was a bachelor and 31 years of age. He had not spoken to Liang Feng of his past but had revealed sociable qualities. He had many friends and appeared to willingly give of himself when necessary.

Observing her studying him with curiosity, not unmixed with a faint hint of admiration he said almost apologetically,

"Liang Feng, I am not averse to women, but I am afraid of possessive women."

In a reminiscent mood he gave a quiet laugh,

"Liang Feng, most women do like to manipulate men, so that men become their subconscious slaves, helpless and dependent."

He smiled to himself. Liang Feng was at a loss to answer. It was the very first time a man had spoken to her about the conflict of the sexes.

Unaware of her embarrassment, Pierre went on pensively,

"I enjoy living alone; there is so much freedom to do what one likes. In Peking there are many places where one is happiest being alone listening to the sounds of nature."

Liang Feng was quick to interrupt him. "Yes, my father said the same, he said he liked to listen to the sound of trees growing, and this he was able to hear only after he arrived here."

Pierre's voice was warm. "When I visit the Fragrant Hills I like to sit in the 'Luminous Temple' at the time of sunset and hear the wind whistle through the pine forest."

The recollections seemed to hold him in deep thought. It was as if he had been hypnotised by those ancient gnarled roots that stood in mysterious dark shadows under the setting sun, secretly holding the continuing history of the land.

Observing the peaceful expression on his face Liang Feng said softly,

"You sometimes remind me of a painting that hangs in your house – with the sage meditating under the pine tree."

His thoughts interrupted, he said,

"Meditation gives me a feeling of being in sympathy with the world." He remembered how he was driven by his inner self to go in search of a tree under whose shelter he could meditate; he had sometimes found the conventional places of worship distracting – for instance he could not meditate amongst the clutter of ornaments in a temple. He gave expression to his thoughts,

"We human beings are always judging people and man-made things, but we accept nature with equanimity."

In his younger days Pierre had been a happy but sensitive and alert child, always questioning the adults around him. This quality had persisted through the years of growing, until his chosen career took him to Bhutan – it was there that his questioning mind had questioned. The practice of meditation had curbed his disposition to form quick judgments of, and control his reactions to, difficult situations. Bhutan had the profound effect of making him a peaceful, compassionate person; his primary concern became the protection of the natural environment for the benefit of all living things. His spontaneity and open minded attitude was child-like. It was Liang Feng's open nature that made him seek her friendship. She understood his appreciation of nature and had herself related to him her joy to be on the summit of the Behai Island and its pagoda. He recalled his visits to the Seven Storey Pagoda in the Fragrant Hills – an experience that never failed to move him. The multitude of bells in the corners of each roof would sway gently as the breeze blew over the hills and the tinkling chimes would blend harmoniously with the soft music of nature around the Pagoda.

Pierre's voice warmed with enthusiasm. "'In the Fragrant Hills I can hear the music of nature. You must come there with me to listen to it." Liang Feng replied quietly,

"I have been there; the bells of the temple seem to echo my thoughts. They sing of freedom to me." Her answer struck him as very unusual. "I wonder how the authorities would look upon that." She laughed. "Freedom is within me and I don't let anyone read my thoughts." Her eyes, softly smiling at him, conveyed her spirit of freedom. The very act of being there alone with him was an act of freedom.

Donald Brown found his friend Pierre a valuable source of advice in countering the anti-foreign feelings amongst the local community. When, one day Donald had expressed anger at the unjustified accusations levelled against his country, Pierre told him calmly,

"You must not take these insults personally, the people are like children, they will hurl insults but forget it the next day." However Pierre made this comment on Chairman Mao,

"The Chairman's drive for changes overlooks one important fact. People need time to get used to reforms and an evolutionary process is necessary. Forced reforms will not succeed."

Liang Feng was delighted to find how easily she could communicate with Pierre. One day she found occasion to speak to him of his art,

"There is something about your landscape paintings that intrigues me. Is the white cloud which appears in most of your paintings something symbolic to you?"

With a thoughtful expression on his face he studied her; no one had questioned him before on the little cloud, and he hesitated before replying. It was something he had felt he could never explain about to others; but now perceiving her keen interest he was moved,

"It is something special to me; it is a symbol of the spiritual awakening in the mind of man."

In a mood of reflection he went on,

"Material comforts cannot bring fulfilment without a sense of spiritual awakening."

Abruptly he stopped, wondering why he was speaking in this vein to a Chinese of the modern era who would certainly have been indoctrinated with the concept that 'Religion is the Opium of the Masses' and that spirituality is not a necessary part of man's life. But with no hint of scepticism she was listening to him with complete concentration.

In a gentle voice Pierre said,

"You do understand what I am trying to say, don't you? One day, you too will need to seek a spiritual life in this society."

These words made her uncomfortable and her cheeks burnt with embarrassment for revealing her inner self to him – a total stranger. She felt that her loyalty to the state and its dogma was being questioned. But that strangeness had never been there when she had approached him in Behai Park. She closed her eyes firmly *as* if to shut out that part of herself from his scrutiny. Then opening her eyes and confronting him directly she said in a matter of fact voice,

"I am not dissatisfied with my life here; it is just that I like to see more individual participation in keeping with the ideals of a true Democratic Communism."

Pierre answered reflectively,

"Yes it is only when all other needs are satisfied that man will be free to look inwards and reflect on the meaning of life."

But sometimes Liang Feng confessed to herself that in her defence of the authorities, she was not voicing her true opinions. This made her feel guilty. She was unhappy that she herself was drawing away from the regimentation imposed by the authorities and reflecting- too much on individual freedom. But the voices around her held her captive with their constant reiteration that 'individualism is bourgeois'. She pressed the palms of her hands against her ears to shut out the inner voice crying "I am different!" and kept telling herself,

"I want to be like everyone else."

When discussing her country with Pierre there were times when she expressed criticism of her country's barbaric past when its citizens were held in bondage. But Pierre would then remind her of the glories of the past dynasties. On one occasion he happened to say,

"Had the Ching dynasty lasted another one hundred years, how much more richness would have been added to your glorious heritage."

With blazing eyes she had retorted,

"How can you commend a barbaric feudal society where a handful of individuals forced a nation to cringe at their feet?"

His obvious amusement goaded her strangely into anger. However calming herself she added less vehemently,

"I have never cared for the old Confucian philosophy, I could never accept its rule of blind obedience."

Pierre waited patiently until her eyes questioned him and then he said in a gentle voice,

"Liang Feng, what is it now – isn't 'obedience' part of the present system?"

She recoiled as if he had struck her; then retaliated, a gleam of triumph in her eyes,

"Of course the Chairman is aware of that. He himself encourages the movement to bombard the headquarters where a few have taken it upon themselves to make decisions."

Yet her rhetoric did not fully convince him, nor did it convince her. His words had pierced her defences of the Revolution. She still clung to her argument,

"But surely you see our freedom to criticise the top party persons? The wall posters do express people's opinion and they do criticise party officials however powerful they are."

Pierre smiled knowingly,

"Yes, I saw a poster critical of Premier Chou En Lai just the other day. It intrigues me as to how posters keep appearing surreptitiously in Wan Fu Chin and the Democracy Wall."

His words renewed her belief in the possibility of individual freedom in her country and she said boldly,

"The campaign criticising the 'Four Olds' began in support of the people. Those trying to stifle their right to have a say in the administration should no longer be tolerated." Pierre was cautious,

"I do accept that the communism practiced here is different to the type of communism practiced elsewhere. Chairman Mao deserves most of the credit for this."

Elated that the Chairman's ideology was understood by someone she would like to consider 'a friend of China' Liang Feng said fervently,

"Whatever the outcome may eventually be, Chairman Mao's intentions are genuinely good..."

"...and, those who carry them out have no genuine intentions," Pierre interrupted, as if completing the sentence for her. Their eyes met and they laughed.

Liang Feng sat back feeling relaxed. In her eyes Pierre was the only foreigner who was making an attempt to understand her nation. She immediately thought of Donald who seemed negative about the Chairman and his schemes, making no attempt to understand the events in the country's history that had led to the present situation. The sentiments Pierre had expressed gave her the confidence to hand to him her copy of *The Thoughts of Chairman Mao*. "Please don't think I am trying to indoctrinate you" she said with a diffident smile.

Although Liang Feng tried to convince Pierre that the Revolution was progressing smoothly, he had his doubts. He was one day at Behai Park with her when a group of young demonstrators with their usual cry of "Down with Revisionists!" and "Down with Imperialists", passed by, many of them hardly old enough to be considered politically mature. The voices seemed louder and shriller when the group passed them and he sensed a threat in the stares levelled directly at the spot where they were seated, but he did not disclose this to Liang Feng. Instead he said, veiling his concern,

"Isn't one Revolution enough in a lifetime?" Relaxed and happy, Liang Feng had noticed nothing unusual. "There is no Revolution. It is more a Movement to eradicate from the Party the remaining anomalies of the old feudal system.

We are only trying to give the people a share in determining how the country should be run."

Pierre was amused to observe Liang Feng resorting to her usual strategy when needing to defend herself against possible scepticism. Her armour was the books by Chairman Mao and the little Red Book, which she always carried on her person. Drawing out of her pocket the book on 'Contradictions' she read out, her voice solemn and serious,

"It is a fallacy to believe that the old society could co-exist with the new," and turning a page, "Revisionism and Complacency could and would lead to the restoration of the old Society."

The single-minded fanaticism and the menace he had seen in the young faces still fresh in his mind, Pierre was negative. "I very much fear that the extremism of those seeking a change can undermine the progress of the Movement."

Just as Pierre had foreseen, Mao Zedong's call for verbal attacks on those who followed revisionist ideas took an ugly turn, becoming physical attacks. Hearing of the daily atrocities committed by the Chairman's Red Guards, supposedly as a measure to reform those capitalists acting against national interest, Pierre was outspoken with Liang Feng,

"If there is injustice in a movement trying to reform society, there will always be a backlash against that movement as well. Only in a just society can there be a Revolution without bloodshed."

Liang Feng was silent.

The Chairman had said, "The movement of opposites existed from beginning to end, and the struggle between these aspects determined the life of all things". To Liang Feng the struggle was necessary but she hoped it would be gentle and compassionate, and then those people straying away from the Chairman's goals would change their ways willingly. She realised that an exemplary leadership was an essential part of such a movement. As she listened to Pierre she realised that in his house she had found a sanctuary to express individual freedom. On one occasion when her gratitude to him overpowered her she had impulsively taken his hand and held it against her cheek. His eyes had looked at her gently and his free arm, going around her shoulders, had for a moment held her close to him. She was surprised at her boldness to reveal her feelings but she was helpless against the woman's need within her for a man's understanding and gentleness. Her affection for him was such that it became increasingly difficult to conceal it.

Sometimes returning from his house she was troubled. She wanted to find someone to confide in. In the study class the students were advised to form 'Red Couples' and share their thoughts. But there was no guarantee that the chosen partners would be trustworthy – they could be informers. She remembered Wang Lee who had caused her much sadness and bitterness by reporting her to

112

the authorities when she had refused to participate in his daily ritual of reading 'The Revolutionary Road for Young Intellectuals'. This experience had made her fearful of communicating freely even with the closest associate.

With Pierre, the protective wall built to safeguard her feelings and emotions was gradually but steadily crumbling; a new and compassionate world opening to her. If she needed a friend, should she not trust him rather than anyone else?

CHAPTER 13

The Purple Bamboo Grove

The crisp dryness of the cold winds of February was interrupted by an unexpected snow fall. Liang Feng welcomed snow with the happiness and excitement of a child. She smiled with pleasure at seeing the children run out of their houses and hold their faces up to the falling flakes. The fall of snow, an infrequent occurrence in the winters of Peking, excited not only the children but also the adults. Groups of people gathered outdoors, relieved to see a temporary end to the harsh dry winds of winter, and glad to remove the surgical masks that had protected them from freezing temperatures. The sight of these cotton masks stretched over the mouths and noses of the wearers were certain to raise the eyebrows of visitors to Peking, but to the residents they were as familiar as their blue workers' uniforms, and signified a safe protection not only from the cold but also from dust storms that ravaged the city in the summer.

Her face free of the mask Liang Feng let her fingers gently feel her cheeks that had roughened and turned red during the winter months. Her attempts to purchase any moisturising or soothing creams proved futile as such goods had disappeared from the shops with the advent of the Cultural Revolution. The use of creams and cosmetics was now considered a bourgeois pursuit and Liang Feng, like the rest of her colleagues, suffered by their absence.

The grey tiles of the dilapidated commune homes, normally a sore and cheer-less sight, were transformed by the camouflage of snow to a magical wonderland. Rooftops and brickwork looked brighter as if after a much-needed coat of paint. Though the sight cheered Liang Feng, yet there was that nagging feeling of isola-tion of her inner self as she gazed at the white stretch before her. Loneliness was stark, white and cold, yet there was beauty in that cold desert.

She longed for the company of others appreciative of the beauty before her who would share her joy. Her thoughts were primarily of Pierre Devon. He had been in her mind since she had been in his house. She was begin-ning to be drawn to him. There was something in him that was solitary as the snow before her. She smiled remembering the companionship she felt with him. Taking a handful of snow she held it against her cheek. She had seen gentleness in his demeanour which was appealing to her own nature. His brown eyes were full of warmth which moved her. She quickly checked herself. It was all wrong of her to think of him in this manner. He was only a foreigner. "One should not build up on people one does not know." But on the other hand there was that inner voice that kept saying, "I feel an affinity with him rarely experienced with others." His biographical data was necessary although the authorities would process all details customary for all aliens visiting the country.

The snow fell gently; it was covering her cloth shoes. She kicked out, leaving a gash in the snow had exposed the warm brown earth beneath. In her eyes it looked naked and hurt. Bending down she gently spread out the snow to cover the exposed wound. It was well camouflaged.

Wang Lee had hurt her. But she had concealed her hurt with an outward cold dressing. That pain had been overcome with a fervent enthusiasm to learn the new way of life. But unfortunately the thought of a new life no longer excited her as it did before. She trembled. The cold wind was blowing on her.

The snow continued to fall at a leisurely pace. The sun shining brightly spread a warm glow on the white surface. The fields before her were at rest. Words of poets sang in her heart. She had allowed them to reappear once again after a lapse of three years. She dared now to remember poet Chou Yang. It was not very long ago, in 1961, that Chou Yang had said, "Artists, poets and authors must break away from situations when everything is stamped with a political view."

Trapped in a magic world of new emotions awakening within her, bewitched by the drifting snow flakes Chou Yang's challenge still echoing in her memory, she now longed for the freedom to give expression to her own personal feelings. Wrapped in deep thought she was startled when a snowball thrown by a child, struck the back of her head. She tripped back in shock, as if her mind had dared too much and was recoiling in fear. What was she thinking? Had the snow ploughed through her mind mesmerising her? Chou Yang was considered a revisionist. His message had been interpreted as bourgeois liberal thought that could undermine the communist state. The authorities blamed him for "throwing open the doors to all demons". However, she was now beginning to respect his courage in criticising the leadership.

She wondered if she herself would be considered one of the 'demons' who ignored the party line, especially as she could not wholeheartedly agree with the authorities' interpretation of Chou Yang's message's meaning, "Worship the foreign and restore the old." Her pacing was abruptly brought to a halt by the sight of a familiar figure approaching in the company of two others.

It was unmistakably Pierre with two of his students, Han and Li. Once again the party's harsh criticism of Chou Yang reverberated in her mind. She felt gripped by guilt as if one of those under the poet's influence. But as Pierre came nearer there was only pure delight that made her say softly to herself, "I like him not because he is a foreigner but because he understands my thoughts."

Liang Feng was tongue-tied as Pierre greeted her warmly,

"Han told me you lived here, and I thought it a good opportunity to visit you. We are on our way to the Purple Bamboo Grove; would you like to come with us?"

Gladdened by his visit she welcomed him and his students. But aware that the residents of the commune who were standing around were observing the strangers steadily, she cautioned,

"I think it would be better if we could leave this place immediately and proceed to the Purple Bamboo Grove."

It was only after they had walked out of the commune and to the road that Liang Feng became conscious of Han's change in appearance, for he wore a Red Guard armband on his khaki shirt. She remembered that he had once expressed to Pierre that his ambition was to be a Red Guard and trek to distant villages in order to spread the new morality of the Chairman's philosophy. She had then not taken him seriously. She wondered cautiously if he genuinely emulated the ideals of the Chairman or he fell into the category of those militant Red Guards the people feared. In line with her speculation the residents, and even those on the roadside, appeared to show anxiety as their eyes followed the group. The sight of a foreigner, whether in the capital or a suburb, always excited the attention of the people, but on this occasion it was not only Pierre who drew their eyes but also Han in his Red Guard uniform.

Han showed pride in his new status as he strode along confidently with his head held high. Han was determined to characterise the concept of the 'Chairman's ideal Red Guard' as against the people's mistaken identity of the Red Guard being a militant troublemaker resorting to physical force.

Taking a leading role in the revolutionary changes within the Shinhuwa University, his peasant background probably encouraged him to support the new proposals in education that favoured a combination of manual work with academic subjects. This policy encouraged the authorities to show more favour to the recruitment of students from the peasants and soldiers who would be adaptable to the changes than those from the middle classes. But this deliberate policy of discrimination alienated a section of the students and the professors.

Although Pierre had welcomed the combination of practical and academic subjects, he began to doubt the sanity of a policy that would close the door to able students. When the conflict intensified the Chairman called upon his supporters to oppose the professors hostile to his reforms. Clashes erupted within the universities among students as well as between student groups and professors. Distressed by this unrest, Pierre could not help voicing his opinions which brought upon him the charge of being an interfering foreigner. The Chairman's own assessment of the situation was expressed openly in his proclamation, "Since ancient times those who created new ideas new waves of thought have been young people without much learning." Students like Han were thus encouraged to spearhead the revolution in the universities. Walking with the group and conscious of the interest he was creating, Han boldly asked Liang Feng,

"Have you joined the workers league?" She was momentarily taken aback by the question. With Pierre's presence the world of reality seemed out of place and so were Han's words. But realising that Han was eagerly waiting for her answer, she said in a voice that was hardly audible,

"No, but I intend joining sometime soon."

She had always felt uncomfortable when being questioned too closely about the present political changes by Han. It was not an easy matter to freely discuss either with Han or any other citizen unlike with Pierre and even Brown. Pierre heard her and broke into the conversation "There is time enough to join any organisation, but Liang Feng has already proved to the authorities that she has accepted gladly the lifestyle of the state."

Liang Feng was grateful for Pierre's support but she could not help feeling awkward that his defence justified her past attitude rather than her present convictions.

Seeking an opportunity to change the subject Liang Feng said,

"Han seems to be creating a stir among the residents here with his uniform."

Han laughingly replied,

"But they have nothing to fear from me."

The news of Red Guards being directed to remote districts in order to propagate the new morality of Mao Zedong had created a flutter in the commune, as rumours were rife that, rather than using persuasion they resorted to acts of violence in spreading the Chairman's message. Han's movements were closely followed with looks of suspicion.

Han had no sinister motive in questioning Liang Feng. The authorities had called upon the youth to join in the political organisations that had been neglected in a climate of political lethargy. Fearing the signs of growing revisionism, Chairman Mao urged the youth to build up enthusiasm for the communist spirit and emulate the courage of the 'long marchers' of the 1949 revolution. Showing this enthusiasm, Han had willingly accompanied his professor to the commune and the Purple Bamboo Grove.

Reminded of the troubles in the university with the drive for modernising the curriculum, Han now turned to Pierre, his eyes concerned,

"Last week a poster appeared in the university criticising the professors, did you hear of them?"

Pierre had been informed of this but wondered why Han should broach the subject at this particular time. The silence made Han insistent,

"Do you realise that some students are critical of you?"

This time Pierre answered,

"Yes I have seen a change of attitude in some of them; and even of some professors. This I suppose is because of my stand on the selection of students."

By this time they had arrived at the Purple Bamboo Grove. Pierre's eyes lit up at the sight before him. Austere in their delicate beauty, the trees stood silhouetted against a still white background, their mantle of snow making only their stark outlines visible – a study of startling and breathtaking loveliness. Pierre stood transfixed for some moments. Then he turned his eyes, meeting those of Liang Feng, standing quite still, just behind him. Her eyes held a gentle understanding of his emotions, and he held out his hand to her in silent communication. As her fingers clasped his, the emotions that had engulfed her when she had been alone that morning in the snow, flooded back almost choking her with their force – she impulsively lifted his hand to her face resting it against her cheek. Seeing them engrossed in each other, oblivious to them, Han and Li quietly walked away.

Liang Feng did not know how it happened nor could she remember the sequence. All she was conscious of was yielding to the irresistible impulse to touch his face gently with her free hand. And then he was clasping her in a close embrace. It had been a long time since she had held someone so close to her. There was a deep joy to feel his warm body like the warm earth she had touched beneath the snow. She glanced up but his eyes were closed.

Suddenly she felt the icy coldness of the snow on her cheeks, as if a warning had touched her. She drew back from him.

Each becoming aware of the other's appearance, with feet buried in snow and head and face specked with flakes, they both laughed shakily. Although it was nervous laughter it helped to conceal the question in their minds as to what would follow now that they had expressed their feelings.

Liang Feng hesitantly looked over her shoulder. Han and his friend watched her. Pierre smiled as if showing indifference to any curiosity on the part of his students.

The two young men stood a few feet away and surveyed them silently for some time. Lee picked up courage to say gravely,

"Anything today could be considered bourgeois, even the display of human emotions can be misconstrued."

Pierre looked sharply at Lee; was there a hidden threat in his remark? Lee was now looking down and kicking the snow. Liang Feng felt awkward to look at either of the students.

As they walked back, their moods subdued, Pierre reflected on what had happened. He was amazed at his own flow of response to Liang Feng's display of affection. During the three years of his stay in the country, despite his genuine

118

admiration of the Chinese people, no indigenous woman had even slightly touched his emotions as a man, or come close in being freely able to communicate with him. Now not only did he feel mentally attuned with Liang Feng but also inextricably drawn to her.

Han wished to continue with the personal discussion he had begun with Pierre on the way to the Bamboo Grove. Seeing no indication on Pierre's part to resume conversation, he spoke out forcefully,

"Pierre you have lived in the world outside these shores, what is it about Peking that makes you want to go on staying here."

The question took Pierre by surprise. "I like the unsophisticated life of the people," he said slowly and then elaborating more on what he truly felt about living in a place that appeared not to have caught up with the 20th Century said,

"This place gives me peace from car horns and traffic that plagues most cities in the world." Feeling he had not expressed himself sufficiently, and becoming conscious of Liang Feng watching him intently again, he said,

"I feel my inner self at peace with the people and the environment here."

Han was not fully satisfied with Pierre's answer. Doubts had plagued him since he had heard some foreign students critical of the rigid lifestyle forced on them.

"But there are many people finding fault with this manner of living and they dare to call me a fool for believing that human nature would be content to remain simple and unambitious under a democratic communist system."

Listening to Han brought a smile to Pierre's lips. It was typical of Han to be honest and even blunt when expressing his doubts. Taking the role of the Red Guard seriously, Han too displayed a naivety that was common to the majority of the youth suddenly entrusted with political responsibilities by Chairman Mao.

In Liang Feng's mind the slogan that extolled the virtues of a continuous revolution was now unpalatable. In trying to be a good communist she had been cruel and harsh to her own self allowing the rhetoric of slogans and propaganda to dominate her mind. But, yet that unquenchable thirst for justice and freedom had not been surrendered while conforming to the system.

Bidding Pierre goodbye she let her hand rest a while in his. Pierre imparted a warm strength; she needed his support to face her inner conflict. Walking back in the direction of the fields she viewed the open space with a renewed joy. It had stopped snowing, and the air felt fresh and free. In the companionable surroundings of nature she felt a sense of freedom, a lack of inhibitions to express her human feelings.

Her attention was arrested by the sight of workers shovelling snow from the footpaths of the commune. Her spirits became heavy once again as she watched them labour, doubting their contentment. Their prematurely lined faces and drab clothing brought associations of a hard life. Facing vigorous weather could be a burden when it was devoid of individual freedom. Overcome with a feeling of hollowness she left the fields.

Heading towards Wampu's house a curious sight made her stop beside the house of old Lin, the artist in the commune. Bent over a clay stove Lin was burning paper. His grandson, a boy in his early teen, with a stern countenance, was directing the work. Pausing to greet Lin, Liang Feng was amazed to see Lin in the act of destroying his paintings. In a troubled voice Liang Feng questioned,

"Why are you burning your paintings Lin? Raising his face from his crouching position and in an accusing voice he said,

"Ask my grandson. He calls my paintings Bourgeois rubbish." Lin's grandson seemed uncomfortable at these words and quickly remonstrated,

"But grandpa, I am trying to help you. You can be punished for possessing these paintings". There was a mixed feeling of bitterness as she witnessed the destruction of something that was creative. Seeing the tears in Lin's eyes, Liang Feng muttered to herself,

"This will destroy his life too."

It was abhorrent that the revolution, in speeding ahead, was bringing unhappiness to many innocent people. Liang Feng had not foreseen this kind of suffering when she eagerly welcomed Chairman Mao's call for democratisation of the party structure. Unable to watch Lin's tears any further she hurried away, leaving the two to their argument. The 'just' revolution was becoming a nightmare, with harsh injustices of the Red Guards threatening the freedom the people enjoyed before. There was a fear that the days ahead would be bleak and devoid of all natural feelings.

Liang Feng was uncommunicative when Wampu that evening served her with her favourite dumpling soup. Observing the unhappy face of her grand-niece, Wampu commented,

"You don't seem to like the food today."

Liang Feng looked up from her bowl, and noticing the anxious expression on Wampu's face that reminded her of Lin, a wave of sympathy engulfed her. Leaving her bowl she put her arms round Wampu saying,

"I enjoy the food very much but I wondered if you and those of your generation could face another revolution."

Wampu's face clouded and she whispered,

"I gave up most of my possessions to stay in this country, but those Red Guards who were not even born at the time of the great revolution are suspicious of us."

Liang Feng's troubled face made Wampu say comfortingly,

"Don't you worry dear, I know how to look after myself under all threats."

But Liang Feng could not help worrying about Wampu. Despite

120

disappointments and disillusionment she had encountered happiness from an unexpected source. Thoughts of a few minutes spent at the Bamboo Grove brought a soft smile to her lips. Meeting Pierre had given her an added desire to strive for that inner happiness that had so far eluded her.

CHAPTER 14

The Red Guards in Action

Aspecial occasion for festivity had been provided by Chairman Mao's unrivalled accomplishment of swimming 15 kilometres of the Yan-si-kiang in just fifteen minutes. In the summer of 1966 every canal and waterway in Peking was vigorously utilised by young men and women emulating the Chairman, although Wampu had expressed disapproval at this rashness and had said sarcastically,

"There is too much excitement for my liking." As she had prophesied, all that adulation was soon diverted to more angry outbursts against the so called Revisionists and Foreign Imperialists.

The neighbourhood committee of the Red Flag commune was suddenly disbanded, and instead a Young Workers Group was formed, depriving Wampu of the fulfilment she had derived by serving the commune. The new committee worked with frenzy. A campaign was launched by which the people were forced to give their time to do manual labour, hardly allowing them any leisure. Leisure was regarded as 'Bourgeois Revisionism'.

Liang Feng was forced to join the revived Youth League and to become a member of the Young Workers group. Those young men and women who had once lived in ignorance of these groups were duly recruited to spread the doctrine of Chairman Mao. Having joined the Young Workers group to prove her loyalty to Chairman Mao, she was able to lessen the suspicion cast on her by her foreign birth. It had further paved the way to achieve her ambition to see Chairman Mao. Holding the book of Chairman Mao's thoughts in one hand and the red flag in the other, Liang Feng kept up with the workers group arriving at Thiananmen Square, to join the celebrations to honour Chairman Mao.

The call to bombard the Headquarters had already begun with some heads in high places coming under fire. Marshall Chenyi was one of the first to suffer this fate and with this there was the simultaneous rise to power of new personalities in the hierarchy. As Liang Feng stood on tip toe, craning her neck amidst a sea of heads around her, mesmerised and roaring the chant 'long live Chairman Mao', she glimpsed him standing on the rostrum of the Forbidden City. With him was Marshall Lin Pio, significantly showing his favoured position beside the Chairman. They were waving at the frenzied youth showering their adulation at the feet of Chairman Mao.

A cold wind blew on her as she watched with mounting fear the frenzied face of her neighbour. Uncontrollable emotions contoured the face and eyes of the young woman Red Guard as she stood gasping for breath and screaming "Long live Chairman Mao". With extraordinary force she brandished the Red book up and down working herself up to a pitch, screaming fury at those obstructing her view of the Chairman. Next moment she had burst into tears, and likewise was followed by most others who had the privilege of catching a glimpse of Chairman Mao.

When Liang Feng knocked on Pierre's door he was surprised to *see* her in a uniform. His eyes teased her,

"Have you come to denounce me?" She laughed back at him.

"I'm not one of those Red Guards who denounces all foreigners." Following him into the house she said,

"My grandaunt Wampu is unhappy at the militant attitude of the Red Guards, she worries that I will become like them."

Pierre smiled; that smile touched her. As on all occasions she met him, there was tranquillity in his eyes and a manner to soothe her. "I could never be a violent revolutionary as long as he influences my thoughts," was the unspoken conviction in her heart.

Pierre's emotions were stirred by her appearance. He had been thinking of her. In fact since he had held her, she had never been far from his thoughts. Her smiling face, the confidence and ease she displayed in her workers' uniform reminded him of Donald's comments of her emotional attachment to Chairman Mao and the revolution. But whenever she came to his house she had shown a greater interest in admiring the arrangements in the house and their associations with the past culture rather than discussing politics. Although, whenever she became conscious of herself being drawn to such objects, she quickly dismissed their value with revolutionary jargon,

"All those things have been achieved with the blood and sweat of the poor."

Today he had something new to show her and, leading her to his study, he stood back and watched her reactions to his painting of the Behai Pagoda. Liang Feng gasped with pleasure. Pierre had captured the serenity of dawn breaking over the hills and against this background the Pagoda glimmered in brilliant white, a symbol of peace.

She walked away from the picture and with a hint of bitterness in her voice and tone was reproachful,

"Old Lin, the artist in the commune, had his paintings burnt by his grandson, a Red Guard. Lin can now paint only in his heart."

He was enraged. Her bitterness reminded Pierre of the injustice suffered by artists and writers. She now saw the painting mocking her in the freedom of his house.

"Such injustices are incomprehensible, why are they betraying their supporters?"

She did not answer.

"Such foolishness will drive the people to rebellion," Pierre said.

His anger gave her some measure of comfort. She was not alone in her disillusionment. Somewhat pacified, she observed him still restlessly pacing the floor. He fiercely turned on her with a suddenness which startled her.

"Why do you come to see me? I'm of no use to you." This unforeseen behaviour gave her courage. She said quietly,

"You know why I come to see you."

He quickly turned his eyes away. He was aware that she was still watching him. But he knew she would not choose to hear what she knew was in his heart. She had once told him that they were both living in opposing worlds. His voice low, he muttered,

"I do not want you to get into trouble because of me."

The emotions which had overwhelmed her in the snow were back again. She struggled against them, forcibly focusing her thoughts on her country and the revolution. Pierre had shown her another world and she needed him. The new restrictions imposed on the people curtailing their little pleasures burdened their already austere life style. The utopian state no longer seemed an attainable dream with the confusion of contradictions. Surrounded by this atmosphere of uncertainty, Pierre's house had become a refuge and a haven.

Within the confines of his beautiful home concealed behind the high wall, so welcoming in its quiet seclusion, Liang Feng was able to relax with a sense of freedom not possible anywhere else.

In the awareness that this home offered a protective harbour from the cacophony on the streets and the atmosphere of wariness and mistrust which pervaded the country, Liang Feng turned to Pierre with a special need and warmth to which Pierre reciprocated. Between them there developed a closeness and companionship in which, while they did not give expression in words to their personal feelings, the silence itself was communicative.

On this particular day their peace was suddenly disturbed by a violent knocking on the door. Fear and uncertainty flashing across her face, Liang Feng questioningly looked at Pierre. Her mind recoiled in dread that anti-foreign demonstrations had forged their way in and she remained rooted to the chair with her limbs numb and her mind praying that they should be in no danger. When the knocking became more demanding it brought Pierre to his feet and took him on to the front door, with his face tense and his eyes alert. Liang Feng's body visibly relaxed when she heard a muffled tone of greeting and heavy footsteps followed Pierre back in to the room. It was only Han but he seemed different, agitated and on guard; and when his eyes fell on Liang Feng there was obvious hostility in his face, although his greeting was civil. In a voice sharp and abrupt, he said to Pierre,

"You are in trouble Pierre; there is a rumour that you are instigating the students to rise against the establishment." Pierre took these words calmly.

"I don't think there is any cause for anxiety on my part. Rumours are best ignored. I have only spoken to the students that they must develop their individualism." Han's eyes narrowed and his voice was brusque. "But can they comprehend your definition of individual freedom?"

Pierre looked at Han sharply. Liang Feng was aware how subtly Han had differentiated himself from his colleagues at the university. Pierre's lips curled in a wry smile and his eyes met those of Liang Feng. She could read clearly his thoughts. One of Pierre's few criticisms of the system was the manner in which young minds were indoctrinated, taking away the possibility of the seeds of any new ideas taking root in them to be nurtured and allowed to grow, enriching their personalities. She knew he had the courage to reveal his convictions.

Pierre felt it best to ignore Han's question and for a few minutes there was an uncomfortable silence. Pierre spoke lightly his face smiling,

"Han relax, stay and have a cup of tea with us."

On any earlier occasion such an invitation would have been gladly accepted. But today his mood was strange. He was seated on the edge of the chair, not concealing his eagerness to escape. Making vague excuses he clumsily stood up and, bidding them farewell, was out of the house in no time. Pierre with an inscrutable expression turned to Liang Feng. "I'm concerned about Han. Events seemed to be affecting all of us."

Liang Feng had remained in silent attention while Han had spoken to Pierre. The information Han had brought disturbed her more than she would care to admit.

She sensed an added danger; to be seen in the company of a foreigner could be misconstrued by mischief makers. She had observed the flush of hostility in Han's eyes to see her in Pierre's house.

As if reading her mind Pierre interrupted her trend of thoughts,

"I wonder if you think it would be best to keep away from my house. There was no doubt that it was how Han felt today."

He was standing by her. Her eyes wide, she looked up at him with a smile. "I do not think I could do that." She paused for few minutes and continued, her voice low but very clear,

"My real self feels only at home here." There was immediate relief in his eyes. He realised that he had lost the closeness with Han which, though painful, he could accept. But he did not want to lose her too.

Confident of his supportive attitude to Chairman Mao's ideology he said,

"I do not think the Chairman would object to anything I have said, after all

I'm also supporting his theory that the young should rise against conventional thinking." Their eyes met in shared amusement.

Liang Feng laughingly broke in,

"Has not the Chairman said, to rebel is justified."

Rising up from her chair Liang Feng walked up to the half-finished painting on the easel. The pagoda was a reminder of the peace her heart longed for. Gazing at the beauty of its outlines she was aware of the yearning to satisfy the spiritual needs of her life. The painting held a message for her and, driven by an impulse, she turned to Pierre,

"I would be so happy to possess a painting like this."

His response was immediate,

"I'm happy you like it, I was doing it for you." His gentleness and generosity aroused a rush of emotions in her, but she quickly checked herself. This was not the time to reveal her feelings with the disturbances of drums beating in the street and the voices of processions marching past shouting slogans condemning imperialists and even foreigners. There was a feeling of resentment against that streak of patriotism within her which pulled her always away from him. She wanted to be alone, and gathering up her belongings she walked up to the door with Pierre quietly following her. It was only at the door that she falteringly spoke,

"I have to leave now."

Pierre was mindful of those conflicting loyalties. He was aware of the world that kept pulling her away from him. He marvelled at the courage which made her come to see him. He put his arm gently around her. She leaned against him for few seconds and firmly drew away from him. The voices in the street jarred on her.

She closed her eyes tightly for a moment to collect her thoughts and walked on up the lane. She was shaken from her thoughts by childish voices.

"Are you alright? You have not greeted us!"

She smiled at their concern and said "I'm alright. The shouting in the street disturbed me." They looked around with curious eyes. To them there was nothing unusual; the noise was an everyday occurrence. It was only the rather subdued figure of Liang Feng that was strange in their minds. Seeing their bewilderment Liang Feng quickly forced a smile. That was enough to make them chatter happily and go back to play.

As she walked her thoughts now dwelt on Wang Lee. She had often felt drained of energy both physically and mentally in her attempts to understand him. He had failed to give her the comfort that derived from Pierre. Wang Lee's involvement with the Tachai Brigade brought a cynical smile to her lips. If he could keep up with their fortitude he could win the nation's acclaim as a glorious member, she thought wryly. But he was as unpredictable as the present times and he might end up being rejected despite his zeal towards his work. There was a pang of pity for him. The present mood could not be relied on.

It had been different for her. The authorities had treated her with more understanding and with kindness than they had shown Wang Lee. They had applauded her interest to learn the new way of life. As for Wang Lee, moulded by political indoctrination from his young days, the mistakes he had made were not tolerated. Her enthusiasm for her adopted nation had shielded her from seeing the drab aspect of communism that was so obvious now to many and this was her shield that protected her.

Her eyes and mind now opened, there was a clamour within her for justice to all those who believed in the true democracy of the proletariat.

Darkness had gradually fallen over the city; like a shadow moving a figure of a man moved fast on a bicycle lighting the streetlights. Strangely fascinated by the sight, in him she saw the spirit of man persevering to cling on to the illuminating and enlightening clarity of light, preventing it from being smothered by the incomprehensibility of darkness. However in the commencing shadows of the lamplight more people had poured on to the street to read the wall posters and to more freely communicate with each other.

The caricature in black and white of President Liu Shaoqi was the new poster her, she joined the crowd by the democracy wall. Liu Shaoqi's wife was caricatured wearing an oversized necklace and dancing with President Sukarno of Indonesia. All attention was drawn to the pearl necklace, a thorn in the communist state that Mao was trying to set up. The crowd that gathered round the poster had their own version of the story. The story was that Madam Jian Quin, Mao's wife had given her the necklace.

"That makes Madame Jian Quin the Capitalist Revisionist to possess such a necklace," was the comment of a disapproving spectator amongst the crowd. Liang Feng was startled by the thoughtlessness of his remark. He would be quick to be noticed by mischief makers. Political activity always increased as night fell.

Hidden behind a mask of passivity in daylight, darkness released their emotions and loosened their tongues. Such emotions were safe in dim light. Walking into her grandaunt's house, Liang Feng saw Wampu preparing the kang for the evening meal. Glad to see her grandniece Wampu hurried to the kitchen with a quick greeting. Today the dumpling soup was made with an addition of a new flavour. Wampu always tried to make their ordinary meals a specialty. A phial of roasted sesame seed oil that had escaped her notice for many months, hidden in a ginger jar, was lifted up lovingly, and smiling with pleasure she sprinkled a few drops of oil on to the steaming bowl of soup now brought before Liang Feng and placed on the kang. But the aroma emanating from the soup seemed to bypass Liang Feng who had a thoughtful and troubled expression as she dipped her spoon into the bowl and held it to her lips. Observing Liang Feng's mood, Wampu quietly climbed on to the kang with her own bowl seeing an invaluable need to speak. She had something important to tell but had postponed those troubled thoughts in the pleasure of entertaining her grandneice with a delicious meal. Wampu now chose her words,

"A group of young people is expected in the commune in the next few days."

Liang Feng heard her but feigned indifference for a moment and then burst out,

"Why should they come here?"

Watching Liang Feng's countenance Wampu spoke hesitantly,

"To teach us poor peasants true communism."

Liang Feng did not miss the sarcasm in Wampu's words and, pushing her bowl aside, she stepped down on to the floor. She was indignant, she could not tolerate the indignity of being watched and scrutinised by new faces in the commune. There had been faint complaints from others that such a visit would become a problem to the meagre food stocks in the commune. Those who had been bold to question such visits when they took place in other communes had been criticised for bourgeois selfishness. There was nothing to do but endure it.

Wampu continued her meal in silence and fed her kittens with tit bits from her bowl. Foremost in her mind was their safety; to find the necessary food for their survival.

Although the two continued to take their food in silence, their minds were preoccupied with the impending visit of the Red Guards.

CHAPTER 15

The Struggle of the Ideologies

"Is this democracy?" Pierre said to himself in amazement. A pitched battle was waging on the roof of the Peking University. The opposing factions were well armed with sticks and missiles. Unsophisticated yet effective were the weapons which they hurled at each other. The students on the roof used mattresses and pillows as protective shields against the ammunitions of stones which catapulted from the opposite roof tops. The gates to the University were closed and a strong battalion of soldiers with faces immobile and unyielding patrolled the road to prevent the crowd from collecting in the vicinity to witness the unusual phenomena.

With time, the people had become more and more committed to the ideologies they chose to believe in and, while superficially professing their loyalty to Chairman Mao, two differing political fractures had sprung up, with conflicting allegiances which had gradually progressed from arguments to bitter feuds and now to open warfare, an example of which Pierre was now witnessing. He sadly reflected on their destructive effects on the citizens and on the progress of the country.

When the skirmish on the rooftops took a serious turn, Pierre's eyes appealed for some settlements to the guardians of the law. But the soldiers remained uncommunicative. They knew their role and the 'limits of the powers' assigned to them. They had no instructions to intervene. Like Pierre they knew that the students had the blessings of the highest authority to rebel against the establishment.

In the complicated educational and political atmosphere within the universities, Pierre had seen students showing a keen interest in politics; not only did they study Chairman Mao's philosophy, but at the same time poured over the literature on communism written by the Chairman's political rival President Liu Shaoqui. Since the theories of the two leaders were now in open conflict President Liu Shaoqui's work had gone underground, but it was surreptitiously circulated by his followers and in fact was considered more relevant to the nation's economic development than the 'Dialectics' of Chairman Mao. Pierre reflected sadly that the intellectual wrangling between the leaders was creating divisions among the students and among the people.

Walking away from the scene of trouble Pierre remembered the words of Chairman Mao, "Without people's democracy, the dictatorship of the proletariat could not be consolidated, and political power would be unstable!"

However, he had not been able to convince Liang Feng that the western style of democracy would enable the proletariat to consolidate the gains of the 1949 revolution. Yet Liang Feng had voiced her doubts, "Democracy as it is practised in the west would bring in capitalism."

In her view this would invariably encourage powerful individuals to control the economy and nullify the democratic freedom of the people. Reflecting on that conversation Pierre felt there was some truth in what she said. There were no ideal systems that would be foolproof against unscrupulous people.

It was the greed of man for power and wealth that has brought disaster to all systems Pierre thought sadly, as he dwelt on the injustices all over the world. Theoretically though Chairman Mao's philosophy appeared to promote justice, but as anywhere else, in practice the faults were glaring.

The system of communism as practised in China was not fully comprehensible to him. He had viewed on many occasions the posters on the democracy wall expressing criticisms of those in authority. This criticism had sharply intensified in the last few months with even the highest officials subjected to veiled censure. The posters had convinced Pierre that freedom of expression was allowed in this communist state as in no other country. He was therefore reluctant to believe the rumours that those daring to criticise were subjected to punishment. This ambiguity and confusion in the political system was under strain and was showing signs of cracking. His mind heavy with a sense of foreboding Pierre hurried in the direction of his house.

Red Guards were thronging the streets. Pierre heard the monotonous rhythm of their drums and he knew a procession of Red Guards was on its way. As he passed it he could see the people on the roadside mutely draw back to let it pass, showing no interest or emotions.

Liang Feng was standing by his house. She had been often on his mind. He was moved that, beside Han, she was the only person who defied the authorities to visit him in his house. But she was still reluctant to discuss the future.

Pierre warmly led Liang Feng into the house. The news of the incident outside Peking University had spread in the city and she expressed her anxiety about the events. They were both subdued but there remained between them the usual quiet relationship. Understanding her dependence on their friendship Pierre gently asked,

"Do you ever give thought to the future?" His eyes were trying to penetrate her mind, but she had no wish to neither delve too deeply into her own mind nor discuss about the future. His words seemed as unreal as the daily incidents of the revolution.

Though Pierre's presence made her forget the unpleasantness of the incidents she did not have the personal freedom to enter the relationship of serious intimacy. She said softly and calmly,

"I do not think of the future, is it important to our friendship?"

When Pierre did not reply she said, her eyes smiling at him and her voice teasing,

"Chairman Mao says the unity of opposites is conditional, temporary, and relative, the struggle of mutually exclusive opposite is absolute, just as development and motion are absolute."

She had succeeded in changing his mood. This time he said lightly,

"It is also said that things which oppose each other also complement one another."

It made her laugh and exclaim in mock surprise,

"But we do not oppose each other, although our different political systems do." Though her voice was flippant there was a note of sadness at the situation they were placed in. Going up to him and touching his cheek gently she murmured softly,

"Love is a wonderful feeling – but with the prevailing conditions, fantasies can be easily created."

For a moment her thoughts flew back to Wang Lee. She could never relate to him. Caught in the web of power politics, all natural feelings had become unacceptable to him, and even during their brief period together the party's principles governed his actions. He however was no different to others with similar political commitment. Liang Feng knew how strongly communist ideology influenced the personal lives of people. She took a deep breath – she had no wish to be like them.

Disappointed by her words restraining him, Pierre's mind dwelt on his own feelings. But he admitted to himself that her words had only echoed his own uncertainties. However, he could not deny that she meant a great deal to him. While earlier, he had enjoyed his solitude, now he waited anxiously for her daily visit. She too had shown no inhibitions in revealing her affections. Pushing these thoughts away from his mind, he put his arms around her, holding her close for a few seconds before releasing her. Deliberately he turned away from her, and to ease the situation said,

"I do not blame Donald when he says he does not understand the people here."

The sudden cry of a female voice, feeble and in anguish interrupted their mood. The voice was crying,

"Comrades please don't take my son away." Startled, Pierre and Liang Feng looked questioningly at each other. They could hear the march of a procession making its way down the lane. A woman's wailing became loud and clear as the procession passed his door. The misery of fellow countrymen upset Liang Feng who, walking away from Pierre, sat numbly on a chair.

Moved by her unhappiness Pierre walked up to her and gently stroked her brow, the only way he could comfort her. Together they walked up to the door and waited till the crying died away. The joy they had experienced in being together could not be recaptured.

Walking back down the lane Liang Feng was surprised to see Chuang Tsu. Chuang Tsu, seeing her friend, seemed too excited to show curiosity as to her presence there. She burst out, relief in her voice,

"I am so glad to see you here, my friend Suyin's son has just been arrested and taken away by the Red Guards."

Poor soul, a sick feeling gripped Liang Feng's stomach. With a furtive glance over her shoulder Chung Tsu muttered, her voice accusing,

"Her son was arrested for possessing a box full of imported wristwatches, and how they dare break into people's homes."

The tone in Chung Tsu's voice surprised Liang Feng. Suspicious thoughts that the wristwatches could be contraband flooded her mind. Chung Tsu's voice complainingly went on,

"What is there for people to buy with the money they save, are they to be only content with a bicycle or a locally made wristwatch."

Liang Feng thought sarcastically, would they not be? She would normally have appropriate quotes from the 'Thoughts of Chairman Mao' for her misguided friend, but she was in no mood to uphold the Chairman's philosophy. But she wondered at Chung Tsu's deteriorating values. It seemed as if the turmoils of the Cultural Revolution had affected Chung Tsu's mind that she should stoop to defend the acquisition of banned goods. Liang Feng sadly reflected on the Chairman's prophetic warning that an economy which offered incentives could lead to the decline of moral values and build up a class structure between the able and the weak, leading to the exploitation of the weaker in society.

Her mind in turmoil, Liang Feng led her friend out of the lane on to the street. The day's events were becoming more and more bizarre. Chuang Tsu, the well trained communist, was showing an approval of capitalist luxuries while her friend Suyin and her son had fallen prey to the temptations of hoarding contraband. Austere communism had failed to curb the ambitions of the people.

On returning to the apartment, Liang Feng and Chuang Tsu were met by a scowling Sheng. He made a characteristic derogatory comment,

"I despise the guts of those countrymen returning now to the motherland."

Liang Feng knew the remark was meant for her, yet she did not retort in her usual manner and chose to remain silent. Angered by the remark, Chuang Tsu was quick to defend her friend,

"It is our duty to be kind to those countrymen now returning."

Liang smiled to herself. Chuang Tsu had come to her assistance, once again assuming an official role. Chuang Tsu was patiently attempting to convince Sheng of the reasons for exiles to return,

"After all one has to experience all systems to choose the best."

In the turbulent history of her country, Chuang Tsu had the benefit of experiencing many political systems. Born to a peasant family before the 1949 revolution her family had undergone tremendous hardships under the feudal systems. Therefore the revolution that had been welcomed by them and they soon enjoyed a freedom that they had not experienced in the old society. But after sixteen years of commitment to the party her loyalty to the system had now weakened. An element of personal ambition had crept in, and hence enthusiasm for the new economic policy of President Liu Shaoqui. She had worked hard and proved her skills to be appointed a Deputy Director of her commune. But the Cultural Revolution was hindering her work, and she had angered hardliners who frowned on the competitive nature of her work. Chuang Tsu was becoming weary of political ideologies which interfered with a progressive attitude to work. To her the Cultural Revolution had become an ill-considered measure that would not lift people up above the level of poverty. Chuang Tsu's support gave Liang Feng the courage to look Sheng squarely in the face, before proceeding in the direction of her room. But Sheng had not been silenced and shouted after her,

"It is time we had a Boxer rebellion to drive out all foreigners from the country."

Stung by this insult Liang Feng could not let his verbal abuse go further. Taking a deep breath she said clearly, her voice contemptuous,

"Chairman Mao is right, he is against narrow nationalism and narrow patriotism."

Liang Feng silently congratulated herself for remembering all the quotations from Chairman Mao's works.

Reference to Chairman Mao upset Sheng. Angered by her disdain he shouted,

"You know so little of our country's politics, all foreigners are ignorant."

He rushed out of the apartment banging behind him the door. Chuang Tsu heaved a sigh of relief at Sheng's departure. She was tired of all arguments. All she now wanted was a quiet life for the moment.

Seated alone in her room Liang Feng was depressed. She could see how adversely the political confusion was affecting relationships within families and between friends.

The same situation was prevalent in Waichia Talou. The workers were becoming suspicious of each other. There were also signs of antagonism between workers and their foreign employers. The anti-revisionist and anti-imperialist propaganda was influencing all her countrymen. A particular significant factor was that the embassy staff of countries branded 'enemies of China' were facing unexplainable wrath from the local people. With the revolution progressing, many other countries too became victims of this animosity; any trivial incident abroad was interpreted as hostile action against the People's Republic of China. To punish foreign residents, blaring anti-foreign propaganda and songs of the revolution were hurled at them using the media. Morning, noon and night, loudspeakers screamed giving sleepless nights to the foreigners in Waichia Talou.

This disturbance intensified, when certain countries refused to allow the flow of political propaganda, such as badges of Chairman Mao and the Red Book, to their particular countries. The Chinese authorities would give reciprocal treatment by organising demonstrations against the embassies of those countries in Peking.

CHAPTER 16

Red Guards Destroy Cultural Objects

The atmosphere in Peking was tense with the internal rivalries on one hand and anti-foreign demonstrations on the other. Those fiery protests against foreign powers were freely expressed on the streets of Peking. Hostile feelings against the British reached the heights of intensity due to events in Hong Kong, a fact Liang Feng was quick to note as it affected her relationship with the Browns. Donald and Sally were now uncomfortable to speak freely before her. It was only Pierre who did not show any change towards her, hopeful that the troubles would end quickly.

There was embarrassing hostility from her own people when she was mistaken for an alien. The children had been the first to show unfriendliness, and one day when she was cycling to Pierre's house one had shouted,

"I hate foreigners." As the remark came from little Lan Kuei who already knew her, the remark hurt her. Jumping off her bicycle she had walked up to Lan Kuei and, giving her a bag of oranges, had said firmly,

"I am not a foreigner". When Lan Kuei remained silent with embarrassment Liang Feng admonished her gently,

"Why must you hate foreigners, there are good people among them too." Not happy at these words Lan Kuei had rushed into her house leaving an accusing crowd of children around Liang Feng.

Witnessing this animosity she was glad her father and she had arrived in the country at a congenial time. Their arrival had been welcomed, but it was not the same for those entering the mother country at the present time. With culture and habits somewhat different to the local people, they faced hostility roused by the Cultural Revolution. The new arrivals, it had to be admitted, were themselves uncompromising and showed an unwillingness to be indoctrinated by the 'Thoughts of Chairman Mao'. The Red Guards, angered by this, harassed them whenever the opportunity arose.

Little Lan Kuei's words kept haunting Liang Feng for many days making her more nervous about her own association with Pierre. Further she feared for his safety despite his reassurances about the sympathetic attitude of his neighbours. He carried on his work in the normal way, greeting the residents down his lane with the same friendliness he had shown them before. But he was sad that his students' visits had completely stopped. Han who was self-righteous in supporting the movement for change was reluctant now to visit him. Since the universities were closed, Pierre had no opportunity to meet his students.

Disapproving of the hostilities caused by professor-student conflicts, more foreign students too had departed.

It was a surprise to Liang Feng when Pierre visited her in her office and, speaking in French, invited her to visit the Summer Palace with him,

"I know there will be more restrictions on my movements soon. This may be the last chance I get." She looked at his keen face and then at the faces of the workers who, having stopped their work, were watching them evidently trying to comprehend their conversation. She agreed hurriedly, wanting him to leave the office before they began to speculate. She felt more than ever before a sense of uneasiness which she could not explain to herself.

Liang Feng walked through the city early the next morning to meet Pierre in Behai Park. A gentle gossamer veil of pink and cream covered the sky. The silent dragons on the city gates seemed to keep guard over the few early risers vigorously cycling across the wide square on their way to work. It was easy to make out Pierre now standing by the Bridge of Perfect Wisdoms, overlooking the island that was once the abode of emperor Kublai Khan. Pierre reminded her of those lofty pines that stood silently on the slopes of Behai. She could never reach up high enough to touch their cones; it was like the distance between the two of them.

Together they passed the door of the Ten Thousand Buddha Pavilion and were sad to find it closed. Pierre said,

"Yesterday I saw a peddycab loaded with Buddha statues of all sizes taken like some garbage to be dumped somewhere out of the people's reach."

At these words her thoughts flew to Wampu's Buddha statue hidden behind the brick in the kitchen wall. Pierre went on,

"It is foolish to destroy something beautiful and good."

She confided in a low voice,

"Wampu had hidden a Buddha statue in the kitchen and when she thinks I am asleep she bows her head in silent prayer. At the start I thought she was expressing appreciation for the food we received, but when I discovered the statue I realised she was a practising Buddhist."

This made Pierre thoughtful to say in a distressed voice,

"That means she will need re-education soon."

Liang Feng said stoutly,

"I don't think Wampu will stand such an education. No one knows about it except myself."

It had taken them more than an hour to reach the Summer Palace. Getting off the bus they climbed the path to reach the many pavilions standing picturesquely on the hill. Fascinated by the rock garden Pierre took out his camera. He loved these rocks which suggested animals in their natural formation. Contented, she sat and watched him, even letting him take her photograph beside the gaping mouth of a monster rock.

Sudden giggles and shrieks rent the air; a group of excited schoolgirls descended on her, surrounding her and begging,

"Tell the foreigner to take our photograph too." Before she could reply they excitedly positioned themselves with arms round each other's shoulders, clustering together around Liang Feng. Seeing this and understanding their words Pierre said in Chinese,

"Stand still, I'll take photographs of all of you". This made them all laugh and wait anxiously for the camera to click. It did not take long for more young people to gather round the group, and Pierre continued to take photographs. In a few minutes it seemed that all those who had come to the Summer Palace had abandoned sight-seeing for the greater pleasure of observing the new camera in Pierre's hand and posing for pictures.

They crowded round him asking many questions on the working of the camera. But this pleasure did not last long. Suddenly a loud command shattered the camaraderie,

"Comrades, leave the foreigner alone." The sharpness cut in with force, compelling the now subdued crowd to disperse in all directions, leaving Liang Feng alone on the rock.

Surprised at this interruption Pierre looked up, to confront an angry soldier barking,

"How dare you take photographs of Chinese people?"

Slinging the camera back on his shoulder, Pierre replied calmly,

"Because I like it." The soldier offended by the foreigner's impudence hissed in a low voice threateningly,

"Don't do it again, you will be in great trouble." Seeing that his words did not have the desired effect and that the foreigner's face remained unruffled, he thundered,

"Give me your identity card." While Pierre calmly searched through his pockets the soldier waited for signs of repentance that could end the affair and he was outraged when Pierre said at last in a gentle voice,

"I shall send it to you if you give me your address."

Liang Feng hastily rose from the rock. Pierre was making the soldier lose control. She walked up to him with an air of confidence in order to resolve the situation. Producing her own identity card, she said,

"He is a friend of our country. I have brought him to show the Summer Palace." He stared at the card and back at her face. Furious at her interference, a Chinese was defending a foreigner. Disbelieving, he listened to her explanation in defiance of his judgment. Exploding in fury he snatched the card from her hand and commanded threateningly,

"Leave this place at once."

The card was in his pocket and she hastily left him. She wanted to escape his wrath. Pierre caught up with her and now, regretting the incident, murmured,

"I am sorry for what happened." He was apologetic and she was quick to reassure him.

"It was no fault of yours." But all the same, she was concerned and added,

"I hope the soldier will forget this incident." Pierre said thoughtfully,

"He won't. He has your card in his pocket." Yet she convinced herself that no harm would come to them as neither was against the movement for justifiable change.

Pierre's face remained calm but she had already experienced a sense of foreboding before coming on the trip. She saw a new danger threatening Pierre. She had not liked the look on the soldier's face. Pierre's friendship had been the most meaningful of all relationships to her but now ironically it would be a source of danger to both of them. The soldier had treated Pierre with malice simply because he was a foreigner; the injustice of this filled her with mortification.

As for her, if she was found guilty of a misdemeanour, she would be forced to wear a dunce cap and be paraded on the streets. The very idea revolted her. Self-denunciation, admission of guilt and the submission to criticism that she was a disloyal communist would shatter her credibility as a faithful follower of the doctrine of Mao Zedong.

Pierre's voice broke into her reverie,

"I wonder why they should pick on people who can be of use to them?" She knew he was referring to himself. He truly loved this country. During the past few days a bombardment of malicious propaganda by the media had imposed new inhibitions on her. She had blossomed out due to her relationship with Pierre. Now she felt stifled and saw herself withdrawing into her inner self again.

Glancing at her troubled face Pierre said,

"How silly to question why I am taking photographs of people; when I said I like the Chinese people he refused to believe it!" This made them laugh and that shared laughter seemed to push away from their minds the unpleasantness of the incident. But she was quick to note others watching them. Their eyes exchanged a message of silent understanding.

Parting on this note Liang Feng and Pierre went their separate ways back to the city. Her parting words to him were,

"I wonder what is in store for us."

Waves of indignation swept over her when she went over the events later on in the day. In anger she did not feel defeated. It was necessary to stand up for her rights. Her friendship with Pierre had reached a point of intensity and she was determined to maintain it even in the face of danger. She tossed her head with defiance.

A crowd was collecting at the entrance to the commune. From a lorry parked by the road, a man was distributing furniture; the goods moved fast. A voice boomed,

"Comrades, the time has come to get rid of the old culture and its bourgeois furniture. We must replace such things with modern proletarian goods in our homes." Briskly he displayed frugal proletarian stools and chairs made with a minimum of wood, more with iron. The revolution had been planned with utmost care, from the very grassroots, to submerge the old way of life. Liang Feng's thoughts rushed to Wampu. The Revolution was on her doorstep, yet Wampu was not to be seen amongst that docile crowd placidly getting rid of the old culture and acquiring proletarian goods. Liang Feng quickened her steps. Wampu was oblivious to the danger. She must be warned.

The Red Guards had discovered remnants of the old culture still hidden in the hearts of the people and carefully concealed in their homes. But this time the people could not escape and the planned methodical cleaning-up process had begun. Chairman Mao Zedong's Cultural Revolution was a step ahead of all other revolutions. Reforms had been begun in earnest, but revisionism, to some extent, had crept back and had been tolerated by those in authority. But this time it would be a methodical clean-up of what had gone underground in 1949.

CHAPTER 17

The Long March to Destroy Remnants of the Past

Winds of change swiftly blew through the whole country. With universities closing abruptly, the students took to the roads in a newly acquired fervour to reach the capital by foot. Launched by Chairman Mao to carry the message of the Cultural Revolution, these 'Long Marchers', the Red Guards, imitated their predecessors who had undertaken a similar feat in 1949.

Armed with the 'Red Book of Thoughts', they brought friendship to some while those suspected of anti-revolutionary acts were targets for punishment. Their zeal to force down the message was intense. Not all citizens welcomed the Red Guard intrusion; they regarded them as an encumbrance to their already burdened lives. They showed reluctance to share their meagre food stocks and were in return accused of revisionist selfishness. Some communes made use of the Red Guards to rid themselves of bureaucrats who, they felt, stood in the way of progress, or those whom they particularly did not like. The Red Guards, the crusaders, battled ferociously with all opposition to propagate the Chairman's philosophy against old culture; old ideas and old customs, seen as a threat to the advancement of the communist states.

These new communists, drunk with power, were a threat to the older generation of post-revolution communists who, having fallen on easier times, or nursing thoughts of better days, were accused of revisionism. In their zeal to propagate Chairman Mao's 'Thoughts', the Red Guards, not clearly understanding the dialectics and contradictions of his subtle philosophy and displaying unimaginable naivety, made the little Red Book their precious guide. One hesitated to wonder whether those abbreviated sayings, taken from the much larger and more comprehensive works of Chairman Mao, were sufficient to promote idealism in those young impatient minds. But it all seemed so easy to the Red Guards, now fervently mouthing the quotations and bulldozing and destroying people's property and lives. Names of places were changed overnight, substituted with more revolutionary sounding names, often used repeatedly for a lack of a wider revolutionary vocabulary.

As the Red Guards continued on their march, overturning people's lives as thoughtlessly as they changed street names, there were those who suffered the changes in anguish, controlling their rage with difficulty. The old suffered most. They were being uprooted from a society that had its roots in the 1949 revolution. They were confused when the same leaders who had not so long ago captured their hearts now accused them of revisionism. Suicides among some became the norm.

At her door, Wampu stood silent and uncommunicative as Red Guards paraded on the commune paths displaying portraits of Chairman Mao. Procession after procession passed through the commune – the air resounding with their cries,

"Down with Capitalism!" "Down with Revisionism!" Revisionism and capitalism seemed to have revived overnight. To the dismay of the older commune members, amongst the young men and women were their own kith and kin, at the forefront of the processions. Within the commune, political classes were conducted with new enthusiasm and a determination to weed out the so-called 'Four Evils'.

As the fervour of the campaign heightened, the marked differences in the ideologies of the two communist leaders were forced more to the forefront. The Red Guards had set up a brand new pavilion in the village school to educate commune members in the Chairman's brand of communism. Liang Feng felt compelled to participate. In this pavilion colourfully decorated with red flags, she spent her weekends distributing the works of the leader. While citizens poured over the philosophy of the Chairman, the daily work in the commune unfortunately suffered, affecting economic progress.

Wampu discreetly avoided any participation in the political activities within the commune. She remained indoors finding companionship in her cats. They had grown in the last few weeks but now posed a problem. Although so far Wampu had ungrudgingly given her share of food to them, they now needed more than she could offer. On many occasions she had gone without meals, saving her share for her pets. To obtain extra rations for cats or for that matter for humans was an impossible task. The only solution was to send the cats out of the house to find their own food. But this, Wampu knew, was a risk, as cats and even dogs were a threatened species. The authorities had emphasised on all occasions that the priority was to feed the people and with the prevalent scarcity of food, only people mattered.

The days when Wampu had enjoyed employment with the neighbourhood cleaning committee had ended abruptly when the committee was disbanded. She had since stayed at home, or sometimes was called to care for little children in the commune. The vigilant eyes of the Red Guard were a constant threat to those elderly people who sought some form of relaxation from work. Forced to be fully employed their labour became a kind of drudgery. Most of them silently suffered anguish at these changes.

May Day that year was celebrated with extra zeal, the programme of activities showing a strong defence of Mao Zedong's line of thought as opposed to the position taken by President Lieu Shaoqui. The latter's emphasis on economic progress was openly blamed by the Chairman and his followers for the revival of Revisionism. On this occasion the Red Guards and the workers were in the fore-front to welcome Chairman Mao in the People's Park. Trekking from all corners of China, fulfilling a cherished dream, they were a sea of heads as they waited patiently for their helmsman. Unlike as in other years the mass of humanity could not be confined only to Thiananmen Square and spilled over to the parks in the vicinity. A further change in the usual scene was the noticeable presence of the military, who despite their passivity, raised speculations about their specific role in the prevailing political struggle.

The People's Liberation Army too, influenced by the new trends, presented a significant change when their well-creased olive green suits were replaced with ordinary cotton khaki uniforms, in keeping with the Spartan uniforms of the Red Guards. Chairman Mao seemed to have achieved his aim of making the army, at least in appearance, truly representative of ordinary people. This however, did not please those sections of the military were concerned about rank.

As such, certain sections of the military were developing dislike for the Red Guard movement. It was not an untruth to say that some soldiers were even growing tired of the lawlessness of many ill-mannered Red Guards although they were favoured and treated with tolerance by Chairman Mao.

Donald Brown who spent a great deal of time critically analysing all aspects of the Revolution had his own comments. He remarked to Pierre,

"I was at a National Day reception in the Peking Hotel when Marshall Chenyi came in, shockingly dressed. He looked more like an ordinary soldier in his creased cotton khaki suit. Throughout the reception he bore an unhappy countenance; it is a great comedown for such a powerful figure."

Almost overnight, changes were visible in the official gatherings of the polit-ical hierarchy, changes resulting from the Chairman's call to the Red Guards to "Bombard the Headquarters and expose the Capitalist Revisionists". Having attended an international celebration at the Peking Hotel, Donald was surprised at the wider cross-section of the party now allowed to grace such diplomatic functions. He spoke of this to his friend,

"I was surprised to see the new faces; those who once would not have been tolerated at these celebrations were there feasting, I should say more fitly 'gobbling down' all the numerous courses served to them."

Pierre had conveyed Brown's observations to Liang Feng and her reaction had been different. She had expressed her gladness at the opportunity the ordinary people were being given to share the privileges the VIPs had enjoyed.

It was that discussion which she had on her mind as she stood with other workers in the park, waiting to greet Chairman Mao. The Red Book was, as always on such occasions, in her hand. Unrestrained adulation for the Chairman was stamped on the faces of the young anticipating the great moment. Liang Feng too was swept away with excitement at the thought of seeing the leader. Suddenly, a thousand voices rose in a chant, "Long live Chairman Mao!" It was a cry that vibrated on every pore and every bead of perspiration of the crowd as they stood in the heat of the sun that May day.

At the sight of the approaching jeep with its hood lowered to give a clear view of the Chairman, resounding screams and applause spread along the pathway of the jeep. Their excitement soaring, the throng roared, as if in a frenzy, "Our beloved helmsman, long live Chairman Mao!" A massive wave of over-enthusiastic Red Guards, breaking the cordon of human hands that had made a pathway for the vehicle, hurled themselves on the jeep. They wanted to see, to touch, their Guide who had inspired them to undertake the long march to Peking. Impatient mobs pushed and shoved, and Liang Feng was unceremoniously hurled against the jeep by the frenzied activity. Her eyes caught a momentary glimpse of the smiling faces of the Chairman and of the Premier Chou En Lai, but that was all she saw for she stumbled, her head heavily striking the metal of the jeep, and she immediately lost consciousness. She had obtained her greatest desire – but at a price.

When awareness returned, Liang Feng found herself lying on the grass surrounded by a group of Red Guards fanning her. Seeing her eyes open their anxious faces smiled with relief. As she showed signs of recovery they had only one question for her,

"Did you really see him?" a question flung at her over and over again. Their feverishly happy faces swimming before her vision, she could only mumble "Yes" repeatedly. Her only need was to get away from them to more sympathetic surroundings.

Rising unsteadily she held on to a post, her head aching painfully. In those young excited faces around her there was no sympathy for the weak. Their voices hailed her, as if her indisposition was a thrilling reminder to them of the event that had taken place a few minutes before.

She managed to escape from the group but had hardly moved many steps before her eyes met an unexpected sight. On the ground lay many others who, like her, had been injured in the stampede, and even those who had swooned at seeing the Chairman in real life. Neither the flowers in the park nor the grass had been spared in this hysteria. They were in shambles, crushed and trodden by thousands of stamping feet.

As swift as the experience, the jeep had passed through, a fleeting dream to Liang Feng. Once the vehicle had disappeared, in her helplessness her thoughts flew to Pierre.

She longed for his sympathy to console the pain of her injury. The anticipation of seeing the Chairman, the dream that had led her to Peking, now seemed unreal, even futile. Yet the happy faces of her colleagues brought a feeling of guilt at this change within her. Whereas her colleagues had swooned in exaltation, she had been knocked down by a surging crowd. She remembered her colleagues in Canton who had instilled in her the desire to see Chairman Mao. Even a glimpse of him they considered the greatest achievement in the life of a citizen of her county. Recalling this, she walked away from the crowds, guilt and unease lying heavily on her mind.

Still clutching the book of 'Thoughts' she proceeded to Thiananmen Avenue and continued numbly in the direction of Pierre's home. At no time had she longed more for communication with him.

Arriving a few yards before Pierre's house, Liang Feng was suddenly brought to a halt, unable to proceed. A uniformed guard was stationed by his door. Confusion flooded her mind, followed by accusations; were the authorities trying to keep her away from him. Although she had been aware of the close watch kept on foreigners who moved freely with the local population, she had not expected that Pierre would fall under scrutiny. She bitterly looked down at her young worker's uniform; it had become an added burden that would no doubt draw the sentry's attention to herself and cause suspicion in him.

Tears rose in Liang Feng's eyes. She felt betrayed by the politics of her country. Innocent people were being victimised while the leaders debated ideology. The pain in her head was becoming unbearable as she bitterly questioned herself,

"Has the dream come to an end?"

While around her the shadows darkened in the evening sky, the need for individual freedom deepened within her. At every turn she had defended the Revolution but now it all seemed so hollow. Donald Brown's criticism rang loudly in her mind, his laughter and cynicism she heard once again. Recollecting that laughter her mind hardened. She would stand up to the authorities she thought, determinedly. Although she accepted that Chairman Mao was still the great leader, something wrong was happening in her country and she had all the right to question it.

Waiting in the shadows she noticed the soldier leaving his post and another immediately taking his place. There was no way for her to enter the house without being questioned. Once again recollections of Donald's sarcasm acted as a stimulating force.

"I will not give in, like Wampu."

Wampu had philosophically accepted the communist regime while the rest of the family had escaped to Indonesia.

Located among the houses of the local people, Pierre's residence had escaped undue attention from the authorities and had become a sanctuary to her. But no longer was it going to provide her with a refuge. The authorities had decided to keep a vigilant eye on it.

In desperation, and now her head aching more, her thoughts flew to Chuang Tsu. Chuang Tsu had always come to her assistance when there was a problem. Liang Feng needed someone to bring relief to her physical discomfort, and Chuang Tsu would also be able to enlighten her with the latest news of the political problems in the country. She quietly turned and walked away from Pierre's lane.

Chuang Tsu was glad to see her. She warmly came forward to greet her, her eyes resting admiringly on the uniform. But her keen eyes were quick to observe the bruises on her friend's forehead and also the unhappiness clouding her face. Placing a comforting arm around Liang Feng's shoulder she questioned,

"What did they do to you at the parade?"

Chuang Tsu's gentle tone consoled Liang Feng who softly said,

"The crowds pushed and I fell, but I did manage to catch a glimpse of the Chairman."

Her voice was full of pride although she had really not experienced such feelings when seeing him. Not surprisingly Chuang Tsu's response expressed envy and longing,

"I wish I had that luck. I have still to see him."

Though Chuang Tsu was sceptical of the Chairman's Cultural Revolution, his personality still enthralled her, as it had done during the time of the great 1949 Revolution when she had been among the poor peasants he had liberated.

The front door banged as Shi Kai Ying burst into the room. She was in uniform. She had been at the parade but her excitement was for a different reason. She cried out,

"Mother, there have been clashes between the soldiers and the Red Guards."

Chuang Tsu remained silent for a few moments, she said cautiously, her tone holding an unspoken warning,

"Now, from where did you get this information?"

But Shi Kai Ying could not be restrained; she excitedly continued,

"My friends said it happened last night in Wan Fu Chien and also in other suburbs of Peking."

Chuang Tsu did not like trouble. She was getting tired of all these divisions which she considered inconvenient for ordinary people like herself. She only desired a peaceful comfortable life after the hardships of civil wars and revolutions.

Liang Feng listened to Shi Kai Ying's chatter. At another time she would have worried at these clashes between the Red Guards and the soldiers but today she was only concerned as to why the army had moved into Pierre's lane. The incident at the Summer Palace was fresh in her thoughts. Her mind was troubled. While the soldiers had taken her identity card and as yet not returned it, they had also been demanding Pierre's identity card. Did the Authorities consider Pierre as creating trouble for them with his influence on the students?

While her thoughts were running through various possibilities, Chuang Tsu had quietly made her sit down and had attended to her bruises. After Liang Feng had been made comfortable, only then did Chuang Tsu turn to her daughter.

"Shi Kai Ying, did you see the Chairman?"

Shi Kai Ying tossed her head, her tone arrogant. "I'm not like others who think that to see him is the greatest achievement in their lives."

Chuang Tsu's response was sharp. "You should not speak like that of the Chairman."

Shi Kai Ying could see that her mother was being cautious in Liang Feng's presence. But she was not afraid. With an insolent shrug she marched out of the room. A few minutes later she put her head in and nonchalantly announced,

"Sheng will not be coming tonight."

It was a great relief for Liang Feng to hear those words. In her unhappy state she would not have been able to bear listening to Sheng's usual tirade against foreigners. So it was with relief she accepted Chuang Tsu's invitation to stay the night in the apartment.

That night lying back in her bed Liang Feng's eyes studied the new posters that were pasted on the walls of the room. No longer were the obnoxious posters associated with her first visit to be seen; in their place were photographs of Chairman Mao and of the emerging new leader Marshall Lin Pio. Leaning back against the pillow she pondered – Sheng, no doubt, was responsible for this shift in loyalties. She could neither comprehend Sheng nor the politics in her land.

CHAPTER 18

Red Guards on Rampage

Inside Weidatalo, Liang Feng viewed with apprehension the new posters and slogans that had appeared overnight on the walls of the building. In a frenzied action a group of young men were putting up anti-revisionist slogans. "Smash the dog head of Russian revisionism" they screamed. Days of angry protests against Russia had continued over the incident of expelling Chinese student technicians studying in Moscow. Watching their angry jerky movements made her heart contract with fear. There was so much hatred burning in their eyes. Her thoughts flew to the guard post by Pierre's front door. With anger building up against foreigners, the authorities' stance towards Pierre too seemed to have changed.

In Weidatalo the local workers made no attempts to hide their anxiety when they came face to face with foreigners. Even the usual polite greetings were now ignored and they shied away from their company, more so fearing those among them acting as informers. Liang Feng's friendship with Pierre too was affected. A strain entered in her relationship with Pierre when she felt frustrated at her inability to visit him. Finally she picked up courage to call on Donald Brown to make contact with Pierre. In that atmosphere of uncertainty and hostility she visited his apartment with some trepidation.

Mr Ma, Donald's cook opened the door but he looked glum and angry that was not his usual demeanour. Today he seemed hostile to her arrival and directed her coldly to the living room to await Donald. Ma's manner upset Liang Feng and it was a relief to see the smile on Donald's face, as he entered the room. He greeted her warmly. Although he had met her on many occasions in the corridors of Weidatalo she had not visited him before at home. Glad to see her and keen to hear her comments on the revolution, he plunged into conversation till such time when he realised that his cook, keeping the door to the kitchen wide open, was showing undue interest in their discussion. Suspecting Ma of eavesdropping, Donald strode into the kitchen.

"Mr. Ma" he said, "could you please bring some peaches from the grocery?" His voice was curt.

Ma was taken aback. He had already visited the grocery in the morning to buy fruits for the household. He did not contradict his master and, removing his apron and hanging it on the door, walked out of the apartment giving Donald a cold stare. Walking back to Liang Feng Donald heaved a sigh of relief.

"I don't know what has come over him, he has become a stranger, shuffling around the house and taking mysterious telephone calls." Thoughtfully he continued,

"I have not yet pulled him up, but I will not tolerate him eavesdropping on our conversation. I have noticed this particularly when the Chinese office staff make an occasional visit here." Noticing Liang Feng's anxious expression, he changed the subject.

"I hope you are not having problems in your work place," his voice was concerned. Liang Feng hesitated then cautiously watching the door, said,

"I am fine. I have come today particularly to inquire if Pierre is in any trouble."

Donald gave a wry smile and returned to his usual tone of sarcasm. "Pierre is finding out now that those whom he thought were faultless are now placing barriers on the freedom he had enjoyed before". He laughed. His quip heightened the concern on her face. She knew he was referring to the new restrictions placed on foreigners as well as on the local population. Seeing her unhappy response, his manner changed,

"I am aware a guard post has been set up in front of his house, but I really don't know whether it is for his protection or to keep an eye on him." He was now genuinely trying to put her at ease; his manner sincere and caring as he continued,

"Did you know that there have been many incidents against foreigners here? The last was when a dissident brandishing a knife tried to attack a diplomat in Wan Fuchien Street."

She was surprised to hear this news; her colleagues in the commune had not heard.

Observing the amazement in her eyes Donald said sarcastically,

"You will no doubt hear of it when a suitable version can be given by the authorities." Unable to restrain himself at this opportunity to express frankly his disdain of the communist system, he went on,

"The time has come when even those friends of China need protection from unpredictable elements."

Donald Brown, a student of Chinese language, was keenly interested in gathering inside information on the turbulent politics of China from the wall posters that appeared from time to time on the city walls. He sometimes concealed his foreignness in a blue-padded coat whilst going on rounds to the city to read wall posters. This novel freedom of expression was freedom contrary to communist practise. It had enabled him to gather information of the power struggle among the top party cadres.

A sudden appearance of a poster critical of Premier Chou En Lai had jolted him. Even the hierarchy was not spared. In his excitement he had tried to return to the place with a camera but to his disappointment the poster had been removed as soon as it had appeared. This political system intrigued and amused Donald as much as the commune system that had captured his imagination during a brief spell at the time of his arrival in China. His interests in the communes had unfortunately diminished after his one and only disappointing visit to a commune. The hard life of the workers in it and their poor standard of living had depressed him. His interest was now diverted to a study of the past history of China. He firmly believed that China's greatness lay with the feudal dynasties of the past. He conveniently turned a deaf ear to the official propaganda so vociferously and convincingly presented to foreign guests that the glorious monuments of the past had been built at the expense of the blood and sweat of the poor and oppressed. He stubbornly clung to his own views, refusing to accept the notion that the poor were seeing better days under the Chairman's reins.

Coming back from his reflections, Donald said,

"Pierre should be safe, although with the sentry keeping an eye on him, his movements amongst his students would be restricted. I told Pierre that the people here are unpredictable." She did not know how to respond to his statement, and changing the subject quickly said,

"Is there a way to communicate with him?" He studied her anxious face for a few moments and, said cautiously,

"If you do so you may be at risk, with the soldiers reporting all activities in that lane."

She suddenly burst out as if talking to herself,

"Why should they be suspicious of him, when he is a friend of the country?" A cynical smile appeared on his lips. "Didn't I say the people are unpredictable?" This time he could not fail to notice the hurt in her eyes and quickly changed the subject. "Liang Feng, do you know that there is a group of so-called counter revolutionaries working behind the scenes to create incidents and then give publicity to them with the idea of discrediting the country?" he asked earnestly. The concern in his tone surprised her.

It was not like him to show sympathy to the problems of her country. Feeling encouraged to talk further about the political upheavals she said,

"I believe the Red Guards are not to be blamed for all the chaos that is rumoured." His manner changed, and rather sharply he declared,

"They are a menace, driving everyone insane with their noise and accusations." Unable to defend the Red Guards to Donald she remained quiet, studying his face.

Donald paced the floor restlessly. He was not unaware of the internal politics. "The official version may be a cover-up of more serious party problems," he said to Liang Feng. Feeling her eyes watching him questioningly, he realised he was treading on undiplomatic grounds and again changed the subject. "I am only worried for the safety of our people here. They are encouraging dangerous anti-foreign rhetoric.

She knew he was referring to the authorities, though he did not directly say so. In her heart there was uneasiness about the authorities as well as the Red Guards.

Donald was continuing his tirade against the Red Guards,

"It is impossible to live here with loud speakers screaming, morning, noon and night, 'Down with imperialists' in to our ears." Here she felt sympathy for him as she too was suffering under all this slogan shouting. Donald still pacing the floor abruptly stopped by her. "The Russian diplomats have already left" he said threateningly. "If this hostility continues, most of the other embassies too will pull out." His voice was thick with anger. "This is a psychological war to drive us out of our sanity, I know those who have already succumbed, and have left the country." His words now sounded like an accusation directed at her. He strode on to the balcony saying,

"Follow me I will show you from where all those hate messages are coming." He pointed his finger in the direction of the "East is Red" commune. Breathing hard he muttered,

"Do you see the new name displayed across the banner?" When Liang Feng nodded her head he burst out sarcastically "I presume they will not spare any place on earth from becoming 'Red' with all this brainwashing."

She saw the loudspeakers fixed by the commune gates and which were hurling propaganda against foreign revisionism turned towards Waichia Talou. While the two stood there, each with their own thoughts a procession of demonstrators came along the road. Red Guard provocateurs in the forefront were beating drums and shouting slogans while the rank and file trekked behind them. It was a very noisy procession. They came to a sudden halt by Weidatalo. They thronged to go there, some shaking their fists and others hurling insults. "Down with Russian Revisionists. Down with all Imperialists, Smash the dog heads Russian Imperialism." The shouting drew the residents to the balconies overlooking the scene of the angry protestors. This added fuel to their fire, and eyes blazing with hatred the demonstrators raised threatening fists challenging the silent overseers continuing to hurl insults at the audience until they were spent. The procession in one voice bellowed, "Long live our great Chairman Mao!" then they trailed away in the direction of further imperialist and revisionist enclaves. With sadness Liang Feng realised that most countries had now become enemies of her country. There was hatred in the hearts of her people. She had got a glimpse of their anger and she feared the consequences of such uncontrolled emotions. She walked back into the room with a heavy heart. Donald followed her without commenting. He was evidently worried about his people. The chorus of hatred expressed by the demonstrators had been like daggers thrust into her. She knew it was unjust to insult all foreigners for the misdeeds of a few governments. There rose in her a new determination to protect Pierre from this hatred. No longer could she accept all those mesmerising slogans submissively. But still holding loyalty to Chairman Mao, she justified her new stance with his own saying "Chairman Mao says that to rebel is justifiable."

Mr. Ma returned to the apartment with the peaches. He ignored both Donald and Liang Feng and set about his work in the kitchen ignoring his master's request to bring in tea for his guest. Irritated by the delay, Donald called out sharply,

"Mr. Ma, is the tea ready?" but there was no response. Sadly realising that she was the cause of Ma's disobedience, Liang Feng stood up to leave. Anti-foreign sentiments seemed to have influenced Ma, and his hostility to her was understandable. Donald was upset by Ma's coldness to his guest; but on Liang Feng's entreaty to refrain from pulling up Ma, Donald closed the door of the living room.

He accompanied her to the door and with sympathy he watched the demure figure going down the steps.

Liang Feng was saddened by Ma's behaviour. That feeling or rejection was proof of her own people turning against her. At another time she would not have cared as much about for Ma's rudeness. But with Pierre kept out of her life, she was more sensitive to trivialities of human behaviour. She longed all the more for Pierre's company as it would give her the sympathy she lacked from her people. Her heart heavy with despondency, she walked slowly to her workplace.

Taking some minutes from work she turned to the pages of the Red Book and read,

"All erroneous ideas, all poisonous weeds, all ghosts and monsters must be subjected to criticism, should in circumstances they are allowed to spread unchecked." Such a time was now before her. It was necessary to criticise herself for feeling lonely and miserable. She was beginning to interpret the 'thoughts of Chairman Mao' to suit her convenience. Were those citations before her losing their power to ensnare her? She had now evidently begun to critically examine her new learning and perceive contradictions. In a low voice she justified to herself that, "the poisonous weeds" the Chairman spoke of could vary with the experience of each individual. She slammed the book down on the table, causing her colleagues to raise questioning eyes. She then confronted their scrutiny with a smile of apology. It was time to leave and she hastened from the room evading any questions.

Outside on the road she encountered a group of Red Guards pacing the road. They, who had felt exalted by their achievement of participating in The Long March to the capital were now faced with indecision, as they roamed the streets aimlessly, counting the hours. Liang Feng no longer found any appeal in the scene alongside the streets. The once picturesque and well-kept avenues had lost their charm. Litter was strewn everywhere and the sidewalks were dotted with hastily constructed toilets.

Liang Feng was jolted from her reflections as a mob charged along the road towards her. Suddenly she was caught in a scene of horror, speechlessly she gazed, as the mob pounced on a man they had been chasing. They threw him on the ground in a frenzied attack; kicking him, and when he became motionless they stamped on him. In few minutes the mob, in their mood of destruction, had kicked the life out of the man. She had never seen such rage in the eyes of her people and a terrible fear gripped her.

Finishing their restless deed, the mob now moved away nonchalantly down the road leaving behind them an unrecognisable corpse. The onlookers who had silently watched the violence hesitantly came forward and surrounded the lifeless body. The confidence and determination Liang Feng had experienced a few minutes ago to pursue her quest of individual freedom was shattered in a moment. Her imploring eyes had pleaded to the policeman in the vicinity directing traffic to intervene, but he had found it convenient to turn a blind eye and had allowed the mob to take the law into their hands. Someone in the crowd whispered,

"He had snatched a woman's handbag and was punished by the Red Guards." Tears stung her eyes, that there should be such brutality and horror.

Walking away from the scene of the crime she wept for the unknown man murdered before her. In anguish her thoughts flew to all the great philosophies, Buddhism, Taosim and even Confucianism that had nurtured China s great civilisation. But now driven by anger and frustration the mob had killed a man in a manner similar to the killing of a field rat. Her unhappiness was making her a defeatist. Her heart cried out to Pierre. His gentleness and understanding was what she most needed at that moment.

Arriving in Wampu's home, she wanted to be left alone. She declined the offer of food and sat in thought on the kang. But her solitude was short-lived; she was summoned to attend the special study class.

In the class Liang Feng sat as far as possible from the eyes of the teacher. The horror of what she had seen haunted her as she mechanically read with the rest the 'Thoughts of Chairman Mao on the subject 'Uproot Capitalist Revisionism'. She wondered if the murdered man was a revisionist; but an onlooker had said that he was a Red Guard from the Shansi province. When the reading came to an end, the class engaged in a debate with the teacher but Liang Feng sat silently. Her eyes studied her colleagues. They were all workers both young and old, not given a moment to reflect on their lives. They were disciplined to follow study classes as soon as they were set free from their daily work. She remembered the time before the revolutionary fervour when people had quietly allowed themselves a much more relaxed lifestyle. But the 'constant revolution' was infringing on that leisure time. Her thoughts flew to the three old men she had once seen with Pierre on the summit of Behai engaged in tai chi chuan. Such congenial scenes had disappeared with the closure of the parks to the public. A rigid life style was now the order of the day.

CHAPTER 19

Revisionists Keeping Pets

The next day, it was Wampu's turn to cry. The neighbourhood committee had received reports of Wampu's kittens. The elderly in the community, sympathetic to Wampu, concealed the truth claiming that the commune had kept a cat to frighten away rats from the grain stores. There were others who, remembering the order received some time ago to destroy all sparrows that ravaged the fields, gave another version that a cat had been reared to destroy the birds. Although the incident died down, there were still rumours circulating of the cries of cats in the neighbourhood at night. No one yet dared to enter Wampu's house to check the truth. They respected her too much. They were however concerned at reports that Red Guards were expected in the commune within the next few days. Fearing the possibility of a discovery of cats, they warned,

"Wampu, we like you. Don't let the Red Guards treat you badly. If there are cats, get rid of them".

Liang Feng had heard these stories and when Wampu, frightened, confided in her, she was determined to help her. With eyes shining in hope she said,

"Wampu, I know of a place where the kittens would be safe from any harm." She was aware that the Browns liked cats and already had one; he would not mind three more especially as they were of beautiful Persian stock.

Concealing the cats in a covered basket Liang Feng, early next morning, cycled to Weidatalo, reaching it before the arrival of other workers. There was no problem in getting through the sentry who simply nodded his assent. His duty was to examine the bags of the workers on their entry and departure through the gates. But these responsibilities were sometimes disregarded when he preferred just to sit in his sentry box and nod his approval.

The first hurdle had been overcome; the next was to deal with the cook. Liang Feng recollected the incident that had been related to her when Sally had presented Mr. Ma with a bag of crystallised sugar for Christmas. The sentry had discovered it when examining Mr. Ma's bag and had ordered him to return it. Mr. Ma would have welcomed this gift as he much preferred the crystallised sugar to the sugary syrup which was the only sweetener available to the Chinese in Peking. To cover up his humiliation at the sentry's insults he built up anger and hostility within himself towards his employer and spread the story that the foreigner had tried to bribe him with capitalist goods. His own children had been his most severe accusers, threatening to report to the authorities that he was becoming 'a capitalist roader'. The recollection of this story together with the memory of her previous experiences of his display of hostility towards her, made Liang Feng wary of meeting him again.

Carrying the basket, she ran up the steps to the apartment on the third floor. Breathless, she rang the doorbell and waited for the door to open. It was the maid who opened it. With suspicion the woman scrutinised Liang Feng and the basket in her hand. At that moment the cry of a cat came from the basket, and hearing it her hands involuntarily went up to her face, and with palms pressed to her ears as if to drown the unwelcome sound she cried,

"What have you there?" Anxiously watching the maid's face for her reaction, Liang Feng carefully lifted the lid; the kittens were huddling together inside. In stunned disbelief the woman looked at Liang Feng as if she had lost her senses. Fear was gradually turning into anger. Liang Feng hastened to explain the reasons for her errand. But the woman showed no signs of acceptance. She knew the seriousness of disobeying the orders. Glancing quickly at her watch she said,

"You cannot leave them here. Ma will put me into trouble." She had to get rid of Liang Feng and the cats, and she added challengingly,

"The master and mistress are in Hong Kong and I simply cannot accept the cats."

Struggling to hide her disappointment, Liang Feng covered the basket. Standing at the open door, biting her lower lip in deep reflection, she wondered what her next move should be. Watching Liang Feng's anxious countenance the maid's eyes softened and she said almost kindly and in a pleading tone,

"The cook is a troublemaker. He has even threatened to report me for eating the food Mrs. Brown gives me sometimes." Liang Feng was amazed. She was aware that despite the order that workers should not consume any food from their foreign employers, those working for eight hours on a frugal meal of boiled kidney beans or manto found it difficult to decline such an offer.

With suspicions removed, the maid had now begun to relate a series of complaints against the cook, trying to defend her stand and hold the visitor's attention. However, the sound of footsteps on the stairs and the fear that the cook was returning, made Liang Feng act fast. Interrupting the monologue she hastily excused herself and rushed down the stairs. A new feeling of reckless courage swept through her. She had to save the kittens; she could not let down her grandaunt. Brushing past a man coming up the stairs she hurried to the bicycle stand. Holding on to her precious cargo she cycled, almost nonchalantly past the sentry who was busy checking workers arriving at Weidatalo.

Her thoughts were full of the risks she was taking. She debated with herself. She and her father had taken a much bigger risk in coming into a new society of which they knew so little. However it had been worthwhile. This consoled her. Only a few days before, news had been received of the massacre of 50,000 Chinese in Indonesia. This news had provoked organised demonstrations in Peking against the Indonesian government.

She was full of determination to defy the authorities. Surely there was no cause for fear; did she not support the movement for justifiable change in the political structure. Even if intercepted, and the kittens discovered, she would only be upbraided and ordered to express self-criticism in public. Those guilty of such misdemeanours were paraded through the streets with dunces' caps on their heads and placards hung in front and back with a string holding them to their necks. . It would not shame her too much to don a dunce's cap. If she succeeded in saving the kittens it would be well worth the humiliation. The thought of herself in a fool's cap brought a smile to her face. Feeling like a martyr she reflected that in that crowd there would be at least one kind heart to congratulate her for her bravery and this thought made her chuckle aloud. The danger, the fear, the hostility of others, were of no account. She was going to Pierre with Wampu's kittens. She cycled fast, often having to swerve to avoid the hundreds of workers crossing her path, going in the opposite direction.

Nearing Pierre's residence she slackened the pace. Seeing the sentry standing beside the door her courage faltered somewhat, but keeping a tight rein on herself she walked boldly up to him. She had made up her mind to deal with him officially. Giving him no chance to question her she said confidently,

"I have a message to deliver to Mr. Pierre Devon from the office in Weidatalo." She submitted her identity card which confirmed her name, designation and work place, thankful that it had been recently returned by the soldier to the office. As the sentry scrutinised the card, she went on in a matter of fact manner,

"Mr. Devon requires a cleaner to work in his house. His telephone does not seem to be working and I have come personally to give him the particulars". It all sounded genuine; the sentry was a newly recruited young man, and he knew why the telephone was not working. Returning the card with a wry look on his face, he walked up to the door and knocked firmly.

Liang Feng's heart beat so loud, she feared the sentry would hear it. Footsteps could be heard inside and the door was opened by Pierre. It took him a minute to notice Liang Feng standing behind the sentry. She stepped forward, impatient for the door to be opened wide enough to get herself and her bicycle in. Discerning a message for him on her face he acted quickly. Guiding the bicycle inside the door he closed it firmly. The sentry, unaware of any suspicious circumstances, even helped to pull the door shut.

All the risks taken that day were forgotten at that moment of being alone again with him. The dangers slipped away as if they had never existed. No sooner had Pierre let the bicycle rest against the wall than he took her in his arms. The uncertainty of not knowing what had been happening to him with the new restrictions placed on his movements, and her own boldness, made her for the moment, tongue-tied. She did not, and could not speak of the turmoil of the last few days. The present seemed all that mattered as she stood secure in his arms. Time seemed to stand still.

The kittens had become restless. The sound of mewing, faint and muffled, issued from within the basket, abruptly reminding Liang Feng of the purpose of her visit. Pierre watched curiously as the basket was placed on the table and Liang Feng gently lifted the coverings. His eyes opened wide with astonishment as the kittens, now revealed, yawned, stretched their limbs and daintily stepped over the edge of the basket onto the table. Glad to be out, they demurely contemplated the faces of the two people having control of their destiny from that moment. Stretching out his hand Pierre stroked their bodies tenderly, making them purr with contentment. Pleased with his reaction Liang Feng gave a quick explanation of the reasons she had brought them to him. It was a decision she had made on the spur of the moment and she mutely begged for his acceptance. With a troubled face she added,

"There are changes daily and I wish the authorities would give us a list of what is bourgeois and what is not. There is so much confusion and unhappiness when people are accused of wrongdoings when they are not even sure of what orders they have disobeyed.

Pierre brought a bowl of milk, and placed it on the floor. With new vigour the kittens jumped down and hungrily lapped up the milk. Liang Feng watched this with surprise as she knew that Wampu had fed them only on a diet of soups, meat and fish. The kittens waited hopefully for more milk, and Pierre seemed more than happy to oblige them with a second bowl. This they drank slowly, seeming to enjoy and relish every drop of it. Liang Feng recognised that their instinct was stronger than what they had been accustomed to. After all, wasn't this what was happening in her own case? Though conditioned to this new way of life, she was instinctively drawn to Pierre. As she glanced at him, so gentle, so calm and so very dear to her, she recalled her intuition about him, at the first mention of his name by Brown. She reached out to him and whispered,

"My instincts brought me to you". His eyes showed silent understanding. She had been very much on his mind but he had kept to himself to save her from unnecessary problems with the authorities. His clasp was warm and gentle, giving her a feeling of comfort and security.

Sudden realisation dawned on her that a long delay would arouse the sentry's suspicions and she quickly drew away from Pierre. His eyes expressed what was in his heart but as usual his words told little,

"I missed you when you did not come". She realised the depth of his concern for her as he added,

"I am reminded of the dangers facing Wampu and you every time a procession passes my house". To cover up the intensity of her feelings towards him she murmured lightly, with a nervous laugh,

"Don't worry about me, I am not a capitalist roader to be denounced." Glancing at the cats watching them silently with wide eyes, Pierre smiled,

"Chinese logic is as difficult to understand as you." Her laughter came bubbling out. Then suddenly she became silent as, with a pang, she realised that it had been a very long time since she had shared laughter with someone. Their understanding was mutual. The people in the commune only discussed food production and their own mundane problems. Young men such as Wang Lee were too-serious, dedicated only to their work. "It's too absurd" she had said to herself many times, unable to bear their over-solemn faces.

Her thoughts flew to the Pagoda. The sight of the Pagoda had given her a strange feeling of happiness – the same kind of happiness that she experienced when she was with Pierre, making her forget the cares of daily life. It dawned on her that it would be many days before she would see Pierre again, but moments of joy they shared, like this, would comfort her. The recollections of the Pagoda prompted her to say,

"I heard the gates to Behai Park are closed, as is the case with all the parks in Peking". Pierre with a sigh said,

"I miss the hills, especially as I am unable to do my tai chi." A note of bitterness too had crept into his voice at the indirect reference to the restrictions placed on his movements. The guard post was preventing his students from coming to see him and he had a constant suspicion of being spied upon wherever he went. His voice was melancholy. "The last time I was at the Pagoda I was disappointed to see the inscription to Peace covered over with white paint.

The Pagoda has no direct influence on the lives of the people – why should such things be vandalised and destroyed." She interrupted,

"But Pierre, the Pagoda does affect people like myself, they are aware of this. Its purity makes me desire individual freedom within a just Communist state." He was well aware of her strong belief in justice and fairplay for all, and that it often made her question what had been indoctrinated in her during the last three years.

Their thoughts were rudely interrupted by the sound of the sentry knocking on the door. Their eyes clung, knowing it was time for her to leave.

Liang Feng walked into Pierre's living room and let her eyes take in all the beauty of the objects that had often stirred pride within her for the glorious past of her country. Pierre followed her and she told him pensively,

"I wonder if I will be able to see you again in these surroundings". Her spirits sank as she reminded herself that an opportunity to see him soon again was not likely to come up. She remembered the man beaten before her eyes in Thiananmen Avenue. She knew if she saw more of such incidents, she too would succumb to fear as others were doing now. It had happened to Wampu. In the last few days, Wampu had changed sadly, losing her independent and authoritative spirit, often whimpering like a lost child.

With hands clasped tightly, Liang Feng and Pierre walked up to the door. The sentry was knocking again, this time hesitantly as if he was troubled at what he was doing. He did not persist for long and walked away leaving them undisturbed. He was new and did not want to overdo his authority. Times were uncertain and he did not wish to get into trouble.

The two within looked at each other. Suddenly there were too many conflicting emotions in their minds to make them feel the wrench of parting. Though they were alone they knew they were not free to experience the normal emotions accompanying such circumstances with danger surrounding them from every quarter.

Liang Feng gently lifted the hand she was holding to her lips. Then with a sudden change of manner she let it drop; grasping the handles of her bicycle she blindly stumbled out through the door. His eyes followed her movements in vulnerability. There was so much he wanted to say but *he* was mute. Then she had disappeared, even before the sentry stepped out of his box.

Liang Feng cycled as if in a frenzy, throwing herself into the stream of cyclists traveling in the direction of Waichia Talou. She let others guide her whilst her thoughts lingered on Pierre. The activity of cycling helped her gradually to overcome the turbulence within her.

Reaching Waichia Talou she got off the cycle and walked quietly up to the sentry. Standing at the gates, she handed him her bag for inspection; he looked at her face, frowning and scratching his head with his right hand. He was sure he had seen her earlier in the day. As Liang Feng waited for the return of her belongings, she smiled in order to take away the suspicion that was slowly building up in his eyes. Dismissing his confusion, he smiled back at her and said,

"I am wondering if I had seen you entering Waichia Talou very early this morning." She laughed back, "Maybe", and wishing him a good day, walked into her place of work.

CHAPTER 20

Anti-revisionist Hospital

The ordinary and happy life of Commune 302 came to a tragic end; the new name could have been partly responsible. Everything that touched a chord of the old culture was attacked as revisionist. 'Red Flag Commune' blazed in bold red characters across the entrance. There was political significance in that new name, carrying more political consciousness, and bringing a different lifestyle to the agricultural workers who once lived in total harmony and obscurity.

Loudspeakers prominent on lamp posts caught the attention of all citizens, intruding not only into their quiet life but disturbing the peaceful country atmosphere. When dawn broke, those broadcasts in the form of songs blasted through the sleepy countryside, rousing and shoving residents to vigorous exercise. They stretched and bent, marched backward and forward, greeting the sunrise with a chorus of revolutionary "East is Red", reminding and moulding the doctrine of the state. Like the constant revolution, that music did not end with sunrise, but continued throughout the day. The day's events ended with readings from 'Thoughts of Chairman Mao' solemnly rendered, solemnly listened to and vociferously declaring, "Long live Chairman Mao, the great helmsman."

Donald Brown stood on the balcony of his friend's apartment watching the demonstrators nearing Waichia Talou. This was as far as he could get to see this revolution. Viewing from a distance he was detached. He kept his emotions in check which was important to his reporting of the events in Peking to his government. But it was becoming truly impossible to maintain his uncommitted composure. The Red Guards were making him angry by invading the bastion of the foreigners. They showed no care for those privileged, like him. Diplomats were nobodies in their eyes, having no special privileges in the equality the great helmsman sought. They had to come down from those unrealistic pedestals as did those in the headquarters of Mao Zedong's country, be abused and harassed, a treatment deserving for all revisionists, imperialists and neo-colonialists.

In Waichia Talou the Red Guards strutted about, pasting slogans and writing in English and Chinese, "Down with all Imperialists and Revisionists". He had seen not only his country, but most countries having diplomatic relations with the government in Peking, coming under verbal attacks. They were treated no differently than those countries that had severed diplomatic relations with Peking. The Chairman was bent on bringing equality to all his subjects and to all nations in the globe.

The procession was before the gates. He listened to their verbal assaults with mixed feelings. He had come on to the main steps of the building after hearing the noise of drums and shouting from his apartment. He had witnessed many scenes of the revolutionary Red Guards by watching from these steps at the entrance to the building as many others were doing now. He could not escape the sound of the drums booming loudly which resounded through the whole Waichia Talou compound.

Making a concerted effort to record this period in China's history he was a guest often of his diplomatic colleague's apartment on the third floor, at the entrance, which gave a good view of the processions on the road. Once he had watched with true amazement the early morning arrival of the workers assembling before the large portrait of the Chairman, rightly placed above the entrance door. He saw them opening the little Red Book and solemnly reading the thought for the day. It was also with amazement he scrutinised their faces blank and brainwashed as he guessed, saying with embarrassing sincerity, "We love Chairman Mao" and "Chairman Mao is always and forever the red sun shining in our hearts".

The demonstrators had noticed him watching them, and the shouting of slogans became louder and demanding. He smiled to himself, but that smile turned sour when they lifted their clenched fists and shook at him and screamed, "Down with imperialists and foreign devils". He turned back to the apartment leaving the mob to finish their verbal declaration of hate.

'Though he was a detached observer, he was sometimes bothered at those threats hurled at his nation and its people living in Peking. But giving credit to his detached observation he was also beginning to notice the well-planned nature of the demonstrations. They knew exactly what they were doing. The faces of the protestors did not show the fire of an unruly mob he would have witnessed in any other land. He would write in his report that he suspected the mobs had the blessings of higher authorities for these verbal attacks to unnerve all of them, and he was not afraid.

Liang Feng had told him with an unhappy face that she was forced to join the demonstrations against the Britishers. He saw in that mob many Liang Fengs who did things they did not like. He remembered the kindness of Chuang Tsu and often wondered what she was doing in Peking with her official role as a Director of a commune in Canton. It would have been good if they were allowed to visit his home, but he knew they shied away from any contact with foreigners with this wave of anti-foreign sentiment. Being only a detached observer of all events he knew he was unable to understand their complex nature. It was just the same with his office staff who he tried to get to know. Their rather expressionless civility was a barrier against knowing their thoughts.

But that civility was now under strain. They were becoming rude and intolerable when the broadcasts screamed that their people were ill treated in Hong Kong.

His cook was a complete stranger making him angry by walking out of his apartment, leaving the food to burn. He knew it was useless to shout at him as he was not the only one who was suffering these domestic protests. In fact all the domestic staff of the British Mission had walked out in protest at the Hong Kong incidents.

He had learned to put up with these inconveniences as he had a strong feeling that they were still safe in the midst of all this verbal hate. As yet there had not been any unexpected attacks that could come with spontaneous anger, to frighten the foreigners. Liang Feng's friendship had to some extent made him tolerate the others' bad behaviour. Liang Feng had been helpful to him and today she was accompanying Sally to the hospital in the absence of the usual interpreter who had walked out of his office.

To an obscure Hutung branching out of Wanfuchin, the car took Sally and Liang Feng to the newly named Anti-Revisionist Hospital. Sally, expecting her first baby, nervously watched the crowds of Red Guards keeping pace with the car, walking abreast with it and peering at the two inside. They were ragged, dirty and tired from trekking to Peking in the long march they had undertaken from all parts of China. Some did not have even wear the Red Guard uniform, but a red armband and knapsack tied to their backs gave them that distinction.

The hospital that was once the privilege of the foreign community and with little publicity also used by the top party people, had thrown its doors open to all the citizens of the country without discrimination. The sick and homeless red guards found it a refuge in a city they knew for the first time. They were coming in hundreds and squatting on the hospital premises both outside and inside. They sat along the corridors with blank childlike expressions waiting for a friendly word of recognition from the hospital staff. But the staff seemed to attend to them only when their services were demanded; they did not show much enthusiasm to those new patients and went about their work with eyes that showed nervous fear and revulsion.

Wading through the rows of Red Guards lying or sitting on the corridor, Sally and Liang Feng entered the doctors' consultation room. Dr. Chao Xing had seen their arrival but she turned her back to them and, picking up a duster from the towel rack, she busied herself wiping the consultation desk. Sally was indignant. She was ignored, and added to that it was rudeness she thought for the doctor to pretend she had not heard her. This had never happened before. Dr. Chao Xing had carried out her medical studies abroad in the United States had always given special attention to the foreign community. She was nervous today, glancing at the Red Guards leaning on the walls of her consultation room watching her with accusing eyes. But today she could not attend to the foreigners or to the Red Guards. She was assigned to the menial task of the hospital labourers, to clean the wards. The special privileges Dr. Chao Xing enjoyed in the years after her return to the mother country had been removed overnight.

Chairman Mao had been indignant at these special privileges that were given to the specialist doctors to buy goods in shops allocated to foreigners. Chairman Mao's accusation that this treatment was creating a small elitist class in the proletariat. He feared their aloofness from the rest of the ordinary people and it was justifiable not to consider their profession socially or intellectually above those toiling masses.

Today doctor Chao Xing had to work as a labourer. There was no reason for her to be polite to her patients. She bent down, taking the pail of disinfectant in one hand, and hastily walked off to join the group of hospital staff standing in their white gowns and reading *The Thoughts of Chairman Mao*. They seemed to be taking every hour off to read and convince themselves of the 'Thoughts'. Sally was furious, so were the other patients who did not express their troubles with the same intensity as Sally. Patients groaned and whimpered while the hospital staff read on without heed. The young man with a red armband was keeping a vigilant eye and ear for deliberate mistakes or faltering in the reading.

It was useless on Liang Feng's part to plead with any other member of the hospital staff. The normal work of the hospital administration was at a standstill until the reading was over. Sally complained bitterly, standing and watching the other patients in her condition. The women with labour pains groaned and moaned as they walked up and down the ward holding their stomachs, trying to ease their pains; their pains were clearly marked in contorted expressions in their faces. Sally exclaimed,

"Don't they give any pain-killers to these women?" Her remark did not go unheard and a nurse said in disdain,

"We expect Chinese women to bear all natural pains." Her own condition made Sally fear she would receive the same treatment. Unhappy at the callous manner of the nurse, Liang Feng consoled Sally by calling her to walk into the next empty consultation room. They waited a long time till finally a nurse in uniform came and sat down in the Doctor's chair. Liang Feng spoke,

"Who will attend to Mrs. Brown?" The question was received uncomfortably.

Today Nurse Meilin had been assigned the 'doctor' work. She was not very happy with this work and avoided as much as possible seeing any patients. In a soft hesitant voice she answered,

"I am new here", and glancing at Sally's hospital card she said quickly,

"Mrs. Brown is still in her seventh month of pregnancy and does not need an examination. If she has any problems bring her back to the emergency section."

She was apologetic. Liang Feng translated to Sally what had been said and since the examination was over they left the room.

They passed through the corridor with difficulty with the crowds pressing on both sides of the wall, wailing and directing hostile eyes at those who had received treatment. They stopped in surprise. Dr Chao Xing was standing with a mop in one hand and the Red Book in the other. Seeing Sally and Liang Feng, she quickly opened her book and read loudly, "Fight self and repudiate revisionism". She smiled to herself and tucking the book into the pocket of her gown she dipped the mop into the disinfectant and splashed it on the floor before them. They quickly took a step back, unhappy to see Dr Chao Xing in a situation that would be embarrassing to her. Liang Feng and Sally walked on leaving Dr Chao Xing to do her work.

In the midst of much excitement and noise in the commune that evening, Liang Feng returned to Wampu's home. The events in the hospital had brought home with force the effect of the Revolution on all aspects of life. With an uneasy feeling she listened to the commune members exclaiming that Red Guards in the commune had discovered capitalist revisionists hiding among them and were preparing to denounce them at a public gathering of the residents.

She did not know what to make of all these accusations except to mesmerise herself with one thought, that Chairman Mao was trying to put things right for everybody. On entering the house it was alarming to see Wampu seated alone and weeping. Her usual smiling face which she tried to keep up for her grand-niece was drawn with signs of more weeping. She had lost her proud bearing and was as helpless as those kittens she had taken to Pierre. Quickly kneeling down beside her Liang Feng said,

"Wampu, are you crying because the cats are gone?" Wampu shook her head, and not waiting to talk stared at the blank walls of the house. They were truly colourless without the pictures of Chairman Mao.

Unable to ignore Liang Feng's question, Wampu blurted,

"Today I heard a rumour that all houses would be searched for capitalist goods." She turned imploringly to Liang Feng for comfort and gave fearful glances at the covered chairs. Quickly putting her arms round Wampu's frail shoulders she said with false confidence,

"Wampu, you don't have to worry, everybody likes you; they know you have willingly given up your old house to live with the ordinary people in the commune."

Those words were comforting. She had lost track of all those past events, but now being reminded of it brought that confidence of the role she had played to help her people, and she smiled and said,

"I love this land, Liang Feng. I am glad I did not go to Indonesia."

Forgetting her worries and realising Liang Feng was hungry after a day's work, she said,

"I must get down and make you a good rice soup" and she pattered to the kitchen. Seated on the kang, Liang Feng gazed at the retreating figure. It had been few weeks since Wampu had given up going to the kitchen. With parting from the cats Wampu had lost interest in cooking and preferred to eat in the community canteen. The aroma of the rice made her hungry but it also brought thoughts of the hidden Buddha statue behind the brick wall by the kitchen fire.

While Wampu sat cross-legged on the kang and began to taste her soup, Liang Feng walked into the kitchen and slowly removed the brick hiding the statue. In the light of the fire she held the green jade statue with a perfectly moulded serene expression, evoking those thoughts so revolutionary in her. She held it in both hands firmly. Pierre had seen the assault on the temples; statues that had stood all through periods of political trouble in the country were now wrenched away and imprisoned with barbed wire before the eyes of all the people, bringing fear to those who had secretly clung to past religions.

Her hands tightened round the figure; she had to protect it from such a fate. There was a likelihood of discovery if the Red Guards searched the house.

Wampu would be in great trouble, like old Lin, for practising her religion without fear. It would be worse than the discovery of cats; it was too strong a force that could oppose Mao Zedong's philosophy.

With measured steps she carried the statue to Wampu. Wampu had finished eating and was lying back in the kang with her face to the wall. She was not asleep but was motionless with eyes staring once again at the wall. She heard Liang Feng in the room. Liang Feng spoke,

"Wampu, what are you going to do with the Buddha statue?" The words shocked her, she turned round abruptly. The statue was in her grandneice's hand; forgetting the question she gazed in wonder. Her face became gentle and calm. She was seeing it after many years in full view. Those occasional glimpses she had under the light of the fire had not revealed the beauty she was seeing now. She had never dared to bring it to the kang for fear of neighbours discovering her secret. Getting down from the kang she walked up to Liang Feng and keeping her palms together worshipped the statue. Seeing Wampu as if hypnotised by the statue Liang Feng kept it carefully on top of the ledge over the kang. She had mixed feelings of sadness for a lost religion and worry that Mao Zedong's philosophy had not made an impact on Wampu.

Watching her grandneice Wampu said quizzically,

"How did you know about my statue?" Her worry was over. Smiling, like Wampu, for the pleasure it gave her too, Liang Feng said,

"It was my luck to discover it". She liked the face of an enlightened human, bringing joy and peace to her heart. The troubled look had disappeared from Wampu's face and becoming talkative and happy at sharing her secret, she said,

"I worshipped only at night when I thought you were asleep".

The joy was over for Liang Feng and there was once again that worrying feeling inside her. Quick to see the changed expression in Liang Feng's face, Wampu said,

"Liang Feng, are you worrying about the Red Guards?" She nodded her head. It was useless talking about it to Wampu who would worry more. But Wampu, feeling the strain of their secret said sadly,

"Even Buddha won't be able to help me now, when they take my statue away." The statue had given her feelings of optimism under trying conditions and it had helped her to accept the social changes with little rebelliousness.

As the authorities relaxed their surveillance of the citizens she had fearlessly slipped back to her old religion which she knew did not make her a bad citizen. Though the temples were out of bounds, the statues hidden in the house gave that serenity of life when her sons had left for Hong Kong. Her sons pitied her, but she had stoutly said,

"They can take away all my material belongings, but they cannot take away my thoughts and my heart." With defiance an angry Wampu had declared,

"I'm no peasant at heart."

Wampu's figure was bent; she had succumbed to fear and loneliness with the loss of her cats. Fear she had not known before stalked her, making her whimper softly. When she did not get an answer she said pleadingly,

"You must save my statue just as you saved my cats from harm".

Liang Feng took Wampu's hand; there was a determination to help Wampu. "I will help you, Wampu. I will keep it in a safe house that no one in this country would dare to enter." She knew Pierre would be glad to keep it in his house.

She smiled. He had given her an equal feeling of calm as the statue. Wampu saw the smile, she was relieved. She looked at the statue. The thread she had woven round the statue for the past years had to be severed, but it did not come without anguish. Parting from the cats had been hard and once again another link to her life had to be destroyed. There was emptiness in the life ahead. Tears filled her eyes, and they fell down her cheeks, and the folded palms of her hands. With those tears she paid obeisance to the statue.

She took the statue to her hands; her crying was over and she smiled with joy. Her eyes busily surveyed the room and, making a decision, she declared,

"I have placed my statue in the highest position in the house."

It stood over the less significant items on the ledge.

Watching Wampu quietly, her own heart was filled with a loneliness to face the future. Wampu was speaking to herself,

"I am displaying you tonight where you should have always been; not hidden away like a sickness in the dark corner in the kitchen."

Holding her palms together and lifting them to touch her forehead she brought them back to her kneeling position. She did this three times. Her thoughts were in prayer and remained motionless as she gazed at the statue for many hours. That night Wampu went to bed with a joyful heart, her old spirit had returned.

CHAPTER 21

Revisionist Art

The attention of the residents of 'Red Flag Commune' was drawn to the preparations of the neighbourhood committee to hold a meeting in the grounds of the commune. The Red Guards jauntily paraded through the streets summoning the people with loud announcements, and beating drums, to hear Comrade Wang, the new leader of the commune. When the gongs boomed the peoples' hearts beat with anxiety and feelings of tension pervaded the atmosphere. No doubt the message had reached all ears and Liang Feng with puckered eyebrows turned to Wampu,

"Did you hear that announcement? We have to assemble in the compound."

But Wampu seemed oblivious to all noises and was gazing in the direction of the kitchen. Liang Feng sighed as she watched Wampu. She had been behaving in an unusual manner since the Buddha statue had been removed from the house. Following the discovery of the statue which had then remained on the ledge above Wampu's kang for many weeks when she finally began to comprehend the threats against people who still clung on to past religions and she said sadly to Liang Feng,

"It's time to part from my Buddha statue please give it to good hands to be protected."

Liang Feng smiled to herself at the thought of the statue now kept safely at Pierre's. It had not been easy to get it across to him, without the assistance of Donald Brown, who passed it on to Pierre. Liang Feng herself had felt sadness to part from an object that had been part of the house as well as of Wampu's life for many years. Once the statue had been discovered Wampu had felt relieved to discuss the matter with her relative and share her secret that brought forth an appreciative companionship between them. But Wampu had not yet recovered from the absence of her revered object and was suffering a loss of memory. Now taking her hand Liang Feng led her out of the house in to the compound.

In the faces of the adults there were anxiety and suspicion as they dragged themselves to the meeting. This was in marked contrast to the young displaying high spirits to comrade Wang's summons.

The raised dais constructed in the centre of the compound gave a good view to those assembled around the Red Guard holding a loudspeaker in his hand. He was one of the Red Guards who had come to live in the commune, now showing impatience by announcing from time to time for the people to keep quiet. There was an uneasy silence and comrade Wang strode on to the dais. His arrival made the Red Guard already on the dais step down and stand to attention.

168

Wang's severe face held the attention of the gathering, pressing around the dais. Wang's hands stiffened as he clenched his fists, his eyes flashed angrily. He appeared to be controlling his temper as he waited for the scuffling feet and mumbling voices to cease. His sharp ears had picked up a hint of indifference from the people to the meeting. He did not care to shout for order, and with cold and threatening eyes he penetrated each one's face. There was immediate silence in the audience.

Comrade Wang chose his words coldly and deliberately so that no one could escape the accusations he was going to pin down on them. He coldly addressed them,

"Comrades, there are still among us citizens who are pursuing revisionist idealism."

The whispers and mumblings of the gathering ceased abruptly. Comrade Wang's voice rose to a high pitch and he lashed out,

"Revisionists are none other than vipers, hiding under grass, comrades, we must bring them to the open and destroy them with force."

He gasped loudly, the only sound in that hushed audience. With a quick change of manner he now sighed loudly, tilting his head with mock sadness," 'It's with great grief that I inform you that Revisionists have not given careful thoughts to the study of Chairman Mao's doctrine."

He was greeted with puzzled looks from the audience who showed no emotions as they studied comrade Wang. Wang cleared his throat, his sharp eyes scrutinised all the faces before him, but the moment of uncomfortable silence ceased and voices began to whisper,

"Who has dared not to study Chairman Mao's thoughts?" each questioned their closest neighbour.

Wampu had heard the words and now stricken with fear she lowered herself to the ground in a faint, compelling Liang Feng to bend down and shield her from the man on the dais. Fortunately Wampu's affliction went unnoticed by those around her. They were already informed that Wampu suffered ill health in the past few days.

With Wang's words becoming incomprehensible to them, there was restlessness in the audience, showing signs of disobedience, daring members to creep away from the rear, muttering that they had enough work to cope with and they had no time to listen to Comrade Wang's far-fetched accusations. Comrade Wang's eyes did not miss them, neither did he seem indifferent to their restlessness and he gave a sharp order for silence. Those who had slipped off were back in their places and the rumblings of unrest stopped. The opportune moment was now before Wang and he triumphantly announced,

"Comrade Lin I order you to come on to the dais."

Shock waves of rumblings once again began. Lin was one of the most respected members of the commune for his artistic talents. Fearless, indignant mutterings of "This is madness" swept through the audience.

Lin hobbled on to the dais, with the aid of his walking stick. In full view of the audience he smiled at them, there were no signs of repentance in his demeanour for whatever he had done. His erect and proud bearing was annoying comrade Wang who pointed an accusing finger at Lin and shouted,

"How dare you paint pictures not suitable for the proletariat?"

Lin gazed at him in puzzlement daring to look squarely at his accuser. There was the occasion when he had burnt his paintings to please his grandson but since then he had concentrated on painting landscapes in and around Peking, which were not impressionist as the ones he had painted before.

Comrade Wang cunningly watched the effect he was creating on the people. He had another role to play other than only denouncing Lin. He had taken upon himself the task of educating the commune folk in the new aspirations of the Cultural Revolution. Clearing his throat, he directed a question at his audience,

"Tell me, for whom should art be drawn?"

The restless crowd saw an opportunity to express themselves and a female voice shouted over the heads of the rest,

"For the people."

She was backed by other voices much lower in tone than hers.

Comrade Wang's face flushed and eyes blazing fury he jumped up from his seat. Pointing a threatening hand at the daring woman he screamed,

"How dare you say that art should be for all the people."

The woman burst into tears. The crowd that had been made silent by his shouting began to mumble in indignation, and influenced by the challenging voice of the female shouted back in a chorus to comrade Wang,

"For whom then should art be?"

Comrade Wang's face that had relaxed at the sight of the woman's tears now angrily glared at his audience. Producing his copy of Chairman Mao's 'Thoughts', he cleared his throat and read profoundly,

"Revolutionary literature and art should be only for workers, peasants and soldiers."

A cheer went up from the audience. They were all peasants and workers, and were happy that Chairman Mao should say art was for them. With the cheers dying down the mood of the audience changed and with angry eyes they glared at old Lin. In their eyes Lin had dared to betray their trust in him.

Comrade Wang continued from the book "Art should never serve the bourgeoisie and the revisionists."

To prove his words that would implicate Lin's revisionist art, Comrade

Wang stepped forward, and with a flourish he unrolled Lin's painting. Eyes that had silently accused Lin now slowly changed. Smiles appeared on the faces of the audience as they gazed at a scene familiar to them before the Cultural Revolution. There was a majestic pine tree sheltering an old man seated in contemplation. In the background was a picturesque pavilion. Proletarian hearts filled with peace and calm, moved by the serenity of the scene. Children, the admirers of the Red Guards, had shouted derision at Lin, but now smiled at Lin and his painting.

A loud rude shout from Comrade Wang shattered the calm. To him, it was unpardonable for the people to smile at such a picture. Old Lin too was smiling, completely lost in the scene he had painted. The anticipated scowls Wang could not see so, losing his temper, he threw the painting on the floor and stamped on it. Comrade Wang's colleagues rushed on to the dais and pouncing on the painting tore it into a million pieces.

The audience was visibly shaken by this ferocity. In distress they remained quiet, while the children whimpered softly. The faces of the audience that had expressed their happiness now clouded with hate and fear. Old Lin was pushed off the dais and once again Comrade Wang took command.

Comrade Wang continued his lesson on art,

"Art divorced from proletarian politics is by no means proletarian Art. Art should subordinate to the revolutionary task set by the party in a given revolutionary period."

He was satisfied with his words; the audience was truly well behaved in bitterness. Wang grinned; he had transformed the people's mistaken views on the subject of art. He called Lin to the dais and said threateningly,

"Now repeat after me,

"I have made a mistake in drawing Art that is not proletarian."

While Wampu remained seated, shielding her eyes from the Red Guard's anger Liang Feng watched Comrade Wang. She could not accept Wang's interpretation of art. Annoyance so far muffled burst out,

"I cannot accept that art is not for all people, beauty can be appreciated by all."

Her neighbour heard her and giving her an understanding smile she whispered,

"These Red Guards are very foolish."

This expression of dissent quickly passed from mouth to mouth till it seemed like warning tremors before an earthquake.

The meeting came to an abrupt end when Comrade Wang darkly hissed,

"Our most important task should begin now to search the houses of our workers and peasants for bourgeois objects of art."

Rumblings stopped and they stared at Wang in stunned silence. They followed him with mute agony as Wang called out to his colleagues to lead the way to the houses of the residents. At the thought of Wampu's chairs a sick feeling swept over Liang Feng. Only a miracle could save Wampu now: that would be only if Comrade Wang did not consider chairs revisionist and evil.

CHAPTER 22

Cultural Objects Forcibly Removed

Within the commune, the Red Guards led by Comrade Wang, a reluctant group of residents trailing behind them, marched in a procession, breaking into houses and forcing out the last visible remnants of a feudal culture. It was the children in the procession who discovered a new game, that of running into houses and destroying people's property. It was they, the children, playing this game, who helped Comrade Wang to unearth bourgeois objects in their parents' homes; they had seen the elders hide valuables under the kang and in dark corners away from prying eyes. It was again the children, who idealising the khaki uniformed Red Guards, ridiculed the elderly. The children, now the new revolutionaries, jauntily marched with the Red Guards imitating their scorn of the old and feeble, the past culture and traditional ideas.

Old Lin had been dismissed from the dais with a flourish of Comrade Wang's hand,

"Lin is an old fool so we are not punishing him because he is showing repentance," Wang said with scorn. Having taken away Lin's walking stick, he preferred to let the onlookers interpret Lin's stooping back as a sign of cringing caused by shame.

Liang Feng and Wampu watched in stunned silence as Comrade Wang with his band pulled out dust-covered boxes of clothes from under their kang. Some Red Guards broke open the boxes and Comrade Wang went through the clothes meticulously, flinging whatever he finished with, on the floor. Disgruntled when he failed to find any bourgeois items there, he kicked aside the boxes and, looking around, headed for the old mat covering and Wampu's most valuable objects. The two women, their hearts thudding in fear stood stupefied and rigid. His eyes gleaming with a sense of discovery, he pounced on the embroidered yellow quilt beneath the mat, hurling it on the ground with revulsion. He stamped and kicked it. And then, his eyes alighted on the elegant rosewood chairs. For a moment he was speechless with hatred and anger. Then, triumphant in his discovery, he yelled,

"Capitalist chairs!" pointing to Wampu's treasured objects.

Unable to bear their grandeur staring in his face he pointed an accusing finger at Wampu and screamed,

"There she is – the Capitalist Revisionist!" He was speechless with hatred and anger. Triumphant in his discovery, he yelled once again,

"Capitalist chairs!".

Liang Feng was numb with horror; what she was witnessing she had not visualised even after seeing the most extreme propaganda films fed to the people about the revolution of 1949.

There was disbelief and shock as she silently watched Comrade Wang hurl abuse at the chairs. For a moment she even wondered if the chairs had come alive.

His energy was boundless. In a show of authority he called out to his colleagues to drag the chairs out of the house. There were gasps from the silent onlookers as the motifs, inlaid in the wood with mother of pearls, gleamed proudly in the light of day. Friends of Wampu who had watched with concern the sight of Wang trailing behind the others glared at her in anger, mixed with envy. They could no longer sympathise with her sickness and suffering. They did not want to remember that 16 years before Wampu had voluntarily parted from her house and possessions. They were ignorant of the fact that recently she had also parted from her cherished Buddha statue and beloved cats. The people's hearts hardened with covetousness at the sight of the chairs. Their hatred of the privileged classes was absolute.

For Wampu, her last links with her past had now been severed by Comrade Wang. Rediscovering the beauty of the chairs in the open daylight she was enraptured by them, even forgetting the people around her and the predicament she was in. She whispered,

"Liang Feng, don't you think my chairs are more beautiful in this light!"

Liang Feng nodded in silent assent as she held Wampu's hand. The sight of their beauty inflamed Wang's fury and he kicked the chairs, bringing tears to Wampu's eyes. Comrade Wang's concern with Wampu's house was now over and calling the children to follow him he with his band burst into the next house in the compound.

In a few hours the commune compound was transformed into a museum of past objects of beauty. Jade figures, silk screens, ivory carvings, ivory chopsticks and many items of precious jewellery had been wrenched out of unostentatious homes of workers and peasants. Cleverly hidden objects that had escaped the eyes of the authorities in the years following the upheaval of 1949 were now exposed. Some of Wampu's neighbours who had been critical of her now dared not look her way; they watched with guilt and dismay as their belongings swelled the haul of confiscated property.

Comrade Wang continued to comb each residence meticulously for cherished treasures and family heirlooms. With mounting indignation and horror they watched their precious possessions piled unceremoniously onto a cart and cycled to the auction house, to be sold presumably to foreigners for it was only they who would be granted the privilege to purchase them.

Liang Feng's arms were protectively round her weeping grandaunt, as they returned to a desolate house. The loss of the chairs had left a void in the room as well as in Wampu's heart. She was not alone in her grief as other members of the commune who had lost their property were grieving within their homes. Their concealed treasures had been a source of secret joy to them and the loss was that of a loved companion. The only ornament allowed in each home had been the bust and portrait of the Chairman, adorning unchallenged the walls of the main room. Liang Feng muttered in anger,

"Beautiful objects are not for us, poor peasants." Picking up reverently the quilt that had escaped the rapacious heart of Comrade Wang, Liang Feng spread it on the kang.

That night lying beside Wampu, Liang Feng's thoughts were on Comrade Wang and the revolution. Wang's extremism she felt was unjustified. Did he not realise that his obnoxious behaviour could sow seeds of unrest in the minds of the citizens about the fairness of the Chairman's philosophy. In fact those Red Guards following the ways of Comrade Wang were a greater threat to the achievement of the Chairman's ultimate goal. If such injustices were meted out to innocent citizens how fearful the future would be under a strong unquestionable party hierarchy. Unable to contain within her the frustrations and anger with Comrade Wang, she decided to visit Chuang Tsu the next morning.

The changed appearance of Chuang Tsu shocked her as she shakily came forward to meet her friend. Chuang Tsu's bouncy smiling face was now thin and drawn. She appeared feeble with hunched shoulders and dragging feet. It was not only Chuang Tsu's appearance that had undergone a transformation, even the decorations on the wall of the apartment hinted at new political loyalties. Before Liang Feng could question her friend, Chuang Tsu whispered,

"I am sorry I ever came to Peking." While Liang Feng silently studied the appearance before her she noticed the absence of the Mao Zedong badge that had always been worn proudly on the lapel of a blouse or coat her friend happened to wear. Chuang Tsu, who once prided herself in looking well before Liang Feng, showed no care for her appearance. Her cotton blouse *was* creased, showing their yellow edges at the neck and sleeves.

Chuang Tsu did not give her a chance to explain her own fears as she was full of complaints.

"I love my daughter but I cannot feel the same about my son-in-law."

As Liang Feng's eyes shifted from Chuang Tsu's face to the posters on the wall she quipped,

"It seems Sheng has shifted his allegiance to the Red Guard movement."

Chuang Tsu's lips curled and she muttered,

"I don't care what he does as long as he does not make life intolerable for me and Shi Kai Ying."

With no one else in the apartment, Chuang Tsu seized the opportunity to unburden herself to Liang Feng. Chuang Tsu expressed her suspicions that Sheng was involved with certain gang wars that had been reported in the newspapers,

"The neighbours feel Sheng is at the bottom of all the harassment they suffer from the Red Guards."

Liang Feng sadly listened to her friend, realising that Sheng had become another comrade Wang, in terrorising the people. The country's inconsistent political system was posing a dilemma to the people and some therefore allied themselves to be influenced and led by people with questionable loyalties. They were now resorting to activities of extremism supposedly carried out as part of a campaign of allegiance to the Chairman.

Moved by the sympathy of her friend, Chuang Tsu led the way to her daughter's room. Standing by the wall she pointed an accusing finger at the pile of torn books on the floor.

"This is what Sheng did today in a fit of anger against me. He tore up the books I read, calling them 'revisionist propaganda.'"

"Fresh tears filled her eyes at the memory of the incident. Liang Feng, seeing the distress of her friend, suppressed her own uncertainty and consoled her.

CHAPTER 23

A Definition of Capitalism

L iang Feng stood by the gates of Behai Park, longing to enter, but the gates were securely locked. All the parks in Peking were now closed to the public. There were thousands of Red Guards descending on Peking. The authorities had taken this measure to prevent them from using the pictur-esque gardens as temporary accommodation and in the process destroying and wrecking them. Due to lack of organisation and lack of foresight, the authorities had neglected to arrange for adequate accommodation for the thousands of long marchers entering the city.

Liang Feng had walked up to the park that day in search of tranquillity away from the tedious and unrewarding routine in the commune. There was a time when she had escaped to the unruffled environment within the parks to enjoy the solitude and inner peace which she could not find elsewhere. She was no different to many others who needed to get away from their highly disciplined lives and for whom the parks and such scenic spots had become a refuge. As the Cultural Revolution gathered momentum the restrictions continued and the people suffered.

These restrictions affected the foreign residents too; they were now confined to Waichia Talou and a limited area in the city and suburbs. Unhappy at the closure of the places he had become accustomed to, Pierre expressed his disap-pointment to Liang Feng,

"These restrictive laws are incomprehensible to me; of what benefit are they to the people?" Liang Feng was aware that he particularly missed his daily practice of going to the Behai Park to do his Tai Chi.

Under this restrictive atmosphere Liang Feng's feelings for Pierre under-went a notable change. With no other outlets open to her as an escape from the disciplined lifestyle imposed by the authorities she clung to her friendship with Pierre. Frustrated at the lack of opportunities to meet him as often as before, her attachment became intense and she set out to seek opportunities to be with him. Together with her increased feeling of rebelliousness against the authorities, and enraged by the frustrations of the people, she was quite willing to defy the laws.

With the rapidity of a pestilence, suspicion and fear spread amongst the people. Faced with heightening murmurs of dissatisfaction, the authorities called upon the people to exchange their thoughts with eachother at the study classes but no one dared to do so. They knew the consequences of such confi-dence sharing; self-criticism could make them a target for punishment. The slogans for self-improvement were chanted daily in the study classes, and with constant repetition their meanings were instilled into the people's minds; yet there were those on whom these slogans had a contrary effect; frustrated, they sullenly nursed their anger in secret. Unhappiness and rebelliousness was the outcome, which made them turn to counter revolutionary activities. There were still others, philosophical by nature who believed that the Revolution like anything else would complete its natural cycle and come to an end, and then a more orderly life would return.

Members of the commune who had been once friendly with Liang Feng and Wampu no longer spoke to them; they viewed everyone with suspicion. Liang Feng's expressive eyes, bigger, oval, were offensive to those who distrusted foreigners, whatever their kind.

Her shoulders drooping with disappointment Liang Feng walked away from Behai Park intending to take a bus to the commune. A procession of demonstrators, were marching towards her on their way to the city; they were carrying placards and shouting slogans denouncing revisionism and imperialism. The sight made no special impact on Liang Feng, these being everyday occurrences in the current political climate, but she was jolted from her passivity when a van, being driven recklessly from the direction behind her, roared past and screeched to a halt throwing a bunch of leaflets at the demonstrators.

There was a scurry amongst the crowd to retrieve the notices as they blew in all directions in the wind. The van sped off in the same sudden and suspicious manner in which it had arrived, obviously having achieved its objective of making contact with a section of the populace that was politically important to them. A leaflet had fallen by her feet, and picking it up with some curiosity read it,

"Heed the words of Marshall Lin Pio. He says – have no fear to expose the Capitalist Revisionists at the Headquarters." Some words of Chuang Tsu echoed in her ears; she had hinted at other personalities and groups working within the 'Movement for change'. A strange feeling of fear and distress gripped her. She had heard rumours of a gang of four led by the Marshall ready to wrench power if and when the Chairman was declared unfit to rule.

The meaning of 'revisionism' was no longer clear to her because many of Chairman Mao's loyal supporters had been branded as revisionists. With so many personalities trying to influence the course of the Revolution, Liang Feng wondered with some misgivings whether the Revolution had lost sight of its original primary objectives.

As she neared the Commune it was no surprise to see yet another procession but her interest was aroused when she noted that it was marching from within the Red Flag Commune itself. The misgivings she had felt a few minutes earlier returned. She suddenly sensed that the drums were louder and the accompanying shouting more violent than usual. She felt menaced by the atmosphere and a swift stab of fear pierced her being. As if mesmerised by the drums her steps led her towards the crowds. She could see three figures being pushed along by screaming Red Guards, their faces lowered in shame overshadowed by fools' caps, and from a distance they seemed vaguely familiar. She edged closer, and then to her horror she recognised Wampu as one of them.

"Down with Capitalist Revisionists in the Commune!" shouted the Red Guards. Wampu's cap was slipping down over her eyes, and she was feebly trying to shake it back by moving her head backwards, in an attempt to see her way on the road.

Faltering behind Wampu was old Lin the artist, and Wampu's friend Li Hua, looking as helpless and bewildered as Wampu. All three had their hands tied behind their backs and the children walking alongside the Red Guards were tormenting the three accused, poking at them constantly with thin sticks of bamboo, seeming to derive much enjoyment from this. Wampu stumbled, and the children beat her with the sticks. At this Liang Feng cried out in anguish,

"Wampu!"

Wampu could not hear her and continued trying to push her cap back from falling over her eyes. Tears welled in Liang Feng's own eyes. A gentle restraining hand was placed on her shoulders; it was a former member of Wampu's neighbourhood committee.

There was bitterness within Liang Feng that such old people had been singled out for unfair punishment. Old Lin, had once so bravely faced his accusers on the dais, but was now bent and helpless as he fumbled along without the aid of his walking stick. He seemed pathetically afraid of his captors who tended to torment him more than they did the others. The committee member behind Liang Feng whispered,

"When Lin refused to call himself a 'capitalist fool', he was beaten with his own walking stick."

It had infuriated the Red Guards when Lin had retorted that if he was a capitalist he would not be in the commune but in the Forbidden City. The man said sadly,

"They broke his walking stick and threw it away. I don't know how Lin could walk without his walking stick!"

Liang Feng saw Lin, with great difficulty trying unsuccessfully to straighten his bent back. Tears of anger and utter helplessness flowed down her cheeks. Li Hua had been selected for punishment because her brother had once served as the Kuomingtang Consul General in New York. She suffered her ordeal with fortitude and a calm face. The tears were running freely from Liang Feng's eyes. These injustices were more than she could bear. She turned to the man behind her, her voice thick with bitterness,

"Isn't this the kind of injustice you suffered in the feudal society?"

"Yes," he answered in a low voice.

Liang Feng's face felt hot with fury as she watched the children's enjoyment as they beat the three accused. She spoke out in anger, her voice loud and clear,

"How can they do this to old people? Are not the elders in the Headquarters venerated because of their age?"

The man behind her looked frightened, and furtively glancing around, he swiftly slipped away from her side.

Liang Feng painfully followed the procession as it made its way along the streets and eventually back to the commune, heading towards the newly erected platform in the courtyard. The three accused were ordered to stand on the dais for self-criticism. The crowd gathered around, a silent audience. A Red Guard leader read out the accusations. Liang Feng's heart was heavy with compassion as she listened to Wampu's feeble voice,

"I'm sorry I was a capitalist at heart. I admit I concealed my chairs from the people."

Overwhelmed with rage Liang Feng blindly rushed away from the scene of the trial. "They dare not touch me" were the words that throbbed in her mind as she locked herself inside Wampu's house. Finding herself in front of the little mirror hung on the wall she stared at her reflection. She saw her blazing eyes overflowing with tears.

Reaching for her sewing box she picked up her small pair of scissors and returned to the mirror. Watching herself as if she were looking at a stranger she began, slowly and deliberately to snip off her hair, strand by strand. She went on doing so until what hair was left was just sufficient to cover her scalp like a cap. It looked untidy and unflattering. She stared at her changed reflection. Through the tears there was a triumphant gleam in her eyes as she muttered,

"I shall never let them torture me." It was that very morning that she had witnessed two of her colleagues being stopped by the gates of Waichia Talou and being molested by three Red Guards who had derived cruel enjoyment from snipping off their long tresses. She herself had managed to slip away unnoticed, taking with her however a memory of the sobbing women helplessly surrendering to the harassment.

Looking fixedly at her reflection Liang Feng spoke out, her voice strong,

"Wampu, your suffering has given me the courage to defy them."

The cutting off of her hair was a symbolic act of defiance against the Red Guards.

Her thoughts again flew to the patron of the Red Guards – The Chairman; his betrayal was impossible to accept. He who had formed the Red Guard movement to fight injustice within the Headquarters is now blind to these acts of injustice were her immediate thoughts. But the reasoning side of her spoke out in his defence once again. "How can I blame him; has he not often said,

"I'm ashamed of some of the Red Guards resorting to physical violence."

Her fingers unconsciously strayed to her hair and her thoughts came back to her own situation as she thought defiantly,

"None would know that she was a woman anymore!"

But this was no reason to be sad. There was a cry of victory within her,

"I have outwitted the Red Guards." Feeling like a new person, she sat on the kang, staring at the deepening darkness in the room.

CHAPTER 24

Earthquake Strikes

W hen Wampu staggered back into her house she was clutching at her chest. Her sick pallor prompted Liang Feng to run forward, her heart beating anxiously, and supporting Wampu with both arms from behind, she helped her to the kang and made her lie down. Wampu was gasping, her breath coming painfully, and her small eyes rolled round revealing startlingly their greying white pupils. When her distressed eyes fell on Liang Feng's concerned face she burst into tears. Tears rolled down her wrinkled cheeks and Wampu stretching her right hand gently touched her grandneice's hair. Her own punishment she had borne without tears but the stubborn will that had supported her courageously through all her suffering over the last few days had at last snapped.

The unyielding nature of the Revolution's power had been most painfully revealed to Wampu. As her fingers trailed through the unevenly cut strands of Liang Feng's hair, the young woman's eyes filled with tears and her own smooth hands gently clasped Wampu's bony fingers. Wampu had lost weight after her cats had been removed, although ironically there was more food in the house. Her head rolled back onto the pillow, pain etched on her face. Liang Feng, taking the embroidered quilt that had missed the scrutiny of the Red Guards, laid it over Wampu gently.

Keeping watch at Wampu's side Liang Feng listened to her groans throughout the night. Her eyes passed wearily over the little clock on the ledge above the kang. Wampu's heavy breathing frightened her. It was as if the wind was passing through a narrow hollow bamboo pipe.

The groaning increased as Wampu lay crouched under the quilt, both her hands pressed against her chest. Anxiously Liang Feng glanced once again at the clock. It was now midnight and she would have to wait until morning to take Wampu to the dispensary. Even then,- would there be doctors, with the doctors being often called up for other work in the commune?

Wampu gave a sudden gasp, and Liang Feng whispered anxiously,

"Wampu, does it hurt?"

But Wampu did not seem to hear as she lay motionless. She had fallen into a coma. Her stillness and death-like appearance made Liang Feng cry out loudly. The fear of death gripped her as she remembered her father lying motionless in death.

Overcome with terror she jumped off the kang and ran out of the house. In desperation she banged on the door of Shu Wang, Wampu's nearest neighbour.

Shu Wang had been recently settled in the commune, and it was well known that her role was to spy on those peasants who had formerly been wealthy. Liang Feng now waited anxiously for the door to open, remembering with awkwardness the sarcastic smile on Shu Wang's face as Wampu and her friends were paraded in the fools' caps.

The window opened and Shu Wang peered out, her eyes coldly surveying the pleading eyes before her. Liang Feng burst out,

"Wampu is very sick" but Shu Wang's lips tightened. She hated all those Chinese now returning to their motherland making more demands of the state than those citizens who had stayed on to resist the landlord class. She had no sympathy for the bourgeoisie and especially loathed those Chinese speaking the language of the imperialists. Liang Feng hoped for some compassion on the face before her but there was none, only a gloating triumph at the opportunity to teach the hated revisionists a good lesson. Her words were sharp,

"Why must you disturb me, I am not a doctor."

It was a victory to prolong the agony in the pleading eyes before her and she continued stonily,

"Anyway you will have to wait till morning to take her to the dispensary."

Watching the suffering of others gave her extreme pleasure for had she not seen her own family treated with cold brutality before the Revolution. Her voice became shrill with anger,

"Why must the bourgeois come to us poor peasants for help?" She closed the door firmly on Liang Feng who stood there helplessly.

Her shoulders stooping in defeat Liang Feng slowly turned away from Shu Wang's door. There was no one else she could call. All the houses were in darkness and only the light in Wampu's house still burned. It was a dark night, as silent as death, and Wampu was all alone in that silence. Frogs croaking in the field became mute, frightened by the sound of her feet. A few stars faintly flickered in the distance, as if saddened by their failure to penetrate the black expanse. Liang Feng forlornly walked back to the house and stood by the motionless figure of Wampu.

Wampu's face was relaxed and the pain seemed to have completely left her. Stooping down and keeping her mouth on Wampu's ear she called out her name softly, but there was no response. She then placed her ear on Wampu's chest. The hollow silence within the body was as deep as the silence outside. She touched Wampu's hands; they were warm but her feet were icy cold. Lifting her eyes away from Wampu's lifeless body Liang Feng looked around the room. The stark grey walls seemed to mock her. Her eyes fell on the empty space left by the two missing chairs; it looked desolate and helpless in its nudity. With a muffled cry Liang Feng rushed out of the house into the black night.

The grey fields lay cold and impassive but the newly harrowed earth softly yielded under her feet, forming light shallow imprints. She kept on walking deep into the night. The faint stars seemed to travel with her. Suddenly in the horizon a faint streak of light streaked across making way for the break of dawn. The suffocating darkness that pressed on her before, now withdrew as a gentle glow spread in the sky. Kneeling down she picked up a handful of earth and pressed it to her face. The scent of mushrooms mingling with the earth warmed her cheeks and hands.

Suddenly she felt a tremor in the earth beneath her. She held down her body to the earth clutching at the soil. She thought her body was trembling and she wanted to control it. However the throbbing increased and she stretched out her whole body against the ground. The trees around her swayed and the newly planted pine trees shook violently as if trying to break away from the imprisoning soil. She heard a voice faintly from the distance,

"Comrades, come out of your houses. The earthquake has struck!" Liang Feng tried to rise to her feet but the earth heaved and swayed rhythmically forcing her to kneel and hold firmly to the ground. As the earth pulsated, pushed and shoved, the sky remained unperturbed waiting for the soft pearly light to colour the grey clouds of darkness. The tremors ceased as abruptly as they had begun. The trees stood firm and straight and the earth was calm and still. Slowly lifting herself up, Liang Feng walked towards the houses that were now dimly silhouetted against the lightening sky.

A crowd had assembled before the houses and as she neared Wampu's residence the voices became distinct. The cries of infants rising above the other voices disturbed her. The people, silenced by the sight of her approaching figure, now gathered around her. Summoned out of their homes by the earthquake they had by now heard of Wampu's condition and had called out to her but there had been no answer. Leading the way Liang Feng entered the house.

Wampu lay motionless as in a deep sleep. Her face was peaceful and the wrinkles had disappeared, giving her a youthful and tranquil countenance. The neighbours, looking concerned, stood beside the kang, their gaze traveling between the supine figure of Wampu and Liang Feng's dazed face. A woman came forward and touched Wampu's body. Finding it cold she kept her ear on the chest. She then looked up and spoke softly,

"Wampu is dead."

The onlookers stood gazing at Wampu. There were no tears. Liang Feng had shed her own tears in the field and now, conscious of the people around her, she simply stared at Wampu's body in complete silence.

The funeral took place the same day. In the heat of the noonday sun of the hot summer's day Wampu was buried in the fields. The neighbourhood committee brought the food and sat round the grave. Wampu was not forgotten; when the food was shared round, Wampu's portion in its bowl was placed reverently on the freshly covered grave. It was all so quickly over, just like the earthquake's tremors in the early hours of the morning. The sun shone brightly over the fields and the new mound which marked Wampu's grave; the rice bowl with her chopsticks across it was diminutive but conspicuous on the rich grey soil. The people did not linger but left without delay. Their time was precious and the fields needed them. Life had to go on.

Painfully Liang Feng watched the people leave; their presence had comforted her. With a pang she realised she was now all alone in the world.

CHAPTER 25

Escape from the Commune

She returned to the house, it was empty and desolate. She slowly walked around touching the little utility items Wampu had used in her daily life. To Wampu they had been of little significance, only the Buddha statue and the antique chairs had held any meaning. The impersonality of the objects around her brought to Liang Feng the sudden realisation that, without Wampu, she was a stranger in this house. Outside, in the fields, she had not felt the estrangement from the world. The bright sun penetrating beneath the soft soil of the grave had been welcome; Wampu was now safe from all the trials and tribulations she had suffered in the last few months. The sun had touched her own body with warmth, lessening the void left by Wampu's remains sinking into the earth. The presence of others in the fields had even temporarily taken away her loneliness. It had been with reluctance that she had returned to the empty house. Closing the window she remained in the dark. The dimness was more comforting to her own gloomy thoughts. Darkness had become a part of her inner self with which she could communicate in the absence of a kindred spirit to share her loneliness.

Her longing to see Pierre increased in the silence of the room. She had lost contact with him in the past few weeks. No longer were there opportunities to even catch a glimpse of him at Waichia Talou. Workers were now strictly forbidden to communicate with foreigners and she was forced to deliberately ignore Pierre's friend Donald as if he was a stranger. There was among her colleagues, a self-appointed leader, who had begun to show suspicion of her association with the foreign community. This surveillance made it difficult to carry on with her duties of settling problems that arose between the domestic staff and their employers. There was despair and bitterness at her isolation from the rest of her community.

She sat dispiritedly on the twisted kang. The earthquake had left its mark everywhere. The wall above the kang had a deep yawning crack. Death had cast its shadow on the house, but the little clock on the ledge still stolidly sat there continuing to keep time but seeming louder than before, its sound dominating the room. She stared at it and then at the blank wall, her mind full of memories. Wampu was determined not to brighten her walls with pictures of Chairman Mao, however colourful. She had firmly refused to hang up even Liang Feng's favourite photograph of the Chairman in his mandarin dress. The authorities had succeeded in taking away all Wampu's cherished possessions but they had failed to break her will.

Liang Feng's eyes sadly wandered in the direction of the kitchen. It had been comforting to hear Wampu's tiny feet pattering about in their cloth shoes as she cooked the dinner. In the absence of the familiar sound the loneliness within her increased. She could not bear to enter the kitchen and rising, she quickly closed its door. She felt imprisoned by grief and a lack of direction.

Suddenly the clock on the ledge beckoned her with its loud ticking and she walked up to it. Its rhythm seemed to echo the rhythm of the thoughts that had abruptly sprung to her mind.

"I must see Pierre" she cried out. His friendship had been strength at times of inner conflict. The need to see him overwhelmed her. With restless steps she paced the floor between the kang and the kitchen door, her thoughts in turmoil. Then opening the door quickly she left the house, closing it firmly against the emptiness within the house, and she walked out into the darkening shadows of the evening sky.

Like a horde of ants with their nests disturbed, humanity had spilled out to the streets after the tremors of the previous night. With night fall their numbers had increased as they invaded all the open and safe places on the streets and sidewalks seeking refuge for the night. Excited groups of people had gathered, vociferous in sharing their anxiety, some voices expressing thankfulness that the tremors had been a sufficient warning of an earthquake. All high-rise apartment buildings had been abandoned.

Liang Feng moved carefully among the anxious people, their agitation making her realise that the earth tremors had made a more frightening impact on the capital than on the suburbs where the landscape was not dotted by high-rise buildings.

The workers of Waichia Talou were leaving for their homes earlier than usual. The guard at the gates did not recognise her as she waited in the shadows, hopeful of meeting some of her fellow workers. Either due to the atmosphere of panic or because of her changed appearance, her colleagues had passed her without perceiving her. She was unrecognisable and this gave her a feeling of security and courage to proceed towards the direction of Pierre's house.

On Pierre's lane the residents had shifted their indoor activities to the comparative safety of the open-air. Kitchens were being set up on the street in readiness to cook the evening meal and bedding was spread on the sidewalks, as the people prepared to spend the night under the roof of the sky. The children seemingly oblivious to the dangers of the earth tremors happily played in the streets though the elders showed signs of anxiety, their eyes watchful and alert.

Unlike normal times the sentry guarding Pierre's door was not at his post. Liang Feng could see him mingling amongst the people, giving helpful instructions to all the residents of the hutung huddling in the anticipation of the predicted earthquake. Taking all precautions to conceal her identity she inched her way, treading softly, until she reached Pierre's door, her heart thudding against her blouse.

The noisy activities of the residents, their concentration focused on their individual tasks, was a protection against discovery. Cautiously she knocked on the door, the minutes seemed to drag unbearably; it was only on her second attempt that the door was opened. Pushing it herself, she darted inside, closing it behind her sharply against the hostile outside world.

Pierre had not noticed in that moment of the opening and closing of his door the person who had so hurriedly entered his house, but the soft feel of the arms holding him tightly, encircling and embracing him, identified the visitor. He responded with an ardour he had not shown before. Liang Feng could not hold back her emotions. The grief at Wampu's loss, her recent troubles in the commune, the suppressed agony of her separation from him for so many weeks, were all now released in a flow of tears. Like a rain cloud it passed over quickly and soon she was smiling tremulously, and attempting to brush away the tears. Her fingers gently trailed over his eyes and lips. On other occasions the slightest sound of voices near his house would arouse fear in her heart, but now she was oblivious to all interruptions and allowed no inhibitions to restrain her from revealing her joy to be with him. Amazed and overjoyed by her display of emotions, he could not hold back his own feelings. Their world narrowed, only the world within this house mattered. They did not need to speak. They had both even forgotten the danger that had shifted into the house with the warning tremors of the earth. Whilst all others had left their homes seeking safety in the street, they both felt perfect security within these walls.

Liang Feng was overwhelmed with the wonder of knowing Pierre. Unlike in her relationship with others, there was no wall separating him from her. Her spirit flew free as it had done only once before – when she had stood at the summit of Behai Park and gazed at the Pagoda.

When she opened her eyes the room was still in darkness. Wampu's fate – the discovery of her chairs and her sudden death – seemed a nightmare which had preceded a beautiful dream. But then it had not been a dream – it had been real. Pierre's face lay beside hers and she touched it tenderly. The need to express love had always been there, suppressed beneath the revolutionary fervour.

Noisy activities outside on the road kept her awake with thoughts of the approaching day. The anticipated earthquake had still not occurred, but it was a long night – dawn was still far away. She could hear voices, still full of anxiety, trying to maintain order on the street.

Pierre too was awake, and sensing his eyes watching her in the dark, she took the palm of his hand and held it tenderly to her cheek. He gently touched her hair and said,

"Did the Red Guards cut your hair?"

"No", she said quietly, "I did it myself. I did not want to give them the satisfaction of bullying me". Remembering her desire to outwit the Red Guards her tone was one of triumph.

Pierre knew well the fate of women with long hair should they meet Red Guards on the streets. Sheng, displeased at the feminism evoked by long hair, was encouraging a campaign against it in the commune. Pierre had seen many a time young revolutionaries grabbing women by the hair before stunned onlookers, and snipping off their hair heedless of the tears rolling down their cheeks; on such occasions Pierre had been powerless to intervene, but had not been able to hide his indignation at their barbarity. Sensing his feelings they had turned on him screaming that he was an imperialist foreigner.

He suddenly remembered that Liang Feng had not been told of his cats. A stab of pain went through him as he recollected the incidents; he could not get himself to speak about it as yet with her. The Red Guards had entered his house on the pretext of searching for anti-revolutionary propaganda and had embarked on a spree of tearing up his books and art materials. They had splashed his paints on the walls and disfigured the paintings hung up, marking out for special attention the painting by Qui Bi Shi. When they eventually left, he had found his cats missing from their basket. After making a frantic search he had called in the sentry to help him, but instead of giving the expected assistance the sentry had questioned him with surprise as to why he should keep pets in the house. The disappearance of the cats saddened Pierre. They had become part of his daily life. Feeding them before his tai chi had become a ritual he looked forward to.

Something else he missed very much was the visits of his students. He was a prisoner in his own house. The sentry's continuous surveillance was an invasion into his privacy and he felt bitter and frustrated. Those who visited him had become a target for suspicion, and when Han was turned away from his door he was enraged, but not surprised. When Pierre angrily argued about the matter with him the sentry had displayed a cool indifference which was impenetrable. Only occasionally did the sentry show a change of mood and such a day had been yesterday, perhaps due to the earthquake, for he had entered the house to warn Pierre, advising him to get out to the garden in case of earth tremors.

Pierre voiced his fears to Liang Feng, his tone gentle,

"I hope the earthquake will not strike tonight".

But with quiet laughter in her voice she replied,

"I would not mind being buried in this tomb".

Her spirit, under strain for so many days by the inability to communicate with him, and almost crushed by the recent tragedies, was now ready to soar above the clouds under which the earth rumbled and the authorities laid their petty rules.

Minutes passed by in meaningful silence. Then her voice spoke out again, low and distinct in the darkness,

"Is it not strange that the earthquake has brought me such happiness?" His fingers stroked her brow in response. There was reciprocity in his gesture. There was a sense of a shared fulfilment.

Suddenly, Pierre spoke again,

"Do you know I am under house arrest?" Shocked by this revelation Liang Feng sat up with a start. In the dim light of the room her gaze picked out the damage done by the Red Guards to his house. His beautiful home had been vandalised! His dragon designed carpet was crumpled, yet showing the dark shadows of paint splashed on it. Slogans had been scrawled on every wall, clearly visible in their black ink. They screamed,

"Down with Imperialists". The windows had been plastered with black paper to keep away the light.

Pierre said with sadness,

"I cannot understand what those young people have against me!"

She could not speak, her mind still stunned.

His voice became reflective,

"I recognised some of them. They were my own students." This had obviously pained him.

Liang Feng turned to him. "Was Han involved?"

"No", said Pierre; "He did try to warn me. He once spoke of students who did not approve of my enthusiasm to combine academic life with work in the farms."

Liang Feng could see his books strewn on the floor, the pages torn and the bookcase itself overturned. All things foreign, even literature, had become loathsome to them.

Sensing the direction of her thoughts he said,

"They came here like a dust storm and made a pile of rubbish out of my books."

She could not find words to comfort him with – had she not herself supported the revolution? That such wrongs could be committed in the name of the Revolution was suddenly horrifying.

"It is such a waste! So many years of progress will be lost if they destroy learning." Pierre's voice was heavy with a deep sadness.

Liang Feng's eyes conveyed her anguish for the wrong done to him while her lips could only blurt out,

"I am so sorry."

Pierre took both her hands in his,

"I am so happy you came. I have needed you." She was moved,

"How I wish I had come sooner!"

She blamed herself bitterly for lacking the foresight to realise the dangerous situation he had unwittingly created for himself – she could then have warned him. She had been too wrapped up in the events within the commune to keep herself informed of the political trends. But would Pierre who justifiably believed he had done no wrong, have heeded any warnings?

The silence broken only occasionally by the beat of a drum, had become ominous. The earth tremors had brought a lull to the feverish revolutionary activities. Now that the anxieties of the impending earthquake had receded, would they be resumed?

CHAPTER 26

Pierre to the Rescue

When Liang Feng opened her eyes Pierre was not beside her and she started up in panic. Her heart lightened with relief when she saw him standing by the barricaded window, lost in thought, a striking figure in his red silk dressing gown. Although her eyes were focused on him, her ears involuntarily picked out the unwelcome voices of people outside the house. The residents had not yet gone back to their homes; the danger of the forewarned earthquake was still alive.

Pierre's thoughts were on the approaching day, his eyes anxiously scanning the dim grey light of dawn falling on his courtyard. Silhouetted against the night sky was his pine tree sheltered by shadows. His eyes strained to grasp the comforting details of its familiar presence. The tree held a special meaning for him because Liang Feng had said "It brings the breath of the fragrant hills to me." In the dusty environment of the city it was truly a refreshing sight.

With the crimson glow of dawn sharply impressing itself upon the horizon, the tree became distinct in detail, and his anxiety increased. He realised he had to act quickly to protect Liang Feng from discovery. Being a foreigner he could evade too harsh a penalty but the authorities would show no mercy to Liang Feng. It was time for her to leave and it had to be done before the crowds outside dispersed to their homes.

He suddenly felt her scrutiny. He admitted to himself that he had been missing her in the days he had been confined to solitude and loneliness. There were also other thoughts mixed with fear of labour camps and re-education which could be her fate as a result of this escapade. Such an ordeal he would not allow. He walked away from the window towards her.

Lying back on the bed, her face smiling in contentment, she studied him, "You remind me of a mandarin in that dress." Her laugh was teasing.

He took her hand in his, but she noticed his glance straying to his wristwatch and her mood changed.

"Is it time for me to leave?" The question was reluctantly asked.

He did not speak; his mind was preoccupied with making plans for her departure.

Liang Feng's eyes dejectedly fell on the cold bare floor now stripped of its carpet, reminding her of the harsh world she had to face outside this house. She did not wish to face that ordeal just yet. Her voice was pensive,

"I sometimes wish I could walk down the street in an old-fashioned mandarin dress. Then, in a swift change of mood and speaking matter-of-factly she added,

"But it is out of the question now. We women are forced to look and act like men."

Understanding the poignancy of that statement, Pierre hastened to comfort her,

"A mandarin dress would not be of much use to you but I have something you will like better." He walked up to the cupboard.

Liang Feng was amazed that she had let her mind dwell on mandarin dresses which once she had rejected with scorn. Yet it was a fact that her taste for beautiful things and, more so, for feminine attire, had developed anew since her contact with the beautiful possessions in Pierre's house.

Pierre was back, with a delicate ivory fan in his hand which he offered her. Liang Feng's eyes shone with delight as she gently opened it out, displaying its intricate carvings, but her voice was deliberately light,

"I feel like an empress, holding this in my hand, yet the palace is now under attack."

Her words made Pierre's eyes automatically turn to the big black characters scrawled on his wall, a grim reminder of the siege. He spoke sadly,

"It is not only the palaces that are now under assault; everything, including learning, has become questionable."

His cherished books, lying in tatters in a corner, were proof of Red Guard brutality.

Liang Feng's mood of delight immediately changed to a mood of recollection. She remembered Wampu who, after ingeniously and skilfully concealing her chairs from the eyes of the authorities for 17 years, had still lost them. All those people now suspected of revisionism had lost their precious possessions overnight. She had seen the confiscated goods auctioned to foreigners. Her people did not dare to purchase them. The treasures of China daily made their way to the Marco Polo Shop in Peking where dollars and sterling gladly exchanged hands.

Understanding her thoughts and strongly disapproving of the sale of China's antiquities, Pierre spoke bluntly. "What fools are these Red Guards, throwing away the country's treasures for a few yuans."

Liang Feng was studying the fan and said,

"In the past this would have belonged to a rich woman of Peking."

Pierre interrupted,

"Yes, I think you are right. It was that woman or a relative of hers who tried to retrieve the fan from the market." Observing Liang Feng's raised eyebrows he explained this statement.

Before Pierre's arrest he had visited the People's (Tundan) Market in the capital.

193

Intrigued by the sight of peddycabs unloading furniture and other fascinating household items, Pierre had walked up to a corner where an auction was in session. Watching the proceedings he had quietly remained at the back, but noticing the foreigner the auctioneer had held up the little fan and called out for bids. Being the only outsider on that occasion, and with no other contenders, he had made an offer of 10 yuans. But to his surprise, and before the bid was closed, a Chinese woman from among the onlookers had agitatedly called for a bid of 11 yuans.

Seated by Liang Feng and telling her this story, he added, regretfully,

"I did not bid again. Her desire was much greater than mine to have the fan".

How characteristic of him, Liang Feng thought, her fingers gently caressing his hand. Pierre's face remained serious and preoccupied.

"What happened to the poor woman?" she enquired.

"The man screamed her down and warned he would report her for her counter revolutionary actions, if she tried to bid over a foreigner."

Pierre was apparently reliving the anger he had felt that day,

"I insisted that the fan should be given to the woman, but it only seemed to make matters worse for her."

The crowd had become abusive, and the auctioneer, ignoring Pierre's protests, had passed the fan over the heads to him. Full of regret and guilt Pierre had searched the crowd for the woman in order to pass the fan to her; it was a hopeless venture.

"I could not find her. She had made a quick get-away, probably fearing the wrath of the crowd, and the auctioneer".

As on other occasions his kindness moved her. He showed a marked difference from other foreigners who were greedily collecting rare treasures at bargain prices, making full use of the Red Guard's frenzy of disdain for past cultural objects.

Noticing her diffidence to keep the fan, Pierre insisted,

"You value the nation's heritage. It would make me happy if you accepted it."

The earnestness of his expression made her smile. She could not refuse his gift.

"I shall cherish the fan but I will have to conceal it from the Red Guards."

Cutting through the harmony of the house and alerting them to the dawn of a new day, there suddenly sounded, over the loudspeakers, a shrill female voice singing "East is Red". Already daylight had gently illuminated the horizon and a second revolutionary song was thrust ruthlessly on them, taking away harshly the magic of their intimacy.

Liang Feng realised she had to leave without delay. The brief respite she had snatched from the bedlam of the revolution was nearing its end. At the thoughts of the hostile world outside, she was gripped by fear and loneliness, and also by the perplexing questions of 'Continuous Revolutions'; but still the infallible advice of Chairman Mao had the power to give her courage. "If the people become apathetic, evil forces would soon take over."

Liang Feng had seen the failure of classical communism in a society filled with hardship and want. She herself was guilty of yielding to the temptations of aesthetic beauty – the fan her fingers held with such possessiveness was sufficient proof of this. Her enquiring mind was once again throbbing – "Debating on ideology would only be practical if there was individual freedom for the people."

It was similar to the message she had fantasised from the chimes of the bells of the pagoda. For a democratic communism to function successfully there should also be a spiritual code included amongst its basic principles. Pierre had no doubt such a code was instilled into his personality; she sensed in him courage to face any crisis with equanimity. He had the optimism to say confidently,

"A Revolution cannot go on forever. Consolidation should be the next step. I am waiting that time, shielding my thoughts from imprisoning events."

With hands clasped they went to the barricaded window. The sentry's footsteps could be heard, pacing the road by the house. The time was opportune for Liang Feng to leave and they parted sadly. In her heart she would not accept an abrupt end to their friendship and so she refrained from wishing him goodbye. Pierre's plan was to invite the sentry into the house to give Liang Feng the opportunity to slip out to the street. It was not a difficult plan to carry out. Liang Feng quickly walked out of the house, pausing for a moment to listen to the door close gently behind her.

The sentry had not shown any suspicion at receiving Pierre's invitation for a cup of tea; in fact he welcomed it after a night of unrest and anxiety. Pierre's easy communication with the local community had won him the warmth of those around him, and the sentry differentiated him from other foreigners treated him with friendliness.

With a feeling of loss and oblivious to her surroundings, Liang Feng walked slowly down the lane, in a daze, herself inconspicuous amongst the people busy gathering their belongings to return to their homes. The morning breeze was cool on her wet face. Her heart was heavy. But soon the sunlight, enveloping her in its warmth, made her lift her eyes, a sense of hope filling her anew, giving her the strength to accept the reality around her. Choosing to be left alone with her thoughts she decided to walk, rather than board a bus, to Waichia Talou.

When Liang Feng stepped into her workplace a crisis was awaiting her. A colleague standing by the door looked at her face with hostility and spoke to her sharply,

"You are dismissed and will not be tolerated in these premises."

Surprisingly however, the news did not shock or sadden her as much as it would have done at an earlier time. But she stood there staring at the speaker for some moments before the words made any sense to her, and then her reaction *was* one of anger. Brushing him aside with scorn she pushed her way into the room.

The self-proclaimed leader of their newly formed workers' group was within, and looked up at her in stony silence. Walking up to him she demanded,

"What reasons have you to dismiss me?"

The man, obviously resenting the disrespectful tone of her voice and noticing that some of the workers were observing Liang Feng with sympathy, raised his voice in anger,

"I have proof that you are a revisionist at heart."

Despite her anger, the words brought a sense of relief – there was no mention of her association with Pierre.

Taking a deep breath Liang Feng demanded,

"Since when have you made this discovery?"

Some of the onlookers smiled, they could not help liking her challenging tone. The workers' leader saw their smiles and was enraged,

"We have information that your grandfather was a rich peasant."

This accusation was a shock and an absurdity and she stared at the man with disbelief. Then recovering her composure she spoke contemptuously,

"But you knew all about my family before I came to Peking."

Her accuser did not want to hear anything more and with a violent jerk pushed back his chair.

"You can leave now," he barked.

The others were no longer smiling. They suddenly appeared pre-occupied and had returned to their work. Upset and angry at their change of manner she swiftly left the room without glancing at her colleagues.

The veins in her head had started throbbing. The injustice of it all was unbearable. She felt alone and hopeless, and in her inability to defend herself she acutely felt her lack of individual freedom. She had just witnessed a display of the autocratic powers of the bureaucracy, and she had, she realised, become its victim. Frustrated and bitter, she walked blindly to the gates of Waichia Talou.

She was almost at the gates when she remembered the Browns; she felt she must see them before her departure. But as she paused with the intention of turning back, the sentry blocked her way, saying sharply,

"I have been informed not to let you enter the building again."

The self-proclaimed leader of the workers had been quick to inform the sentry of her dismissal.

Leaving the premises she walked towards the street and stopped to look back at Waichia Talou. It suddenly dawned on her that she did not know where she should go now, or to whom she should turn. In that moment of indecision she heard the strains of 'East is Red', the carol of the Revolution coming from the opposite direction of the peoples' commune. Before a decision was made, her feet automatically turned in the direction of Chuang Tsu's apartment.

CHAPTER 27

Bombard the Headquarters

In late summer 1966 the Cultural Revolution made headway with great intensity. The political atmosphere was heightened with tension when Chairman Mao called upon the Red Guards to 'Bombard the Headquarters', to weed out the revisionists. This was a period of mass starvation due to the failure of the commune system of agriculture. Lieu Shaoqui, the head of state, and his followers, who saw the failure of the agricultural policy, had to attack Mao surreptitiously. It was during this time that Jiang Quing, Mao's fourth wife, was wielding more influence on Chairman Mao. She gave her full support to Chairman Mao's bands of Red Guards to attack those who disagreed by showing signs of returning to the past, so-called revisionism. The Red Guards were let loose like hound dogs to destroy anyone who was deemed to be an enemy of the Chairman's ideology for the country.

Sheng's eyes screwed and with mischief; watching bands of Red Guards roaming the city. He was standing by his window in deep thought. His desire for revenge was increasing day by day and he planned his political strategy which he thought fit to be kept a secret from his wife and mother-in-law. Liang Feng's presence in the apartment was making him more secretive and angry. He did not like to see her influence on his mother-in-law, and now he heard her voice consoling Chuang Tsu.

Striding out of his room he glared at Liang Feng standing beside the sad faced Chuang Tsu. In his eyes they appeared a pair of conspirators hatching a plot against him. Chuang Tsu had been upset by new regulations governing the arts.

Chuang Tsu sniffed softly into her handkerchief; it was large and comforting to cover her round face. Giving a furtive glance at Sheng she whimpered,

"I have suffered enough under all this political bickering."

Sheng interrupted sharply,

"I have had enough of your complaints," his anger making her gulp down her next words. The *People's Daily* lying on the table caught his attention and he forgot for a moment Chuang Tsu. His temper under control he began to read the news items. Suddenly his lips curled in a twisted smile. The reports seemed encouraging: factional clashes had occurred between Red Guards and employees in government departments and even in the theatre. Unable to keep the news to himself he announced grandly,

"The production of 'Bartered Bride' has been banned from public viewing."

Chuang Tsu's sniffling suddenly stopped and she burst out wailing,

"What are they doing to us poor peasants? A play we were once allowed to see is now considered not good for us."

Sheng huffed. Jabbing at her eyes and watchful of Sheng, Chuang Tsu slowly dared,

"Anyway Chairman Mao is wiser than us poor peasants."

Sheng was too engrossed in the news to pay attention to her sarcasm.

Liang Feng's eyebrows puckered. She could not understand why the authorities wanted to make everyone unhappy. The sight of Chuang Tsu's sickly face with tears pouring down in self-pity, made her glare at Sheng for his cruelty to Chuang Tsu.

Sheng enjoyed seeing his mother in law in tears. It was his nature to bully the weak but so far he had not been successful in imposing his authority on Liang Feng.

Sheng had more news for them and turning this time to Liang Feng he said,

"There has been a clash between the workers and the Red Guards in the motor transport workplace."

Just conveying the news was not his mode, he took pleasure in making others unhappy and seeing an opportunity to make Liang Feng miserable, he said with insolence,

"We must encourage these clashes to get rid of undesirables."

At all times Liang Feng had taken his hints and abuses calmly, but now his triumphant guffaw irritated her into saying with disdain,

"That's not what Chairman Mao advocates."

Her disdainful aloofness was a sore point with him and in fury he turned on her. He threw the newspaper aside and threateningly stamped up to her,

"What does the Chairman want, does he want to keep all of us in this state of poverty, and does he know that debating his philosophy would not solve all problems?"

He could not strike her and banging the door loudly he stamped out of the room.

Liang Feng had sat motionless during Sheng's ranting. Now she quietly wondered why he should parade openly his loyalty to Chairman Mao if he did not agree with him. In anger his hidden motives were coming to light. Under her breath her nervous voice kept saying,

"I am not afraid to tell him the truth." But for a moment she had been unnerved by his fury. Sheng came back in the room and was still seething. With a desire to crush his over-bearing manner, she quietly said,

"For your information the motor transport workplace problem has been settled. The workers had realised the Red Guards were trying to help them; they have become friends now."

Driven by irritation, she had once again made a political speech. This time Sheng's anger was devastating. Taking up the People's Daily, he tore it into shreds. What he cultivated was disorder and revolutions and not peace and harmony. He rushed out of the apartment in a blind rage making Chuang Tsu jump from her chair and clutch at Liang Feng's hand.

Sheng had acted like a tiger caught in a trap. Deciding to reveal Sheng's problems, Chuang Tsu cautiously began,

"Before the present Cultural Revolution Sheng had been involved with the movement to democratise the party structure."

Liang Feng interrupted,

"I am surprised to hear this, his autocratic behaviour does not divulge his enlightened past."

Chuang Tsu sighed "I understand how you feel, but his character underwent a complete change after he was punished."

"What did they do to him?" Liang Feng inquired with a softening feeling towards him.

"He was sent for re-education, when he came back he was an angry young man."

"He still is," Liang Feng uttered with consternation.

"The authorities who punished him have been dismissed now, but Sheng insists on revenge."

The door suddenly jerked open. Sheng was in the room and he said with bitterness in his voice,

"I shall never forgive them. I have my own plans to take revenge."

His sudden appearance no doubt was made on hearing Chuang Tsu's words. This frightened Chuang Tsu out of her wits and she began to whimper. His irritation had not subsided with his outburst and now turning to Liang Feng he shouted in her ear,

"Aren't you bothered about the events in Indonesia?"

Taken aback she stared with disbelief at Sheng. Interpreting her silence for aloofness Sheng ranted,

"We must demonstrate our contempt to all foreigners, blood should not go unrevenged," he sneered.

In Liang Feng's ears those words sounded unreal, the hatred in his heart was unbelievable, yet his vicious slanting eyes reminded her of a fox waiting for the moment to get at the bones, the left-overs of the lions' battle for power.

Unable to bear Sheng's hostility, Liang Feng rushed out of the apartment. She hid herself in a dark corner of the staircase. At the thought of the incomprehensible nature of politics and human beings, tears of anger rose in her eyes. To be cooped up in the apartment between Chuang Tsu's friendship and Sheng's

200

hostility choked her. Her thoughts rushed to Pierre, who's warmth touched her; so different to Sheng's display of hate. An uneasy feeling crept over her at the thought of her friendship. Sheng's determination to avenge all foreigners hung like the Sword of Damocles above the heads of all the innocent non-Chinese. It was fortunate she was not influenced by such propaganda. How could the residents in Waichia Talou be blamed for the atrocities committed by their governments, was her own unspoken indignant reply.

The Revolution had embittered everyone. She was beginning to hate the Revolution and all politics. She had not yet been given an opportunity to criticise herself. It would have been the best chance to have told the authorities that they were driving good citizens against the system. She would never succumb to threats as Wampu had done.

Liang Feng remained on the steps showing no desire to go back to the apartment. Sheng's anger frightened her. The enveloping darkness around her gave her a sense of security to reflect on her own views of the present troubles. It was also not safe to continue with her friendship with Pierre.

His friendship was gentle and sympathetic. Behind a camouflage of fervour for Chairman Mao's philosophy she had suppressed her own gentle nature that had now responded to his understanding. The sudden gush of Revolutionary songs in the commune jolted her reverie. The words of praise for Chairman Mao were familiar to her ears. The song was interrupted with an unwelcome announcement,

"The time has come to raise our heads against revisionism and imperialism."

Wasn't this the same message of unforgiveness and hatred that was thrust on the people, she deliberated bitterly. It was this message of revenge that influenced Sheng to act cruelly.

While the leaders engaged in bitter political bickering the Revolution had caught in its web innocents like herself and Pierre. Even Han had not been spared. Compassion brimming in her eyes, she whispered,

"Poor Han, he was the only sincere Red Guard I happened to meet".

Han had left Peking without informing any of his friends including Pierre. His colleagues had made him feel uncomfortable about his friendship with Pierre. In fact they had laughed at his naivety to believe that a democratic system could prevail under communism. It had been Pierre's influence that had made him believe that such a system was possible. Yet with rising criticism of imperialism and foreign influence he had left Peking, not wanting his friends to know he was keeping away from them.

She held her breath nervously, hearing Sheng's footsteps thundering down the steps. He was gone in a minute down the stairs and into the street. Heaving a sigh of relief she wiped her tear-stained face. "I must never allow him to see me in tears," she whispered to herself.

He was a bully who derived satisfaction from the weakness of the others. His violence had made Chuang Tsu a mental and physical wreck. She wondered what effect the revolution would have on people who could not stand up to bullying, which was evident in the trials of self-criticism.

Rising up from the stairs she slowly traced her steps back to the apartment, and that ever-present courage made her say loudly,

"I shall not yield to injustice."

But that courageous thought quivered at the sight of the crouching figure of Chuang Tsu who had succumbed to brutality. Placing her arm gently on Chung Tsu's shoulder Liang Feng whispered,

"There will be a time when justice will prevail in this land," but as the words escaped her lips she wondered how long she would have to wait to see the dawn of such an era.

CHAPTER 28

The Revolution Reaches a Climax

Summer in Peking is unbearably hot. It was a time when most residents living in modern but cramped two-roomed apartments, temporarily abandoned them for cooler environments such as pavements and open spaces. However 21st August 1967 was such a day when a local crisis arising from problems in international politics combined with the heat to drive more people on to the streets. In an atmosphere that was uncomfortable enough to keep tensions high, mobs marched militantly against the British Mission.

By this time most diplomatic missions in Peking had faced some form of protest. Against this tense atmosphere the British Government in Hong Kong had banned three Chinese-language daily newspapers. On this day in retaliation, all forces in the People's Republic of China were rallied to condemn 'British Imperialism'. The streets were mobbed; demonstrators were parading placards and vociferously hurling slogans and insults. They were blind to all reasoning; the mobs hurled insults at foreigners who could be mistaken for British subjects. Emotions were running high roused by the media.

In Peking, radio and loudspeakers at every street corner took up the task of keeping the public informed in detail of imperialist aggression not only in Hong Kong but all over the world. Special study classes had been organised to drive in this propaganda. The domestic staff of British diplomats in Waichia Talou were well informed of these unfriendly acts of the British Government and deemed it reciprocal to walk out on their employers.

Liang Feng was restless and angry. She had been pushed against her will by a bullying leader to join in the protests against British imperialism. Hemmed in from all sides by a mass of humanity she remained helpless in resistance. Her thick cotton blouse and heavy blue trousers added to her discomfort. They clung to her body while beads of perspiration ran down her back and legs. She used her little fan in an attempt to work up some cool breeze from the heated still air.

Her thoughts went back to the time when she had worn a comfortable skirt and blouse as the majority of women had done in the heat of summer. But the Cultural Revolution had not spared them even that facility. Making inroads into fashion, it was now decreed that women too should keep to the pattern of men's clothing and wear blue trousers and white cotton shirts in summer. At least in the mode of dress the weaker sex has not been discriminated against, she muttered bitterly, fanning vigorously.

These rigid stipulations in fashion were further reinforced when women were forced to keep their hair cut short like the men. Liang Feng's hand lifted up to touch her hair. This recalled the traumatic experience of her retaliation against the Red Guards, and although the fan in her hand reduced the discomfort from the heat it could not appease her bitterness. Her face contorted in anger at the sight of Sheng thundering across the road, instigating and herding more citizens to shout slogans of hate.

Waichia Talou, in Jianguamen Wai, was totally besieged by angry demonstrators. In silence Liang Feng stared at the building that had been her place of work for the past number of months. Her eyes watched helplessly the residents making their way to the windows and balconies to witness the fury of angry demonstrators. The sight of their enemies goaded the mob around her to shout louder insults. Liang Feng's eyes anxiously scanned the group on the balcony facing the main entrance. She quickly averted her gaze. Their faces were showing a mixture of curiosity and anxiety. Donald and Sally Brown were not to be seen on this day as, unlike at other times, the demonstrators were rather fierce and rowdy, shouting 'Sha, Sha'. The British mission and their government were singled out for vociferous condemnation for actions taken by the Hong Kong government against propaganda from The People's Republic of China. Unhappily her heart cried out against the betrayal of the friendship they had offered her. They would not know she had been forced against her will to join in the demonstrations.

With the shouting increasing to a high pitch, the onlookers on the balconies of Waichia Talou retreated indoors leaving the mob to face empty balconies and windows. The demonstrators who were tired and bored and standing at an advantageous distance, away from the screaming leaders, dared to slip away and sit on the pavement and stare aimlessly towards Waichia Talou. But Sheng's eyes did not escape this show of disinterest and he used his tongue like a whiplash as he pounced on the deserters, bringing them hastily to their feet. He screamed an order to march to the British Chargé D'Affaire's building in Jianguamen Wai.

The demonstrators ran behind Sheng trying to keep pace with his running feet. When Sheng stopped, the mob paused. When he shouted frenziedly, their pace quickened. When he lashed out his slogans, they mumbled. Heat and boredom were slowly encroaching upon their revolutionary fervour. The rank and file followed sheepishly behind Sheng, although from time to time they pulled out fans from their pockets, concentrating their efforts vigorously to work up some cool breeze.

The most sacrilegious act committed by the Hong Kong government was now read out. The Hong Kong government had dared to smash a bust of Chairman Mao. Roused from lethargy the mob waved vigorously the Red Books, violently shouting for revenge against the British Mission. The arrows of heat striking down from a blazing sun were not kind to the mood of the mob. They were now angry and restless, sweat pouring down their faces. Once again the fans came out of their pockets and although some relief was obtained from the heat, those delicate objects failed to cool the tempers of the mob. Dramatically as the new fans unfolded, scenes of the revolution on them fanned the imagination of the crowd to be alert and be focused on their goal.

Red Guards sprang from the gentle fans, revolutionary fervour increased. Any hearts in which patriotism could have wavered were quickly overpowered with new zeal, the crowd waved the Red Book shouting, 'Down with foreign imperialists,' and almost with the next breath a fervent chant 'long live Chairman Mao.'

Chuang Tsu accompanied Liang Feng, panting and dragging her feet. Sheng's loud voice although jarring on Liang Feng's ears was apparently influencing Chang Tsu's thoughts. Slowing her pace Chuang Tsu turned to Liang Feng,

"Is there any truth in what Sheng is saying about the foreigners?"

Surprised, Liang Feng stared back at Chuang Tsu. How could she amongst that crowd, explain that Sheng's conduct was more questionable than the foreigners he was condemning. She herself was totally indifferent to the propaganda and suspected Sheng's motive for creating trouble and hate in the hearts of the people. She was convinced he was not speaking out in loyalty to Chairman Mao or to the nation. Without answering Chuang Tsu she walked on, regretful that Sheng's propaganda had obviously succeeded with Chuang Tsu. On all occasions when Sheng had expressed his contempt for foreigners, Chuang Tsu had solidly disagreed.

"You can't blame all foreigners for misdeeds of their governments," she had said remembering Donald Brown's kindness to her. But now under the onslaught of Sheng's propaganda Chuang Tsu was showing signs of confusion.

The mob was now in front of the British Mission. The moments when their enthusiasm had wavered under the heat were now forgotten, their revived spirits were further invigorated on the threshold of enemy territory. They jeered loudly. The Red Book, the bible of the Cultural Revolution, was lifted up and brandished vigorously in a show of strength to those within the building. Some voices cried "Sha Sha" meaning "Kill Kill".

Twilight had fallen. Bands of crimson bound the horizon, choking the atmosphere. Any signs of a cooling breeze to tranquilise the air or the hearts of the demonstrators were slight. Languishing in the heat and humidity, their tempers were overwrought. Shuffling feet and a restless stretching out of hands above their heads signified a call for more action. More demonstrators had arrived from all quarters of Peking. The crowd massed by the Mission gates determined to take revenge against the Hong Kong authorities. For the last few hours their feelings, worked upon by their leaders, were about to burst into a display of action.

Shrouded in an uneasy calm was the British Mission. Within the building the personnel of the Mission remained behind windows and doors, cautious not to be seen by the mob, yet keenly observing the events, no doubt recorded by television cameras hidden behind heavy curtains.

Yet not all that mob was in a wild mood. Away from the eyes of the leaders there were in the rank and file, those sitting on the pavements, resting their tired feet. Preoccupied with her own thoughts Liang Feng remained silent in the shadows. Her ears battered by slogans of hatred, the whole scene seemed unreal to her. Chuang Tsu stood quietly by her side, showing the fatigue that was a symptom of her mysterious illness.

Sheng and his colleague, tired of making speeches, moved closer to the gates of the Mission. Liang Feng glimpsed Sheng climbing the gates and waving the flag shouting "Down with British Imperialists".

A voice shouted an ultimatum to the British Government,

"Lift the ban on Chinese newspapers tonight."

Encouraged by that authoritative voice the mob began to chant,

"Down with British Imperialism".

Liang Feng had now lost sight of Sheng. He seemed to have joined those pushing vigorously at the gates. The crowds behind her were surging forward, forcing her along with Chuang Tsu to quickly get on their feet and move.

There were wild screams as the gates were flung open and a raging tidal wave of humanity dashed in to the premises of the British Mission compound; wave after wave of the maddened mob rushed towards the building. Those who were unable to push in through the front gates scaled the walls in vigorous haste to get into the prohibited territory. Only when she was flung on to the gates by the screaming mob behind, did Liang Feng know where she was. Terror now clouded her eyes as she struggled against being pushed inside. Clinging to the gates she watched in horror the demonstrators destroying everything they could lay their hands upon and one by one the cars parked in the compound burst into flames.

With the crowds running into the building, the inmates of the Mission abandoned the building and rushed out from side entrances to get away, only to be chased and harassed by screaming demonstrators. It was then that Liang Feng saw smoke rising from the building and soon a burst of raging flames spluttered and crackled. Pulling herself away from the swinging gates, Liang Feng turned onto the street. She did not want to remain there any longer and, fear taking over from exhaustion she began to run away from the scene. She was not alone in her desire to flee, there were others too hastily hurrying away.

The action of setting the fire came as a shock to many citizens unprepared for such violence when they had set out on the protest march. The shock and horror in their faces spoke of their confusion and lack of direction. Things seemed to have got out of control. So far the demonstrations against foreign powers appeared to have been carefully monitored, with no individual acts of violence being allowed. The rules and regulations governing the organised demonstrations had suddenly snapped resulting in a show of individualism that had so far been kept in check by the authorities. Human nature, unable to withstand the onslaught on emotions, had refused to be contained within a specified boundary. The fire was an expression of their frustration, anger and roused emotions. In the thoughts of many observers of this event was that the authorities had failed to anticipate such an act of violence. Her mind in turmoil Liang Feng's thoughts flew to Pierre. He had often said in warning. "The authorities do not seem to understand the gravity of tampering too much with human nature."

That night the unanswered question in the minds and hearts of all citizens and foreign residents of Peking was "Who started the fire?" The memory of Sheng amongst those forcing the gates to open and letting in the demonstrators Liang Feng nursed alone.

Gathering her straying thoughts Liang Feng hastened in search of Chuang Tsu who had disappeared in the pandemonium. She had almost given up her search when a voice, feeble and familiar, struck her ears.

Chuang Tsu, in a dazed condition, mumbling "Where is Sheng?", was straying away from the crowds running away from the fire.

Recognising her voice Liang Feng rushed towards her and took her hand. Their eyes met in sympathy, comforting each other. Sheng, who seemed to have acted as a leader of the mob, had disappeared leaving the crowd to their own fate. Sheng's influence on Chuang Tsu when being mesmerised by slogans now seemed to have weakened. Her hold tightened on Liang Feng's hand as she whispered,

"I hope Mr and Mrs Brown have not suffered any violence."

Liang Feng pressed her hand warmly. It was good to see Chuang Tsu back to her normal compassionate self.

Looking out of the window from the apartment Liang Feng stood in silent thought as the sky darkened and a red glow became visible in the night sky. The Mission was still burning. In Jiang Gowen Street the troops were arriving in anxious haste. Silently and deliberately they combed the streets.

That night the people did not sleep; their ears were glued to the darkness around them. Only the sound of dull heavy boots echoed during that troubled night with an occasional command breaking the uneasy silence.

Liang Feng closed the window and walked into Chuang Tsu's room. She was fast asleep. The agitation she had displayed in the street seemed to have calmed, her body curved comfortably hugging the thin pillow.

CHAPTER 29

Counter Revolutionaries

Next morning the residents of East is Red commune woke up to a strange silence. The revolutionary songs and speeches heralding the dawn of a new day, which for the last two years had become part and parcel of people's lives, were now mysteriously absent. There was an eerie silence, a silence that was unfamiliar and therefore giving rise to suspicion and apprehension.

Chuang Tsu was resting. She had cushioned a chair with the aid of old pillows laid against the back and the seat. She was tired of a Spartan life and was now indulging herself in the absence of harsh words of criticism from Sheng. The apartment was pleasantly quiet and inactive. Shi Kai Ying had disappeared on the fateful night and so had Sheng. Her daughter's disappearance was received with stoical acceptance. Chuang Tsu only wanted to get away from all the noise and take a deep nap. With an expression of contentment, she was trying to catch up with two years of disturbed sleep. Chuang Tsu remained motionless on the settee with pillows around her when Liang Feng entered the room and spoke her name.

Unlike for Chuang Tsu, the silence was making Liang Feng uneasy. She was disturbed by fears concerning the fate of the people inside the British Mission at the time of the attack. The authorities maintained a stony silence and had not yet taken any action against the mobs that launched the attacks. Liang Feng was more worried for Shi Kai Ying, than her mother. Seeing Sheng in a new role too worried her.

Chuang Tsu's eyes flickered. Liang Feng once again called out her name and said,

"Chuang Tsu, have you had any news of Shi Kai Ying and Sheng?"

Hearing the name of Sheng was enough to jolt Chuang Tsu from her doze. She sat up in her chair agitated, she looked round the room; her heavily hooded eyes lifted their lids painfully and stared at Liang Feng. She exclaimed,

"Has Sheng come back?"

"No" said Liang Feng; there was repressed anxiety in her tone.

She was uneasy at Sheng's disappearance and his words of hatred against the foreigners. She preferred to know his whereabouts than speculate at what other revenge he planned while hiding.

Feeling her nerves making her more irritated with Chung Tsu's lack of interest in the night's events, Liang Feng said,

"Chuang Tsu, aren't you worried for Shi Kai Ying?"

Hearing the name of her daughter Chuang Tsu whimpered and sniffed into her handkerchief.

"I knew that husband of hers would get her into trouble." With sad eyes she continued,

"Shi Kai Ying behaved badly to her mother after you arrived in the apartment."

Those sad eyes smiled kindly at Liang Feng as she continued to reminisce,

"Poor girl, Shi Kai Ying thought I loved you better and began to take the side of Sheng against me."

Liang Feng did not speak and Chuang Tsu, becoming her old self, declared with more authority and confidence,

"Shi Kai Ying is a foolish girl to believe that Sheng can influence a Revolution."

Liang Feng remained silent as she reflected at what Chuang Tsu said. The next words of Chuang Tsu really surprised her.

"I wonder," said a matter of fact Chuang Tsu, "if Sheng was trapped in the fire."

After a pause she added reflectively,

"But there have not been any announcements of the discovery of bodies in the rubble."

Concealing her distress at Chuang Tsu's callous indifference, Liang Feng walked up to her friend and rested her hand lightly on her shoulder. Moved by this action Chuang Tsu became silent. She had always been fond of Liang Feng, yet could not comprehend her zeal for the revolution. In order to come to terms with those doubts that had placed restraints on her relationship with Liang Feng, she murmured,

"I hope you will not think unkindly of me if I say I was never a great supporter of Chairman Mao."

Liang Feng said thoughtfully,

"I considered you a loyal follower of the Chairman when I first met you. Yet, later, I feared this zeal was waning under Sheng's influence."

Chuang Tsu smiled weakly. She wanted to explain the complicated nature of her country's politics.

"I like Chairman Mao but I prefer the economic policy of President Liu Shaoqui. This idea of incentives he advocated won me over."

In a voice that begged Liang Feng to have sympathy for her misconceptions, she confessed,

"No one likes to work only for the state; all human beings have aspirations to improve themselves," then pleadingly she admitted,

"I like money and comforts, especially in my old age."

Feeling she was beginning to understand human nature and those currents which made people selfish and ruthless and exploit others, Liang Feng said sadly,

"But what people forget is that the unequal distribution of wealth and exploitation of the weaker in society will lead to revolutions."

Chuang Tsu listened intently, trying to understand this explanation, but she was too old now to sacrifice her own needs for the good of the others. After all, she thought, there is only one life to enjoy; communism was based only on material principles.

Liang Feng's explanation now sounded rather hollow in her own ears. She too had been attracted to beauty and to material objects. She, like Chuang Tsu, was guilty of deviating from the austere communist way of life. She had searched for love and individual freedom in the regimented life of the commune; strangely her devotion to Chairman Mao had been founded on the appeal of his intellectual idealism; it had reached out to her own search for a true spirit of freedom within the human being.

Chuang Tsu rose shakily from her chair and walked over to the photograph of Shi Kai Ying hanging on the wall. She took it in her hand and, gazing at it, murmured,

"Poor Shi Kai Ying, she met Sheng when she came to study in Peking."

Seeing Liang Feng watching her intently she went on reminiscing,

"He was not a bad worker but he always made trouble for the authorities till they got rid of him. He is too political minded and confused. When he suspects persecution he becomes intolerant".

Liang Feng said thoughtfully,

"Chuang Tsu, when did you suspect he had sympathies with the counter revolutionaries?"

No longer feeling the need to hold back the political leanings of the family, Chuang Tsu answered frankly,

"I knew it all the time. Sheng kept things hidden from me and also Shi Kai Ying. How could I advise him?" She looked pleadingly at Liang Feng and once again she cried, "You know how he terrorised me".

It was a confused household. Sheng and his mother-in-law had different aspirations. Chuang Tsu had come to Peking to propagate her economic policy based on incentives. These incentives and earning extra money had simultaneously given rise to the seeking of foreign goods that were officially banned in the country. A practice had developed among the authorities to send all those connected with it, including Chung Tsu's friend, for re-education to a camp. It was this worry, in addition to Sheng's harassment, that had driven Chuang Tsu to ill health.

Liang Feng had arrived in Chuang Tsu's apartment at a time when Chuang Tsu had lost all interest in 'doing Good' as she referred to her actions. Liang Feng now watched with sympathy the haggard face of her friend as she walked over and hung the photograph on the wall. Chuang Tsu, silent, walked back to

210

her chair. She suddenly seemed tired of everything and staggered on to the chair. Heaving a sigh she fell onto the comfortable cushions. Addressing no one in particular she said,

"I am thankful I can sleep in comfort now, without those screams from the loudspeakers".

In a few minutes Chuang Tsu was fast asleep. Liang Feng did not like to see Chuang Tsu retiring to sleep at daytime. The unusual quiet made her nervous. She felt isolated and friendless. Since meeting Pierre she showed no desire to open herself to any of her countrymen who, since the outbreak of the revolution, viewed with suspicion even their own families. There had been a time when she thought she was perfectly happy, but all that had now changed. She could not envisage a future in which the political upheavals would be peacefully resolved.

The spectre of the fire brought memories of a mob that had gone mad. The anger and frustration was devastating. Liang Feng winced; she remembered the angry young woman Red Guard flinging away her hand that had clutched her helplessly. The next moment she was thrown on to the gates by a frenzied mob and the woman's eyes blazed with hatred for her weakness. The woman Red Guard had willingly and triumphantly let herself be swept into the territory of the hated imperialists. She had a fleeting glimpse of the woman, vigorously waving the Red Book high above the heads of the sweeping mob. Her own book of 'Thoughts of Chairman Mao' that had been her most precious companion in her journey to Peking was lost in the race to get away from the fire.

Neither Sheng nor Shi Kai Ying made an appearance in the apartment after the fire. With mixed feelings Liang Feng listened to rumours that circulated the commune in the absence of official announcements. It was with gladness that she had greeted the information that the Red Guards had come to the assistance of some of the Britishers caught between the fire and the screaming mob. But on the other hand she had heard accounts of militant Red Guards who were now taking a prominent role in the movement.

As days passed Liang Feng felt imprisoned in the company of Chuang Tsu and the apartment, although the apartment gave comfort and security in the absence of Sheng. Chuang Tsu was indifferent and insensitive to the world around her, seeking to doze even in the daytime in a chair she had comfortably cushioned. But when days dragged on to weeks, the disappearance of her daughter was met with anxious inquiries about the fire. Each time she caught the attention of Liang Feng she recalled incidents in the life of Shi Kai Ying in Canton before she had married Sheng.

Chuang Tsu had fallen asleep once again on the chair. Liang Feng feeling restless in the silence of the room walked up to the window and walked back into the room. She did this many times. In the street below guards of the People's

Liberation Army kept close vigil. Since the fire the military was conspicuous, giving special protection to the foreign community and at the same time keeping a watchful eye on the local people.

Liang Feng walked into her room and pulled out the fan she fiercely guarded. It reminded her of Pierre and his kindness. A slow smile appeared on her lips remembering the moments she had stolen to be with him. Since she was no longer allowed in Waichia Talou, she had no news of him, yet the satisfaction of knowing he was in the country gave her hopes of meeting him in the future. She had kept away from Wampu's commune since her death. Wampu's grave by now would have gone under the plough she reflected sadly. Life is impermanent, all great philosophers had discovered, Pierre had reflected thus while he watched the sun swallowed up by dark evening clouds. It had thrown a shadow on that moment of being together, and now, with a sense of great futility she folded the fan and thrust it into the pocket of her padded coat.

Leaving the apartment she walked in the direction of Pierre's house. Winds of change seemed to have battered the Hutung and the house. The Hutung was deserted with no sign of any life other than the two solitary sentries standing guard. An atmosphere of desolation pervaded the once active neighbourhood. Only the pine tree in his garden stood unchanged, steadily rising above the gloomy scene. There was detachment in its beauty, a cushion to protect it from the effects of change the rest of the lane had been subjected to. A sense of bitterness rose within her and was soon accompanied by a feeling of guilt at her unfair judgement. In detachment she had sought to escape changes that brought unhappiness. At a time when she had felt isolated, the trees like Pierre had been the catalysts, drawing out feelings within her for a world of compassion.

Liang Feng's steps drew closer to Pierre's house. With mounting nervous fear she saw the changed appearance of the door. The brightly painted door was cruelly distorted with splashes of black characters that accused him of being a foreign spy. She did not know how long she had waited debating with the injustice that had fallen upon him.

The sentry had seen her coming down the lane and now-staring at the door. He quickly came forward to intercept her. But he soon relaxed as the unhappiness in her face struck him. Walking up to her he said curtly,

"'Why are you loitering here?"

She did not reply, she had not heard him. The despair in her face made him say almost kindly,

"No one other than the residents is allowed to enter this lane."

There were many questions to ask but she could not speak and stared at him mutely. He took a step back, she seemed deaf and helpless, and leaving her alone he walked back to his post.

212

As Liang Feng recovered from her deep shock, she felt heaviness in her head that was painful. Despair had imprisoned her in blind fury and desolation. Blood rushed into her face and her thoughts came in flashes blinding all her powers of reasoning. Her hands clenched and she walked briskly and blindly in the direction of Thiananmen Square.

Her eyes pitched into the Red fort; within that was the Forbidden City, only the roof and the rostrum were in view. In that magnificent rostrum the leaders would stand and address the citizens including her who would be forced there, against her will, to pay respects to those who would profess to have freed them from arbitrary rulers.

The touch of warm tears on the cheeks turned anger to bitterness; she said to herself desolately,

"I am like one of those cringing slaves kowtowing to infallible emperors." Turning her hack angrily to the Forbidden City she walked towards Behai Park.

Hidden among the trees and rock, only the upper part of the pagoda was visible to the street even though it had lost its plaque bequeathed to peace. It could still inspire beauty and serenity.

The Red Guards had failed to remove the pagoda from the landscape. Her tormented heart recovered gradually thanks to the silent tranquillity of the sight before her eyes. Gently, as night fell and the view faded from her sight, Liang Feng traced her steps towards the city and Wan Fuchien Street.

As usual the citizens had made their way to Wan Fuchien Street to read the latest news of the revolution, information that would surreptitiously appear and be read under the dim lights of the street. There was more excitement than on any other day as the people pushed each other trying to read the new posters that had appeared on the shop windows and walls. With her heart beating anxiously Liang Feng hurried with the rest to where an excited crowd had gathered. She halted. Pierre's face stared from the poster on the wall before her. Slowly reading, her heart was strangled by the figure of 48 below the photograph.

Pierre was to be expelled in the next 48 hours from Peking and indeed from China. An audible cry of anguish escaped her lips,

"I must see him".

She wrenched herself free from the crowd around her. Disbelieving the words she saw, and staring at the watch in her hand, she paused to recollect her thoughts. Before his expulsion a trial was to be held at the Peking municipal grounds. Blindly Liang Feng rushed along the street, there was nowhere else to go but to return to Chuang Tsu's apartment and wait for the dawn of the next day.

The world of beauty and compassion that Pierre had opened to her was to be closed in the next few hours. Although he had been under house arrest, his presence had given that ever-present optimism in her heart to seek opportunities to meet him once again. She wrung her hands in desperation – that anticipation would now be futile when he would be thousands of miles away from her. She had reached the door to the apartment. A chilly feeling imprisoned her; the poster informing everyone of Pierre's expulsion had appeared at the time she had been gazing at the white Pagoda.

CHAPTER 30

Winds of Change on the Horizon

The residents of Peking were once again suddenly pulled out of their beds in the early hours of the morning. Loudspeakers that had ominously gone silent during the last few weeks had begun a barrage of propaganda aimed at the 'foreign spies' and 'imperialists'. Mounted on wooden carts and fitted on bicycles the drums began to roll in, the Red Guards screaming their slogans.

Hastening to the window Liang Feng's eyes anxiously followed the crowd walking on the sidewalks and spilling on to the road. Her mind was preoccupied with the impending trial that would take place in the next few hours.

She had waited impatiently, counting every minute for the appearance of dawn. She was determined to make her way to the grounds of the municipality.

The increasing noise of the people outside had startled Chuang Tsu out of her sleep and she staggered into Liang Feng's room holding her head with both hands complaining,

"This noise is giving me an awful headache."

Liang Feng remained silent. Her mind was too preoccupied with anxious memories of the fire that had engulfed the British Mission few nights ago.

The day had marked, so far, an end to mob rule. Whether it was auspicious or inauspicious to the ongoing Cultural Revolution was debated by different sections of the Peking population. The processions criss-crossing the streets of Peking, shouting derision at foreigners, "Down with foreign imperialists" and "Down with foreign spies", had suddenly stopped.

It seemed that, although unexplained, the advance of the Cultural Revolution had been suddenly arrested.

The crowd did not look ruffled as they nonchalantly walked in the direction of the trial grounds. There was a screech of a vehicle braking and a bundle of leaflets was thrown at the crowd. The people rushed to get their hands on it, they knew this was some important news the authorities were letting them know. It was a popular mode of conveying news to the public. Although there was less enthusiasm in the crowd, they began to realise that once again the revolution was activated. Some sighed and others hid their emotions with blank faces.

Watching what was going on from the window, Liang Feng quickly stepped out of her room. She glanced at Chuang Tsu who was seated, rocking herself back to sleep on the chair and muttering,

"When will all this end?"

On the street, a stream of citizens carrying flags, were already hastening in the direction of the Municipality. Joining them, Liang Feng picked up a leaflet from the ground and with mounting despair began to read the accusations against Pierre. He had been accused of photographing military installations that were out of bounds for all foreigners. This was considered a serious act of espionage. A helpless cry of indignation arose in her in defence of Pierre. Her eyes kept on going over the words as it dawned on her that he had taken photographs of his students at the park at their request. He had given the students their pictures as soon as he photographed which made them so proud and happy.

She wondered if those innocent acts of friendship were now called unfriendly acts against the Republic of China. The more she reflected, the more incredible the accusations appeared. She had known Pierre better than the authorities denouncing him. She was convinced of his innocence; he was a genuine admirer of the Chairman. In his eyes the Chairman was trying to unify a country left in tatters by foreign powers and corrupt warlords.

With a sense of hopelessness and helplessness her eyes appealed to the crowd as if to tell them that they were accusing an innocent man. She walked with the procession to the municipality.

The crowds seemed more curious than hostile; the rage and anger that had roused them to brutalities were absent. Her fingers clutching the leaflet, she quickened her footsteps following the procession increasing its speed to get within the sight of the municipality.

Despite her distress Liang Feng became acutely conscious of the soldiers standing conspicuously on either side of the road.

Since the fire at the British Mission there had been a pronounced increase in the number of military personnel placed on guard by embassies in Peking and Waichia Talou.

The military no longer were aloof observers of Red Guard activities but at all times kept a sharp vigilant eye on all citizens.

Slipping quietly to a position closer to the Municipality where trials were being daily conducted of those accused of counter-revolutionary acts, Liang Feng waited anxiously for Pierre's appearance. The chanting of anti-foreign slogans by Red Guards had already begun.

She held her breath as a convoy of military vehicles arrived amidst jeers from the crowd. The impassive faces of the soldiers looked nervous. One shouted for order. When the vehicle came to a grinding halt soldiers leaped down from the vehicle, their rifles pointed in the direction of the assembling crowds. A path was quickly cordoned off for the accused.

Pierre Devon along with two Chinese nationals was accused of acting against the Revolution. They were conveyed in an open lorry to the municipality. Throughout the journey they had faced a hostile crowd shouting derisions at foreign spies.

Pierre stood up hesitantly before descending the steps of the lorry. There was silence other than a shrill voice hurling a command to the people who had gathered to watch the trial. Pierre was surrounded by screaming Red Guards. His eyes were moving in the direction of the crowd as if looking for any known faces.

In the hands of his captors Pierre managed to retain his tranquillity but Liang Feng noticed a hint of pain crossing his eyes when confronting the screaming young demonstrators pressing on him. Her mind, numb, she had followed the proceedings with almost a stranger's aloofness. At the sight of Pierre, her eyes blurred; unrestrained tears flowed down her cheeks. Her view was momentarily obliterated when the Red Guards thrusting their fists at his face screamed out fiercely, "Down with the capitalist imperialists".

Pierre managed to stand his ground, being taller than most of the crowd around. Gazing above their heads, his eyes questioningly passed over the faces, sometimes lingering. Standing in her corner Liang Feng wondered helplessly whether his eyes were searching for her. All she could do was to stand there by the steps and hope that by some miracle he would turn her way. A sudden cheer from the crowd made her gasp; Sheng, in gloomy black shirt and black trousers darted across the dais like a threatening black cloud with an ominous plan.

Sheng had disappeared on the night of the fire and nobody in the family knew about his whereabouts. But some rumours making the rounds in the commune were as ominous as his clothes. Chuang Tsu had been worried about her daughter's disappearance which she blamed now on Sheng.

Thrusting his lean body forward, raising his right hand with a flourish, Sheng yelled, his voice sharp and clear "Down with foreign spies! Down with Revisionism and capitalism!"

He seemed to have worked himself up to a frenzy of screaming platitudes that had the desired effect to keep the audience spellbound and giving him added energy to thrust an accusing finger at the foreigner on trial.

Liang Feng, holding her breath fearfully, watched the actions of Sheng with suspicion. There was mounting fear that he would do something unpredictable. A few days before, a similar black-clad figure had been seen at the forefront of the group of Red Guards ill-treating three British diplomats to stand trial for the misdeeds of their country.

They had been brought on to the steps of Waichia Talou and compelled to listen to a tirade of accusations. Not satisfied with mere verbal attacks, the Red Guards had attempted to wrench from them subjugation to their leader Mao

Zedong. A large portrait of the Chairman had been thrust before the helpless diplomats with accompanying screams, "Bow your heads to our great leader."

Enraged by the diplomats' aloofness, some Red Guards had daringly jostled them from behind, causing one of them to trip and fall on his knees. The mob had then flaunted the portrait of the Chairman before the fallen victim. There had been thunderous cheers by the spectators at the seeming act of penitence of a hated enemy.

This almost ritual form of punishment was to be inflicted again, this time on Pierre.

An oversized portrait of the Chairman was thrust at his face, forcing him to lose balance and take a step back. The commanding picture seemed to have a mesmerising effect on the crowd, almost as if the Chairman himself was present. Grasping the portrait, Sheng pulled it away from the hands that clutched it and himself pushed it against Pierre's face, his voice ringing out, "foreign spy, bow your head to our great leader."

Pierre stood his ground, an inscrutable smile playing on his lips as his eyes rested on the portrait. Liang Feng could read in that smile the amicable tolerance Pierre had always shown towards 'those misled young people' – his name for the Red Guards. Sheng's overheated countenance revealed that he did not like that smile and his voice became shriller, "We are not afraid of paper tigers!"

Sheng was obviously not satisfied, incensed by the unaffected demeanour Pierre displayed. Now emboldened, he took a step forward. Grabbing Pierre's arm he pushed him onto his knees. Indignation gave Pierre strength to brush off Sheng's hold on him and hold his ground.

The accusations against Pierre were now formerly read out. He had been caught trying to take photographs of places that were barred to foreigners, in fact where signs had specifically stated "Foreigners are not allowed."

Pierre faced his accusers calmly although there was a glint of quiet anger in his eyes, perhaps due to bitterness that his genuine support for a democratic communism had so soon been forgotten. Liang Feng, already aware of the new restrictions imposed on individual freedom, thought that these were charges arbitrary and far-fetched.

The torture of the prisoners continued. The two Chinese captives were even less fortunate than Pierre. The Red Guards turned their attention to their nationals who were not spared any sympathy while unrestrained aggression against the foreigner was held back. Some young men resorted to harassment, prodding the two nationals with sharp sticks of bamboo. Their crime was harbouring counter-revolutionary thoughts. Unable to vent their anger fully on Pierre, the frustration made the Red Guards more brutal towards the hapless Chinese prisoners. Distressed by their callousness, Pierre quickly stepped down and offered his arm to help one of the accused onto his feet. Pierre was overwhelmed with anger, but as he glared at the jeering crowd his anger became mixed with pity. Amongst those mocking faces he could recognise some of his students.

He surveyed this crowd for Liang Feng. Although he feared her controversial nature, he was confident that she would survive and wait for him. These were comforting thoughts which brought a smile to his lips.

Sheng saw that smile and his fury increased. With a lightning leap he sprang forward and delivered a hard blow on Pierre's face. Stunned, Pierre staggered; his hand went up to his face. Blood was dripping from his lips. At the sight of the blood there was a momentary hush among the onlookers, and the cries then resumed. But this time it was in a low key. Mixed with these cries were also cries of concern. The mood had changed from triumph to fear.

Liang Feng, who had seen that action, had shouted in protest at Sheng's brutality, her cry being taken up by anxious protesters calling the soldiers for help. They were there in no time; rushing up the steps and pushing the crowd back violently, they formed a protective circle round Pierre and the two other accused.

Suddenly, in panic the people were rushing off in all directions. Sheng meanwhile identified as the culprit, was being dragged away, his cries of protest smothered. Liang Feng had forced her way forward to get near the prisoners but was now thrust back by the suspicious soldiers. In order to keep away any potential trouble-makers, the soldiers began forcefully driving back the entire crowd of onlookers as well as the Red Guards. In the ensuing commotion Liang Feng momentarily lost consciousness.

In that quick moment of recovery she had heard the sound of a pistol being fired. She reached out blindly, crying out Pierre's name, but she could not go any further, being smothered by the crowd. However, vaguely she caught a glimpse of an army vehicle racing towards the crowd, bundling into it the people on the steps; with numbed feelings Liang Feng watched the vehicle being driven off the grounds. Only when it was out of sight did she make a move to leave the scene.

Despite the bitterness, her predominant feeling was one of relief that Pierre was at least still alive. In silence she walked back to Chang'an Dajie. Passing the gates of Sun yat Sen Park, her feet halted. The setting sun was casting many shadows among the silent trees. The grass seemed unusually green and luxuriant in its growth, bringing a sad reminder of the laws that were keeping away feet that once walked among its beauty in the years before the Cultural Revolution. It looked as if the beauty of the park in isolation was tinged with sadness.

There had been a time when she escaped from her mundane life to the park to live her dreams. In a time that allowed no other relaxation other than revolutionary songs and revolutionary drama, she had, like Chou Yan the poet, now despised by the authorities, found a beauty, even a meaning to life, in the solitary surroundings of the natural environment. Chou Yan's words had inspired her to courageously hold to the belief that artists and poets should have individual freedom to express themselves without political interference. She remembered the numerous occasions she had been with Pierre among the pine trees of Behai Park. It was where her feelings for him grew more intense under the silence of the majestic pines.

With a desolate feeling she dragged her feet towards Chuang Tsu's apartment. Chuang Tsu greeted her with a welcoming smile and taking her hand directed Liang Feng to the comfortable sofa in the room. There was a bright glimmer in Chuang Tsu's eyes, which she had not seen for a long time.

Unable to restrain her emotions Chuang Tsu cried out,

"I have some good news". Clutching a radio transistor in her hands and keeping one ear to it, she declared rather grandly,

"A counter-revolutionary incident had taken place at the trial of the foreigner."

As she said the last word she looked sharply at Liang Feng, expecting an answer. But Liang Feng's expression remained impassive as she studied her friend. Chuang Tsu's excitement did not seem real to Liang Feng, who was in a numbed state of lethargy that had seeped in since the trial and its aftermath. Noticing the dull stare in Liang Feng's eyes, Chuang Tsu became concerned and gently asked,

"Are you ill? Did something happen to you at the trial?"

Without waiting for a reply Chuang Tsu burst out,

"I am sure this will cheer you up; Sheng had planned to attack the foreigner to create an international incident to bring discredit to our nation." In a self-righteous tone she added,

"I always knew he had a heart of a brute, I'm glad he no longer can intimidate me."

With a sigh she sat down beside Liang Feng.

Liang Feng's mood changed to sudden anxiety as she recollected the terrifying experience at the steps of the municipality.

"Was any one hurt?" were the only words Liang Feng could utter anxiously.

Seeing her words had brought some colour to Liang Feng's face and enjoying the effect she was creating Chuang Tsu said loudly and abruptly,

"Sheng was shot dead by the guards; he deserved this for his nasty twisted heart."

All this was said in a callous tone that upset Liang Feng. A surge of pity for Sheng engulfed Liang Feng as she considered the 'system' was more to blame for his anger and frustration. He had clashed with Chuang Tsu as he had begun to suspect her harbouring capitalist dreams. Getting up from her chair Chuang Tsu went to the kitchen to make some tea for both of them.

Left to her Liang Feng muttered,

"I don't know whether to laugh or to cry".

What had happened was so unreal – more like a dream.

Liang Feng walked up to the balcony. The evening sky stretched before her, overwhelming in its silence and intensity; a power wielding force over all humanity which now, in its customary undaunted manner, flaunted its crimson banner in the horizon. Her eyes were helplessly drawn to it. A sharp pain stabbed her. Pierre would be soon gone, forced to leave a land he had often said was 'home' to his spirit. He had told her,

"My heart is happiest when I am here, amongst the fragrant hills, with you".

These words gave hope for his return some day. Such a time would come she thought. The sudden halt in the Red Guards' activities in the last few days gave her hope of changes that would come in her country in the future.

Liang Feng turned her back to the red brilliance in the sky. Thoughts of democratic conditions, where they would allow a free flow of ideas and new ideals that would satisfy the hunger within so many hearts for individual freedom flashed in her dream of future China. Whatever political events overtook the land, she would still value it for its beauty that was an inspiration to her; and was it not here that she had met Pierre, a free thinker.

Liang Feng had no immediate plans. She had lost her job as a translator at the Waichia Talou office. She was also glad to get away as it carried too many memories.

She would remain with Chuang Tsu until they heard from Shikai Ying. This would suit Chuang Tsu, who did not like the severe winters of Peking and did prefer the warm climate of Canton. But to her, the cold Peking winter had once brought the warmth of an unexplained happiness. Her eyes softened remembering the snow-covered Purple Bamboo Grove.

Chuang Tsu hurried back into the room still holding in her hands the transistor. It had been her constant companion since her cherished books had been destroyed by Sheng in a fit of cultural fanaticism.

She was excited as she announced to Liang Feng,

"A very important announcement will be on the air in a few minutes."

She sat beside Liang Feng in high expectations to hear about Sheng's demise. The broadcast began as Chuang Tsu increased the volume in the transistor. The measured words came out,

"Only the competent authority has the right to take actions against foreigners living in China."

The message was repeated firmly to the nation many times.

Rather disappointed at not hearing about Sheng's incident Chuang Tsu went back to the kitchen to resume her tea making.

A wry smile appeared on Liang Feng's lips. It had taken the fiasco of the fire at the British Mission and the trial to make the authorities consider action on all demonstrations. Pierre's constant words of reassurance had been "conditions have to change sooner or later". There had been confidence and optimism in his voice and manner, as he said it standing by the 'Bridge of Perfect Wisdom'. Within the Cultural Revolution the wheels of change were turning already.

Darkness gently curtained the sky. The friendship she had shared with Pierre was securely closeted in her heart. Just like the eternal stars that disclosed their radiance only at night so could she discover happiness whenever she relived those moments of happiness.

Hope stirred in her. Pierre had a vision of the future events in the land he considered home to his spirit. She believed his words.

Acknowledgements

I thank my son Yasantha Monerawela, who has helped with suggestions, graphics and encouraged me to proof read and publish my novel at a time when China is always in the news.

I also wish to thank my dear friend, the late Amala Dissanayaka for typing out the manuscript and proof reading from my original hand written manuscript; Gill Graham Maw my contemporary in Peking and a good friend from 1965 who allowed me to use the photographs she had taken of the Cultural Revolution; and Sir Alistair Hunter for his invaluable comments and corrections to make the incidents and time scale authentic during the Cultural Revolution.

Dedication

I dedicate this book to my granddaughter Tarita and my son Yasantha